The Last Hundred

The Last Hundred

Jim Ellis

Acknowledgements

Dave King for editing The Last Hundred, contact Dave@davekingedits.com.

Thanks to Cynthia Wiener, Libby Jacobs, and Miriam Santana for their support and encouragement; and a special thanks to my Good Lady, Jeannette.

"Jock never surrendered; not in 1865 or 1886, Cap'n. It's 1927 and he's fighting with his Chiricahua down in the Sierra Madre. A real Bronco Warrior."
—Joe MacIntosh, Scout.

Chapter One

The Apache call the Sierra Madre the Blue Mountains.

The range of nine thousand-foot peaks runs for a hundred miles from the Sierra el Tigre south to the Basvispe Valley. Three rivers bisect it: the Rio Aros, the Rio Bavispe, and the Rio Yaqi. The Rio Bavispe guards the isolation of the Sierra Madre. The continental divide flanks the range on three sides. The mountains mark the border between Chihuahua and Sonora.

Hidden deep in the mountains are small fertile plateaus. It is hot in summer, but the temperature can fall to freezing when the sun slips behind the ridges. It isn't a landscape for timid men – it's a vast, menacing land dominated by mountains and sharp rocks, precipitous cliffs, snakes, jaguars, and wild cats. It is a place for retiring armadillos and badgers; the benign white-tailed deer, brightly plumaged parrots. It was a killing ground where Apaches fought Mexicans and Americans with no quarter asked or given.

And it was home to the last free, independent Apache, who dovetailed with this wild place, snugger than a mortice lock.

Jock MacNeil, formerly of the Confederate Navy and Stand Watie's Mounted Rifles, stood at the cliff edge of the rancheria, raised his arms to the sun and sang the Morning Song. He was giving thanks to Ussen, the God of the Apache, for the heavenly gift of the love he'd known with his wife, Miriam, and for the lives of their son and daughter.

Jock wasn't a man who received divine grace on his knees. Ussen had given the land to the Apaches, even though the White Eyes took it from them, and their Government broke its promises. Ussen had also given Jock back his spirituality, replacing the primitive Catholicism which had slipped away when he was in his early teens, now nearly six decades past. Jock's voice, strong in the low registers, wavered on the higher notes, but strengthened as he offered his gratitude to Ussen for his protection from enemies and the bounties of the rancheria.

Suddenly, the heat of the sun vanished. A crushing sensation pierced Jock's heart, and he grew cold. Perhaps this was his time to die, and he hoped it wouldn't be painful. Slowly, his thighs gave way, his arthritic knees collapsed under him, raised arms dropped to his sides, and he fell to the ground. He lay, twitching and shaking, his legs jerking so violently that he thought they might separate from his body. A foam of saliva gathered at the corners of his gaping mouth and hung on his cracked lips.

But Ussen hadn't called Jock to the Happy Place, not yet. Ussen was sending the power. Jock could feel it. He was being asked to give another service for his people.

Suddenly, his soul left his body. He could feel a distant attachment to the shell lying on the ground, but he was transported to the old northern homeland. Homesickness and nostalgia swept through him as he saw his younger self with his wife and family, in beautiful Oak Creek Canyon. Oh, that sweet, happy time, that lost paradise.

Then the *chin-a-see-lee* touched his soul, and he was in the Parjarita Wilderness, the place of deep sorrow, reaching with crooked fingers to touch the earth where the bones of his beloved, Miriam, and their son and daughter lay in the grave he'd dug.

He sensed danger nearby and looked up. An aged man sat beside him. Jock suspected he knew him, though the old man's face was blurred. Farther back, a group of Apaches waited. The young men and women looked at him expectantly, and the old people stared pleadingly, and he did not understand why this was so.

Then he was once again in his body.

Jock gradually recovered. Presently he got to his feet, wiped the saliva from his chin with the sleeve of his calico shirt. Kusuma the old woman, who looked after him – and who was younger than he –stood by the side of his wickiup and beckoned him to breakfast. Jock wasn't ready to eat and subdued his desire for coffee, pretending not to hear her calling. He adjusted the ties on his long moccasins, doubled over and fastened them at the knee. He admired Kusuma's deft work on the curled-up toes, which protected his feet from thorns and cactus spikes. Jock felt around the leggings, smiled as his hand rested on the pair of Derringers hidden there. The Derringers were old and well-preserved, each one primed with two .44 rounds; fatal at close range. If he were cornered and disarmed, he might fight his way out, or shoot himself if it came to that. Jock adjusted his long breech clout, unfastened and fastened the buckle of a leather Mexican Cavalry belt, and played with the position of the sheathed Bowie knife hanging at his left side.

"Jock," Kusuma yelled. "The coffee'll be cold."

He tried to walk confidently to his wickiup, ignoring the torment in his knees; but Kusuma was not fooled and spotted his ill-disguised limping.

Jock sat in the arbor of his wickiup, facing the sun and thinking. He liked to sit here when he had a decision to make. The vision from Ussen had added to his power, and he felt stronger, confident that he could do whatever Ussen desired of him.

Kusuma poured more coffee. Jock took generous swallows, washing down the last of the stewed hoosh made from the fruit of the prickly pear. He liked to watch the women gathering the fruit – using two sticks to save their hands from the spikes – then rolling the fruit on the ground to remove the barbs.

"You're going north again?" Kusuma said.

"Yes."

"What if you're killed? Take Jim, or one of the warriors."

"Jim's in worse shape than me. He knows what to do when I'm away. I don't need a warrior to protect me; my power to go north comes from Ussen."

"I'll prepare food and water for your journey."

"Pack some hoosh."

Hoosh kept him regular. Piles did not go well with long days in the saddle and were he to get wounded up north, Jock didn't want enemies laughing at his stained breech clout. Or if he were killed, he didn't want his soul to know the White Eyes' contempt for an old, fiery-bottomed Apache.

Although he was troubled by what lay ahead of him, Ussen's mercy worked on Jock. He looked around, and a smile of satisfaction creased his habitually stern expression at what the band had achieved.

It was good to be up in the high places, deep in the old Apache heartland where Juh and the *Nednhi* Apaches roamed in the old days. The dome shaped wickiup behind him was built well, the best willow poles supporting the brush cladding and the roof of shingle-style bunches of bear grass, fastened with yucca strings. A wavering ribbon of faint blue slipped out through the smoke hole in the roof, drifting northwards in the southern breeze. Inside lay his weapons, the few belongings, and the comfortable grass and brush bed covered with a deerskin robe where he eased his old bones when the arthritis was acute. It was a sturdy permanent home, warm and dry in the winter and cool in the summer, not like the temporary, rickety shelters used in the eighteen-eighties when the Apache were on the run, pursued by American and Mexican soldiers.

In the small fields below him, corn and mesquite beans grew. There was lush grass for the horses, sheep and cattle. Water was plentiful, and a small stream was dammed, creating a pool for the animals to drink. Game was abundant. In autumn, berries were to be had for drying. Agave grew in the valleys and the women gathered it to make tiswin, a weak beer. The women and children risked the fury of wild bees to harvest honey. Lower down, aspen and scrub oak flourished; higher up, firs and oak grew thickly. Through that high forest was a secret path up and over the ridge which Jock had cut; an escape route if the stronghold were attacked. Food, weapons and ammunition were cached up there beyond the ridge. Stones were carefully positioned along the approaches to the stronghold, and a boy, a girl, an old man, or woman, could send an avalanche down on enemies. For now, his people were safe.

But now the power was on him. Today was the day to go north and overcome the sense of danger lurking in his soul. Unexpectedly, regret tugged at his heart, and his throat swelled. Perhaps Ussen was sending him up there to his death. Perhaps he might not see his beloved rancheria or his band again, but he kept his anguish hidden beneath an iron mask.

Cherokee Jim was crossing the open ground separating their wickiups. Jock waved him toward a folded blanket, and Jim sat down, resting his arms on his knees. He handed Jock a long, thin, dark Mexican cigar and simultaneously, they bit off one end. Jock held a hot ember to Jim who drew on his cigar until he was satisfied it was burning well. Jock lit his own cigar, and they smoked contentedly.

"You're all right, going north?" Jim asked.

"I'm fine. I want to visit the grave of my family. Oak Creek Canyon too. We were happy then."

Jock let himself drift back more than sixty years to Miriam, his beloved wife, a petite slip of a girl who was fifteen when he first met her. She'd had an ebony complexion and walked so proudly, and she was so beautiful. As her face came back to him, he thought his heart might break. Tenderness surged in his heart as he recalled reviving her from near death by drowning, remembered his anxiety as he set the broken bone in her right arm; the relief in her lovely face when he made her drink laudanum to relieve the pain of her wound.

Kusuma, who looked after him, was good company; a gift from Ussen and he held her in great affection. But he was often lonely, and though he had Jim's friendship and the companionship of Kusuma, sometimes he craved the affection that came only from women. As leader, Jock might have insisted upon the company of younger women, but he knew he was ugly to the young, and he kept his honor by respecting all the women of the band. It was a respect which grew from his love for Miriam and their children.

The two men sat quietly.

Young voices came to them from the edge of the village and they turned to stare. A few older children in two lines, twenty yards apart, hurled rocks from slings at each other, dodging and weaving the flying missiles. One girl finished nursing a bloody forehead where a rock had struck, then slung a stone at her adversary. Jock nodded and saw Jim nodding, too. Simple games like these were preparations for the warrior's path. The noise and youthful energy reminded Jock of his own son and daughter, but they'd been murdered before they could learn to fight.

Jock chewed on his lip as he remembered finding their dead bodies, the top of their heads a bloody mess, where the scalp hunters had cut and wrenched away the hair. He looked up at Jim. "Might go to my secret stronghold in the Dragoons, look at some of our old places. The last time, maybe. Ussen has strengthened my power. I must overcome something dangerous. I saw some of our people, young and old, and I think I'm to help them, but I'm not sure. Ussen will show me when he is ready; He will protect me."

"I'll come with you."

"I need you here."

"You know," Jim said. "Once, your hair was copper, as mine was black. The hair on your face is no longer red, now it is white. But you are too young to die up there, maybe?"

"I'm seventy-seven years old, Jim, and you're well past eighty. Time we both thought about dying." His knees ached from sitting still, but he was too proud to stand first. "Take care of things, Jim?"

"I'll do that, Jock. And I'm coming down the mountain with you."

Jim reached for Jock's fifty caliber Sharps Rifle and, squinting out of his best eye, took the weapon apart, methodically cleaning and oiling it. Jock checked and cleaned a pair of Confederate Cavalry pistols, and the Derringers. He took a .45 Colt automatic pistol and shoulder holster, with extra ammunition for security.

Jock didn't want trouble and wouldn't look for it. But he wouldn't run from a fight either. He'd face enemies if they came at him.

Satisfied that his guns were prepared, Jock looked around again. It was a fine rancheria, and he was glad his Chiricahua had added farming to their raiding skills. Jock liked the Sierra Madre, especially the Sonoran side of the mountain, more fertile than the Chihuahua slopes. His band had been happy and safe since before 1920, raiding in Sonora and Chihuahua, fighting Turahumari who scouted for the Mexicans, trading with a couple of villages to which Jock gave protection from bandits. And there was the small mine where they extracted enough gold to pay for new weapons and supplies. Jock had strived to live well by serving his people, but he worried about the small numbers of warriors and young women and the survival of the band. And it grieved him, that given the resources of the rancheria, they couldn't grow by much.

Perhaps that was why Ussen wished him to go out again.

Deep in his heart, Jock was haunted by the knowledge that these were the twilight years of the free Chiricahua; they were a shadow of their former selves, their power broken by the wars with the Americans. The Apaches had been battered to defeat by the forces of Manifest Destiny as a horde of White Eyes surged west, bringing civilization, establishing ranches and putting up fences, building railways, erecting telegraph poles, and stringing wire, digging mines and settling the land. Jock kept a special loathing for those Apaches who scouted for the military. He knew that the Apaches could have survived for many more years had they remained united. From time to time, he dreamt that they would never have been defeated by the White Eyes.

For a moment, long discarded Catholic beliefs haunted him, and he worried that Ussen's power was less than the sound and fury of the Holy Trinity worshipped by the White Eyes. But without Ussen's guidance, the band would not have survived. Jock had learnt that the God of The People eschewed the pomp, the thunder and lightning of God the Father, Son and Holy Ghost; Ussen's power worked through mystery and nuance, guiding Jock, allowing no man to sully the honor of the People.

7

One time on San Carlos when the People were bottled up on the reservation, an agent by the name of Reyes refused rations to Sigesh, insulting and striking her. She was the wife of Capitano Leon, a great leader Jock had followed. Jock confronted the man.

"Fuckin' renegade," Reyes said. "You and your nigger squaw. I'll have you arrested."

Jock pistol-whipped Reyes, the barrel of the Confederate Cavalry pistol fracturing a cheek bone and breaking his nose. Then Jock blew Reyes' brains out.

No, if the People were to retain their dignity, they needed to be free.

But how was that possible in 1927? In the last few years Mexicans had begun settling in the Sierra Madre, threatening the rancheria. It was only a matter of time before Mexicans and bounty hunters found a way to attack, and the band might be reduced by the fighting or threatened with destruction. Jock would devote all his power to avoiding that calamity and trusted Ussen to help the band survive and move ever deeper into the Sierra Madre. But a sense of an ending of things hung over him and dampened any optimism.

But he would wait and listen for the coming again of Ussen's power which had allowed the band to flourish in desperate times. He would show Jock a way forward.

"You're going to wear that old jacket?" Jim said. "I thought you'd thrown it out."

Jock brushed the sleeve of the patched and darned waist-length jacket of steel gray wool. He fingered the rolling collar. The braid had worn thin and few buttons remained, not enough to fasten the jacket; and the cuff buttons had long gone.

"It's an officer's jacket. Captain Semmes himself gave it to me when I signed off the *Alabama*."

"I know."

"If I meet any Americans, I want them to know what I am and where I'm from."

Jim finally rose and Jock followed. Kusuma led out his stallion, packed and ready for the journey. Jock stood by it, confident and proud of his appearance, satisfied he was dressed suitably for this journey. An Apache would feel Jock's spiritual strength, perceiving that he was *enthlay-sit-daou* – one who endures and remains calm, clear headed, and courageous whatever danger he faces. Mexican peasants and vaqueros would see that he was well-armed and dangerous and stay out of his way. But to the White Eyes, dressed as he was in high moccasins, long white breech clout, blue calico shirt and red bandana, with the antique weapons, and the Confederate Navy jacket, he was just a shabby old fool from another age; a renegade who'd gone over to the Apaches.

"Tell everyone I'm going north," Jock said to Katsuma.

Jock mounted his horse, and the agonies of arthritis fell away. Confidently working the reins, bringing pressure with his knees, thighs, and heels; offering a soothing whisper in the stallion's ear. Jock and this horse knew each other well.

Jim mounted a black gelding and followed Jock through the two lines of his followers. Jock absorbed the silent respect of the old people, but the warriors and the young fighting women raised Mulberry bows and rifles overhead, pumping them up and down; their cries of 'Yiii, Yiii' making Jock proud.

Jock felt young again and reined the horse round to face his followers. With rifles held overhead they steered the horses back in dignified dressage to the start of the trail down the mountain, Jock filling the air with the cry of She Wolf, and Jim singing out the Old Rebel Yell that in the days with General Stand Watie had scared many a Yankee shitless.

They camped at a quiet place before the aspen and scrub oak faded, close to the start of the Sonoran desert, sitting in darkness and sharing a meal of beef jerky and water. Neither of them wanted to risk a fire so far down the mountains.

"Traveled far, Jock."

"You too, Jim."

"I remember the stories about the ocean back in the old days," Jim said. "I saw the water at Galveston, and one time we went down to the Sea of Cortez, but I never saw the ocean. You've crossed it. You've come further."

"You're right Jim. Scotland is a faraway place."

Jock's White Eyes name was John MacNeil. He was born in 1850 in Westburn, a tough seaport on the River Clyde on the west coast of Scotland. Jock's family were Highlanders from the island of Barra. When he was thirteen, his mother died, and in despair his father killed himself, leaving Jock an orphaned apprentice blacksmith and farrier.

Wrapped in his blanket, Jock remembered going to sea soon after his father's death, signing on as Galley Boy aboard the *Jane Brown*, a schooner trading in home waters. His job was to assist the cook, a slovenly man. Jock smiled. Before long, his skills surpassed the cook's, much to the delight of the small crew. Because he had experience looking after sick and injured horses, and because the steward was usually too drunk to deal with them, Jock began to treat crewmen who were knocked about and felt poorly.

Jock let a hand warm his thigh, gently rubbing heat into an old injury, a legacy of his seafaring when he fell into the hold of the *Jane Brown* and convalesced for a month ashore in the care of Doctor James Gunn, a retired Royal Navy surgeon. Gunn had taught him to clean and dress wounds and bruises and to use the cautery and the suture needle.

James Gunn had washed the wound in Jock's leg with alcohol. It stung.

"Keep still, Jock," James Gunn said. "An Irish surgeon told me about this when I was in the Royal Navy. I don't know why, but the spirit reduces infection. Use it on your patients."

He never forgot James Gunn's advice.

Jock marveled at the direction his life had taken; when he was fourteen, sailing back and forth across the Irish Sea, he couldn't have imagined the path he'd choose, or the life he'd lead.

Jim rubbed his stomach and pulled the blanket closer. "Wish we'd a fire. Could've had rabbit and biscuits and coffee. This damned cold's hurting my arm." Jim pushed back the sleeve of his calico shirt, rubbing his left wrist which had been broken in a Civil War battle. "You fixed this old arm good, but it still reminds me."

Ach, Jim wanted to pick over old times, keeping them awake half the night. Jock's shoulders slumped, weighted by fatigue. Tomorrow, he faced a long day on horseback crossing the Sonoran Desert. He was in no mood for conversation but forced a vigorous nod.

"Then you found 'The Cause'," Jim said.

Jock needed to stretch out; his backside hurt from several hours in the saddle, and his knees sent out warning stabs of pain. Jock was so tired he risked an attack of piles and suppressed an urge to evacuate, leaving the motion dormant until early morning.

The hell with it. He stretched out, tucked the blanket around him. "I was rated Loblolly Boy, helping the Assistant Surgeon on the *Alabama*."

"We met outside Galveston, and you bought the Hawken Rifle before we headed north to join Stand Watie. 'Ol' Rebel Soljers', eh?"

Jim kept talking, but his voice was growing more distant, odd words dropping out of the chatter, marring the sense of what he was saying.

And then Jock drifted into sleep.

Chapter Two

Both men said the morning prayer to Ussen, facing the sunrise, arms raised. The sunlight dispelled the chill and Jock was glad of the warmth as they ate their cold breakfast of beef jerky and water. Jock wanted a firm grip of his surroundings before he'd risk a small smokeless fire to brew coffee and prepare hot food.

"I brought this." Jim held up the wooden-handled cartridge loader, a device resembling oversized pliers with crooked handles. "Make ammunition for the Sharps."

"I'll find a place for it." Jock packed the cartridge loader and the accompanying capper and bullet setter in the saddle bags. "Thanks. Extra bullets for the Buffalo gun never go wrong."

They embraced in farewell.

"You'll be back in the stronghold tonight," Jock said.

"Yes. Take care out there; watch out for the White Eyes."

Jock watched as horse and rider diminished and prayed to Ussen that Jim would have a quiet ascent of the mountain. It would have been good to have Jim with him on the journey, because Jim was an unnerving adversary and knew how to deal with enemies. But Jock knew he had to watch his last friend from the old days slipping into the thickets of aspen and oak. He knew the risks of the way the last free Apaches lived: at any moment they could be killed by enemies. The band needed Jim with them more than Jock did. It grieved him that his friend of more than sixty years might die and he'd never see him again. But Ussen had willed it.

Jock hoped that it was Ussen's will that they'd meet again.

It was the morning of the second day and Jock rode across a prairie of short yellow grass. He relaxed in the warm air and dismounted to gather dried yucca wood. He favored yucca, so easy to start a fire with and burning smokeless. He'd chance a fire and have hot food that night.

Jock remounted and wheeled the chestnut, riding a short way to admire a flowering creosote bush –from a short distance, because he disliked the smell. Ahead, he could just discern the shapes of meadow foxtail and remembered the days, forty and more years ago, when the People rode freely across this land. Riding on he passed agave plants used to make the distilled spirit, clandestino or lechuguillaby, an opaque, heavy flavored spirit. In his younger days he'd tasted it; but these days he drank little or not at all, and never in the company of Mexicans, who'd been known to get Apaches drunk and then massacre them.

Jock felt good that morning as he rode north-east towards the Rio Bravo and Texas. The desert was beautiful, and he was at one with the land; his arthritis had eased, his bowel motions were soft and regular, and he'd stopped worrying about an attack of piles.

The tranquility of the early morning was shattered by the report of a heavy caliber rifle and the whip-crack of a bullet shooting past his head. He wheeled the chestnut around and was faced by an open motor car leading a posse of horsemen across the plain towards him. Mexicans most likely; hunters after game but prepared to scalp an Apache and collect the bounty money.

He'd let his guard down, swept away by the beauty of the desert. He was far too old for that kind of mistake.

Jock leant low in the saddle, and with knees and heels urged his horse around and into a gallop towards a dip in the ground, four hundred yards to his front. Jock had first mastered the dread of combat serving the Confederate cause, and his fighting skills were honed to perfection by his life as a Chiricahua. So he set aside his anger for allowing himself to be surprised by adversaries and drew from deep within himself a calmness as still as the eye of the storm. He drew the pair of Confederate Cavalry pistols from the saddle holsters as he rode, turned in the saddle and fired a couple of shots at the Mexicans. Jock was at long-range, but the shots might distract them.

The arthritis in Jock's knees stabbed painfully as he dismounted, guiding the stallion to the prone position just below the rim of the hollow ground, a maneuver learnt while riding with Stand Watie. Calmly, Jock rested the Sharps rifle across the saddle and laid a few rounds from his bandolier beside it. He got out the long glasses –his eyes weren't so sharp now that he was closing in on eighty years.

The pistol shots had killed the man now lying on the ground. One down and seven to go.

The Mexicans and Americans –surprisingly, he saw three of them dressed in khaki and stiff-brimmed campaign hats –stopped, and stupidly crowded around the car, not even taking cover. From the exaggerated movements and loud voices carried to him by the breeze, it seemed some members of the party were drunk. Perhaps the drink had given them the confidence to attack an old, lone Apache.

Jock wanted no trouble, and hoped they'd withdraw, and he'd get on his way across the Rio Bravo. But if not, he was ready. He was weary of being despised as an Apache, abhorred and feared for becoming a Chiricahua: loathed; a renegade in the eyes of Mexicans and White Eyes. Jock was ready to kill them all for their bias and stupidity.

From the car came a burst of fire from a Browning Automatic Rifle, aimed from the shoulder of a man in a campaign hat who stood in the rear of the car. The rounds flew harmlessly over Jock's head, but the gunner might find his range eventually, so Jock got him in the scope sight of the Sharps, and matter of factly killed him with one round to the chest.

Jock ejected the spent cartridge and reloaded the Sharps, then reloaded the Colt pistols and again examined his pursuers through the long glasses. They appeared to be rattled and frightened. Jock waited, keeping the Sharps trained on them.

The head of a pinto pony came up over the edge of the plain; then a man's head with black hair, bound with a familiar red bandana, streaming behind. A Chiricahua. The unexpected appearance of this lone horseman made him euphoric and although he could deal with his tormentors, he was certain with this newcomer's assistance he could destroy his adversaries. Ussen had surely sent this rider, and together they would triumph.

The pony came into full view, and no sound came from its hooves which were shod in short buckskin boots as they sent up spurts of dust. He got to within one hundred yards of the Mexicans and the Americans before they sensed the rider's presence. The Chiricahua worked the bow beautifully, and four arrows were in flight before the first one hit. Two Mexicans went down, one with an arrow through the neck, the other pierced in the torso.

Jock put two rounds from the Sharps into the radiator, immobilizing their car.

Jock executed an old cavalry maneuver; bringing the stallion's head up by the reins, getting into the saddle as his mount rose and he holstered the Sharps. Drawing the Colt pistols, he galloped towards the enemy while they were confused by the attack from both front and rear. His new ally killed one with his Winchester rifle and Jock got another with the Colt pistols. The one remaining Mexican and two Americans scattered. Jock met his new ally at the car and dismounted – gasping at the arthritic pain in his knees – and unholstered the Sharps.

"Hold the horse's head," Jock said.

The riders moved fast, but Jock got a Mexican in the scope sight and was satisfied when his sombrero lifted as a round smashed into the back of his skull, and he flew out of the saddle.

He looked up to find the Chiricahua gathering the horses near the motor car.

"You shoot well," the Chiricahua said.

"Two of your arrows missed. Let's get those two Americans."

In a few minutes, they were in rifle range and brought the horses to an abrupt halt. Jock nodded to the Chiricahua, and they dismounted. This time he held the horses steady. The Chiricahua rested the Winchester across the saddle; with two rapid rounds the American riders were down. As they rode over to make sure they were dead, the horses drifted back to where the bodies lay. They were two officers, a Major and a Lieutenant in Army uniform; Arizona or New Mexico, maybe Texas National Guard, riding with these hunters.

So somebody must know the hunting party was out, but it was unlikely there would be a search party looking for them for several days. Had these two got back to where they'd started, there would have been a posse chasing them before nightfall.

"Kill the horses," Jock said. "They might find their way home."

The Chiricahua cut the horses' throats and they collapsed in fountains of blood. Jock regretted leaving good saddles, but it wouldn't do to over-burden themselves with loot. But they took the ammunition and the guns and returned to the massacre at the car.

"I didn't want trouble, but I guess we're a war party now."

A thin smile creased Jock's face at the memory of an old Indian killer's words back in the eighteen eighties, "Apache war parties come in all sizes, from two to two hundred."

Jock dismissed his first thought of burning the car and the supplies they couldn't carry; smoke spiraling into a clear sky would draw attention. They took flour, coffee, sugar, and meat from the supplies.

He told the Chiricahua to keep a piebald mare to carry the loot and had him hold the horse's head and whisper and soothe the animal. When the animal calmed, Jock removed the horseshoe nails and discarded the iron horseshoes which would leave clear tracks, then smoothed the hooves with a file.

"Put these on him." He handed the Chiricahua a spare set of buckskin boots. "Can you jerk beef?"

"Yes."

Quickly they cut beef into thin strips and hung it to dry from the saddle of the pack horse. Then they cut the throats of the remaining horses; releasing more gushers of blood. Jock hated doing it, but he couldn't let them drift back to where they'd come from.

Jock's love of horses dated back to when he'd been an apprentice blacksmith, but his life among the Apache, had supplanted that affection with a matter of fact approach to the treatment of the animals. The People could make a horse run faster and farther than any cavalryman, then let it die or kill it when the beast could not go on. A warrior might cut its flesh for food, use the intestine to carry water, then steal another mount. Jock took care of his chestnut stallion, as he did his other mounts, and this noble creature served him well. But he wouldn't hesitate to ride it to death or to cut its throat. The life of the Apache demanded this utilitarian attitude to horses.

"What about the car?" the Chiricahua said.

They slashed the tires and poured sand into the engine sump. Jock knew how to wreck a car from the days when the band rode with Villa, back in 1913. He gave the Chiricahua a side arm and holster. Jock valued the power Ussen had given him to see ahead, but he sensed danger from the White Eyes and was wary regarding what might be in store for them. He decided to take the BAR, its magazines, and the pair of 1897 model Winchester pump action shotguns, and loaded them on the pack horse.

The massacre wouldn't go unnoticed. Posses', the Mexican Army, and bounty hunters would be looking for him and the boy now. Americans could be waiting for them on the border. Calmly, he accepted that Ussen was testing him, and the young Chiricahua too, but Ussen had just provided them with plenty of fire power. The presence of this young man was a boon sent by Him, and he was glad, filled with hope that he could complete Ussen's work and return to his beloved rancheria.

They were ready to leave the wrecked car, the bloody horses and the bodies of the men they'd slain. Unless someone came by soon, the vultures and coyotes would reduce the corpses to carrion: shards of dried flesh hanging on bare bones. The desert was not kind to the dead.

Jock turned to face the Chiricahua. "Who the hell are you, and what are you doing in this wilderness?"

"I'm from the reservation near the Sacramento Mountains. Silver, the Holy Man, had a vision of this place and the attack on you. I know that you are Jock, Chiricahua Apache. Silver knows many things. He told me the stories about the Bronco Apaches, like you, and Masai and the Apache Kid, who hid out in the Sierra Madre and never surrendered. Silver knew of your coming for the last time and shall sing about you, maybe. He sent me to help you and to bring you home safely."

The Chiricahua had come a long way to find Jock. And that was quite a speech for an Apache.

"Silver? Is that old devil still alive?"

"Yes. The Americans let him return in 1913 from Fort Sill, where he was a prisoner of war for twenty-seven years. He is eighty years old and wants to meet you again."

Jock liked the look of this boy: long, thick black hair kept in place by the red bandana, lean and well-muscled, his long off-white breech clout was held up by an old US Army webbing belt with a bowie knife hung in a scabbard. There would be a knife, or perhaps a small pistol concealed in the breech clout. The long moccasins doubled over at the knee with the round, turned up toes, sewn round a piece of leather for protection against thorns and cactus spikes.

"Good moccasins," Jock said. "Just like mine."

The Chiricahua smiled, revealing white, even teeth.

He was well mounted on the pinto pony, with an old, but good Mexican saddle with the big horn. A Winchester rifle sat in a saddle holster, and the unstrung bow in a buckskin case and a quiver of arrows hung from his shoulder.

Once, Jock had looked as good and he had a fleeting image of his elegant, younger self – and the winsome looks Miriam gave him when he came to her father for her hand. Forty years now she'd been gone...

Well, he knew well enough the old and wrinkled face he presented to the world in 1927. If Miriam came back from the dead, still in the bloom of her early middle years, would she love his aged face and withered body? But then were she alive, she too would be diminished by the years passing, and would no doubt still love him.

"You're bleeding," Jock said, catching the boy's arm, examining a graze from a bullet.

The Chiricahua winced as Jock spread the wound. A deep graze, nothing more, but it needed closing and dressing to reduce the risk of infection. Jock sat the Chiricahua on the running board of the car while he got the old Confederate medical kit from the saddle bags. Jock trimmed loose skin from the edges of the graze and dabbed iodine well into the wound; the Chiricahua grimaced, but made no sound.

"I'm going to close the wound and bind it."

The Chiricahua nodded as Jock put on the wire rimmed glasses traded from a Mexican and threaded the fine, curved needle with silk; he put in six close sutures.

"Where'd you learn to do this kind of thing?" the Chiricahua said.

"When I was a sailor a naval surgeon, James Gunn taught me."

"You were a sailor?"

Jock ignored the question. He covered the wound with lint soaked in iodine and bound it tightly with a strip of calico. "It'll do, I'll take out the sutures later. What do they call you?"

"Joe Eagle."

"What's your Chiricahua name?"

"Joe Eagle."

He deserved a better name, but for now, Jock would think of him as 'The Boy'. He glanced at the sun; it was about midway through an eventful morning. Tiredness was forgotten as a savage euphoria took hold. Jock was exultant mounting the chestnut, prancing the stallion around the carnage, then pulling the beast onto its hind legs so that it neighed a protest.

Jock turned the animal's head to the north-east. "Let's get far away from here. Keep deep in the back country. Sooner or later, there'll be a posse out."

They rode at a pace the horses could maintain for many hours, stopping only to water the animals. They were silent most of the time, keeping watch for pursuers or a posse of vigilantes with an excuse to murder them.

As the euphoria dimmed, Jock realized the encounter had shaken him to his very roots. Of course, he was satisfied at the hammering of those damned fools in the hunting party. But Jock admitted to himself that while a solo triumph was likely twenty, even ten years ago, it had been the boy's intervention which made the difference between winning and losing that day.

Jock had wallowed too much in the past cherishing the renascent love for Miriam and the children. Passion for Miriam even stirred his ancient flesh, making him so happy and very horny. He laughed quietly. If he stayed that way, they'd end up dead.

But that had been changed. This journey was like the old days and events had made them a war party. While the boy was capable, he was a young, and it would fall to Jock to lead them through the troubles that awaited them.

That night they camped in Mexico at a quiet place hidden by scrub oaks and mesquite on the shores of Lago de Guzman, a spot Jock knew from the old days. He lit a small and smokeless fire from dry Yucca wood. Jock made biscuits while the coffee was brewing.

The boy chewed silently on biscuits and jerked beef. Jock moistened jerky in the remains of his coffee and nibbled cautiously on a biscuit.

"Why are you wetting the jerky?"

"My teeth are few."

Jock moistened another strip of jerky and tentatively chewed on it, his tongue searching for hard bits that might threaten his surviving loose molars. The boy smiled.

"You're amused? It's ahead of you should you live so long. Then you'll smile, gap-toothed, out the other side of your face."

"I apologize for my rudeness, Old One."

Jock dismissed the boy's apology with a wave of his hand, but he was glad that he'd shown the traditional respect for the aged. "Just call me Jock."

"We're not far from Tres Castillos?"

"It lies to the west."

The boy wanted to talk about the old raiding days when the People were in their glory, but Jock was not in the mood to discuss the massacre of Victorio's band.

"A victory the Mexicans called it, but it was murder. I met Nana afterwards when he raided to avenge Victorio. He killed many Mexicans and White Eyes."

Jock told the boy about that raid. He wanted the young man to know that when they could, the free Chiricahua attacked the White Eyes. The boy, reservation-bred, may not have experienced it.

"You've heard of Pancho Villa?"

"Yes."

"When he raided Columbus, New Mexico, a war party followed him."

In March 1916, Villa brought five hundred Mexicans north and sacked Columbus. They took about a hundred mules and horses from the US Cavalry, killed eighteen Americans. Villa lost eighty men and then crossed into Texas.

"It was the Chiricahua that attacked Glen Springs. We killed a White Eyes and wounded soldiers. Then we raided San Ygnacio and rubbed out the soldiers there."

"My father knew it was Chiricahua from the Sierra Madre."

"The Americans said it was Villa. They were afraid to admit it was Chiricahua."

They sat by the fire a while. The boy had retreated into silence, hard to read. What was on his mind?

"You've chosen a hard path, son," Jock said. "Not much future in it. If the Americans catch you, they'll kill you. The Mexicans'll sell your scalp. But thank you for coming to my aid this morning."

"It was my duty. I chose the warrior's path."

"Then I'll teach you the ways of the true Apache. Maybe your arrows won't miss, and you might live a little longer."

Jock took the first watch and let the boy sleep. The young buck's need of rest was greater than his own. Jock sat, back resting on a boulder, the Sharps Rifle across his bent knees. The blanket was wrapped round his hunched shoulders, and the glowing embers of the low fire kept him warm and alert, watching over the boy. He fell into a shallow sleep and Miriam came to him. She was whole, unblemished, free of the scalp hunter's wounds; lovely, ghostly in her white buckskin dress.

"Oh, Jock, my husband."

It had been several years since Miriam had last come to him and he was filled with happiness, his heart aching with love for her.

"Stay awhile," he said. "Lay by my side."

"No, my love. Another time; and soon. You shall need your strength in the days ahead. Do not worry, I bring Ussen's Power for you and the boy."

Miriam laid her hands on Jock, touching his chest and his arms; then his legs and knees and he knew that he would be strong.

Jock reached out to touch her, to keep her from going, even if only for another moment or two, but Miriam laid her fingers on his lips.

"No, my love; wait for me."

And she vanished into the darkness.

It was another day's ride to the Rio Bravo del Norte and the border. There would be little sleep as they waited to cross in the dark hour before dawn when the Americans and Mexicans should be sleeping.

Jock and the boy rode steadily that second day and were not yet pursued. Jock was pleased by the boy's bravery and fighting skills. When he was the boy's age, he was a disciplined sailor and medical assistant on the *CSS Alabama* and a little later skilled in field craft and soldiering, taught by his mentor, Cherokee Jim when he'd enlisted with Stand Watie.

If only his son, Runs With Horses had lived to become a warrior.

Now – and the irony wasn't wasted on Jock – he, a renegade Chiricahua would put the finishing touches to the boy's warrior apprenticeship. Though they'd yet to speak of it, this young buck understood what he must do to win. Jock felt that he could rely on him to watch for danger and talk as they rode.

"Tell me about your life."

The boy was born in 1910 at Fort Sill, Oklahoma on the military reservation. His father was a Chiricahua prisoner of war. The family were allowed back to Apache country in 1913 – not to their true homeland, but squeezed in on the Mescalero Reservation in New Mexico, near Mayhill and Ruidoso. Silver, the Holy Man, taught him some of the old ways out on the Sacramento Mountains when he came back from the Indian School in Phoenix.

"I hated that place. They tried to turn me into a White Eyes. I am Chiricahua."

The boy's life at the school was regulated by the disciplinarians of the Bureau of Indian Affairs. Whistle blasts and bugle calls controlled the inmates. Their hair was cut short to fit the tastes of the White Eyes. They were obliged to wear a uniform, and hard shoes. Boys and girls were marched everywhere.

"They said our religion was bad; that we must stop believing in Ussen. I went through the motions of becoming a Catholic, but, I kept the hatred to myself and they were pleased with me."

"I was born a Catholic. It didn't stick for me, either."

They talked for a while, and Jock discovered that the boy learned to work metal and that he had a gift –his green fingers transformed the school garden into a tasteful composition of vegetables and flowers. When he returned to his people, he assumed responsibility for the family corn field and garden, planting mesquite beans, chilies, potatoes, celery and onions; and he pleased his mother by establishing a fragrant rose bed.

The boy had left the school eighteen months previously in 1925. The reservation wasn't much, but he was glad to get back to his family. By outwardly pleasing the School Superintendent, the boy had disciplined himself to keep his Apache identity and shake off the dead hands of the Bureau of Indian Affairs, deflecting attempts to make him a patriot. The bureaucrats didn't understand that patriotism as they knew it meant nothing to Apaches, who loved their territory alone.

"What about you, Jock? You were once a White Eyes before you grew wise and became one of the People."

"That's true. I'm seventy-seven years old. It was a long time ago, even if it sometimes feels like yesterday."

They rode hard and lay up at a quiet place nearby, but hidden from the border. The boy gathered dry mesquite for a smokeless fire. There would be no sleep as they waited until just before dawn to cross the river into Texas. The border crossing might be difficult, and Jock decided they might as well eat some decent food. Both of them wanted coffee and looked forward to roasting the rabbit the boy had killed with the bow that afternoon. He had deftly gutted and skinned the carcass.

Jock had flints and a steel, and matches, but used a bow drill to make fire. He liked to keep his hand in for the day when those other aids might not be available.

"You know what this is?" He held up the drill.

"No."

"Then watch; learn something."

Jock rapidly rotated the wooden drill through a hearth piece, over a pile of dry yucca bark placed in a hollow in the earth. Soon the bark smoked, and Jock coaxed live flames.

"Next time you can make the fire."

The boy slowly fed the dry mesquite into the fire and Jock prepared the mix for biscuits. Jock passed a sharp stick through the rabbit, and they took turns roasting it. And Jock talked about his early life.

Jock MacNeil's father, a blacksmith and farrier, moved from the island of Barra in 1850, seeking a better life than he could find in the Western Isles. He settled in Westburn, where they were Catholics in a Protestant land; that they were Scots didn't matter to the Calvinists of Westburn who lumped them with Irish Catholics. From an early age, Jock knew prejudice and resentment.

Jock's father worked hard, and the family survived, but dreams of paradise on earth floundered in that dire Westburn slum, the Old Vennel. Yet Jock had the benefit of schooling until he was near thirteen, and valued his literacy and numeracy, accomplishments he used well in later life.

It was the diphtheria which suffocated Jock's mother; and when she died, his father sought relief in drink and lost his grip on life. In despair, he put Jock's younger brother and sister into an orphanage, assuming his eldest son would watch out for them. Later, enveloped by melancholy, he threw himself into the West Harbor and drowned. The police said it was an accident but Jock, already a shrewd observer of men, knew otherwise.

Jock MacNeil might have surrendered himself to charity and, like his brother and sister, found himself at the mercy of priests and nuns. The iron in his soul anchored him to the grim realities of Westburn, and though grieving the loss of his mother and father, Jock, showing a maturity beyond his years, declined to have anything to do with the Catholic Church. At thirteen he might have been made a ward of the court and been driven behind the grim walls of a Catholic institution, but a kindly Protestant neighbor, a blacksmith, took him in, keeping Jock at school for a few months and giving him a job in the forge as an apprentice blacksmith and farrier. This man's goodness was Jock's sole experience of Christian charity. But, after some months he knew that these arrangements couldn't last. Jock took up space in an overcrowded tenement flat; he was a drain on the meager resources of the blacksmith, his wife, and their four children. So Jock went to sea.

The blacksmith, secretly glad that he was leaving, did the best for Jock that his circumstances allowed: he gave him five shillings from his savings to start the journey and a small, well-thumbed, leatherbound King James Bible. For a time, Jock turned to the Good Book, but the way Christians behaved quickly drove him from it.

When Jock left to follow the sea, he had the shabby rags he stood in, his mother's sash of fine blue linen, and a pewter quaich that had belonged to his grandfather. Jock had sold his father's pipes, as he himself played badly, but he kept the concertina. Jock made it all into his bundle, in a MacNeil tartan shawl, and hung it from his shoulder.

The boy was impressed by the story of Jock's self-confidence, and his willingness to take responsibility for his life. But he was wary of the way, alien to the Apache, he'd summarily abandoned his siblings to the care of the Catholic Church. He didn't quite say as much, but Jock could see it there.

Ah, but then the boy couldn't see the tender-hearted Jock, or his cherished memories of childhood; the artless days of laughter shared with poor Irish neighbors; the barefoot children playing; the busy hawkers and wifies wrapped in tartan shawls; the warm sense of belonging to the Old Vennel. Nor could the boy know of the happy times with his mother full of life, his father making money at the forge, and their loving family. Jock fondly recalled family walks after Sunday Mass in the quiet streets of the affluent West End. But nostalgia for the idealized past did not assuage his guilt at forsaking his brother and sister.

"It was bad, selfish, abandoning them, but I had myself to worry about." It was difficult to acknowledge the guilt and regret he harbored after so many years. "I never saw my brother and sister again after I joined the Confederate Navy."

"I've never seen the sea," the boy said. "What's it like?"

Jock looked at the Boy and smiled, pleased by the response to the pain of his old emotional scars.

"It's like the desert, always there and always dangerous."

Jock waved his hands representing the motions of a ship under sail in heaving waters that bring sea sickness; short grey, drab seas, choppy in foul weather. Then, leveling his palms, in the passage of a vessel through smooth blue tropical ocean, the color of the sky.

"On my first voyage to Ireland it was rough, and I spewed my guts up. But I liked a calm sea. I cooked and helped sick and injured sailors."

The boy smiled and touched his wounded arm. "So that's why the biscuits and the rabbit were so good."

"Later on, I joined the Confederate Navy; Loblolly Boy, helping the Assistant Surgeon."

"I wondered about that gray uniform jacket."

"An officer's jacket. Captain Semmes gave it to me when I served on the *Alabama*. I've looked after it. But it's like me, often repaired."

They crossed the border south of Ciudad Juarez, undetected by the Mexican posse. There were riders showing many lights on the Texas bank, but they were easily avoided in that dark hour before dawn.

But though Jock and the boy were careful to leave no trace of their passing, keeping mostly to hard ground, the river bank on the American side was soft sand, and someone with experience picked up their trail. Seven riders pursued them after they'd forded the Rio Bravo. The posse threatened the plan, to cut across the corner of North West Texas and into New Mexico. The riders had to be Americans. They must have figured seven against two was good odds.

Jock, no longer concerned to avoid a fight, left a clear trail.

"Let's see if they take the bait. If they do, we'll set an ambush."

The posse wasn't careful and followed the trail. Jock and the boy rode the horses hard and got far ahead of the riders. Jock knew this corner of Texas from the old days.

"There's a creek just ahead; dry at this time of year. Hide the horses and get back here. Stay off the trail."

Jock had the long glasses on the posse. One rider ahead reading sign; behind him six riders in American uniforms. Cavalry? Texas National Guard? They'd find out soon enough, the riders were now less than a mile away and coming up fast. The tracks were clear; all the posse had to do was follow them.

"We'll hide in the sand," Jock said. "You go twenty yards up the trail. I'll stay here. We'll use the shotguns, perfect for this close work, and pistols. When you hear me firing, come out."

Attacking front and rear. It would be unexpected and confusing for the enemy, who would expect two fugitive Apaches to keep running.

The Boy licked his lips, and Jock suspected he was worried at the prospect of close-in fighting, perhaps fighting hand-to-hand.

"Concentrate on what you have to do. You know how to use the shotgun; I showed you. It'll be over quickly. There's no room for doubt: we'll kill them all."

Jock waited until the boy had covered himself in the light, drifting sand. He listened to the wind moving through low scrub oaks and mesquite; a Gila woodpecker tapped busily; a hummingbird with vivid plumage hovered, sucking from a mesquite bush. Then he dug into the sand himself. It was a good setup.

Jock waited until he heard seven sets of hoofbeats pass him, then came out of the sand, aimed the weapon, and fired three rounds, downing the rear riders. As he worked, the boy came up, wraith-like from the bowels of the earth, sand flying from him. He shot two more out of the saddle. Jock shuffled forward as fast as his arthritic knees allowed and they fired simultaneously, killing the last two riders, then they shot the milling horses. It was over in less than a minute.

They reloaded the Winchesters, and Jock walked among the stricken riders. One man, not in uniform, groaned in agony from the bloody wound on his back. Jock turned him over with his foot. He was in his seventies, but younger than Jock, and like him, a survivor from the frontier, paying his dues now for negligence, for spending too much time in bars cadging drinks, playing the Old Indian Fighter.

"I knew it was you, Jock, you fuckin' Red Nigger," he spat through bloody foam.

Jock looked at him for maybe ten seconds before the killing craze, the *hesh-ke*, gripped him and he fired twice at the man's head. When the flies descended on the bloody mess which was once his face Jock walked away, then turned back, and fired the shotgun into his groin ruining his vital parts. He went among the bodies and fired more rounds, reducing heads to a bloody mush before the boy got a restraining hand on Jock's shoulder.

"Jock, Jock! They're dead!"

"*Dah-eh-sah*; dead. That was John Injun, a murderer of women and children; an Indian killer, a seller of Apache scalps to the Mexicans. Our people hated and feared him."

The boy looked at the mess of John Injun's groin and vomited up what was left of last night's rabbit.

"But you defiled him," the boy said, wiping away threads of puke hanging from his mouth.

Jock rammed the shotgun into the boy's gut.

"Listen, you damned fool, that man took part in the Camp Grant Massacre. Whites from Tucson brought a bunch of killers, Mexicans and O'odham. Wouldn't tell you about that at the school."

Camp Grant: with the warriors out hunting, the O'odham slaughtered the rest. The people they missed were picked off by the whites of Tucson and Mexicans. These vigilantes murdered more than one hundred Arivapas and Pinal Apaches, butchered all but eight women and captured twenty-seven children. To have his people killed while under the protection of the US Army; that was Chief Eskimizen's reward for trying to live in peace with the White Eyes.

Jock thrust the shotgun harder into his gut, and the boy stared at him, shocked and afraid. But the *hesh-ke* was still on Jock, and he didn't care.

"I defiled him to take his power and keep him in the dark place forever. He cannot pass to the other side when his body is corrupted. Don't judge me ever again, or I'll kill you. I didn't ask you to come, you wanted the warrior's way. Did you think it would be warpaint and victory songs around the campfire? They started this round, and I'll finish it. They meant to kill us; torture us, cut off our heads maybe. A quick death was too good for them."

It was a long speech for Jock, and it helped to calm the killing rage.

"I'm sorry, Jock." The boy slowly pushed the shotgun from his belly as he backed away.

"Leave if you can't deal with it, but they'll kill you for sure."

"I'll stay. I can handle it. I'll learn."

"You're in this up to your neck, son. It started when you came south to find me. I don't know yet if we're *Schicho*, friends, but we're bound by *nah-welh'-coht kah-el-keh*. You understand? You're a free Apache."

The boy understood. Silver had evidently taught him the law of *nah-welh'-coht kah-el-keh*; the duty to take as many of the enemy down as possible. A warrior, even if wounded, or threatened by the guns of the enemy, must give his life for the sake of a fellow warrior, and the safety of the band. Jock had absorbed the law, and now the boy could not escape it.

Jock told the boy to pack the posse's ammunition and arms while he butchered the rear leg of a horse for jerky. *Thlee*, the odor of horse, overpowered the stench of dead men. He put on the wire framed glasses and removed the main intestine, trimmed and cleaned it; filled with water and tied at both ends it would be an excellent water carrier. They would need more water where they were going.

"We'll burn everything we can't carry. The bodies too, except John Injun's. Cut off his clothes and leave him naked. I want them to know what they're up against."

Jock hadn't spoken so many words together in years. He'd not looked for trouble, but the Mexicans and the White Eyes had left him no choice. Now they were dead. Back in the rancheria he'd played with attacking the cavalry and dismissed the idea as foolhardy. But Ussen sent them power and gave them victory. Just one old renegade Apache and the boy, and they'd vanquished these trouble makers.

But perhaps their triumphs came too easily. A preparation for greater troubles that lay ahead? Trials that would stretch Jock and the boy to the limit?

"Take the horses back to the Rio Bravo." He'd want any pursuer to think they'd gone back to Mexico. Jock cut a branch from a scrub oak. "On your way back, wipe out your trail. Tie the branch to the saddle horn and trail it behind the pack horse."

That would fool the Americans, as long as they didn't have an Apache scout with them. And Jock was sure that at this stage, in Texas, they wouldn't.

Jock searched thoroughly, salvaged what he could from the American's belongings and was surprised to find sticks of dynamite in the saddle-bags. He packed them carefully, perhaps he could make use of them later. Jock decided to lay low for a while; let the fear and panic of the White Eyes subside before heading northwest to his old stronghold. On the way they'd lie up and make a cache of food, blankets and ammunition.

Jock got out his buckskin bag of sacred pollen, the Tule or Cattail that the People called *Hodentin*, and threw a pinch to each of the four winds, seeking additional blessings from Ussen. They would need it.

Chapter Three

As Jock and the boy disappeared into the San Andreas Mountains, a force meant to destroy them was gathering south of the border at the small town of Samalayuca. Neither the Mexican nor the American Government wanted to acknowledge that there was trouble with Apaches from the Sierra Madre. So word went out to the local authorities: deal with the hostiles, but keep it quiet. Hire a few good men, organize a force, then locate and destroy the renegades. The Americans would pay the bills, but the attack had to happen south of the Rio Grande. That way, any fighting could be denied, rejected as a concern for the Mexican Government. No one could suggest that American politicians couldn't control Apaches.

What the authorities most feared was a repeat of the rows which broke out in the press and among Tucsonians, and along the border when the Bronco Apaches continued raiding for years after Geronimo surrendered in 1886. The authorities wanted no rumors of an Indian War, or the appearance of latter day Masais or Apache Kids terrifying the citizens, with the newspapers demanding the Army do something. This way, if the Apaches were destroyed, well and good. If things went belly up and the Apaches mauled the force, the authorities would deny having anything to do with a border rabble stirring up trouble, hunting Apaches for heads and scalps to sell to the state of Chihuahua.

The inhabitants of Samalayuca watched disinterestedly as hard, shabby men – most on horseback, some driving ramshackle cars, and a few impoverished enough to be on foot – passed through the town to the camp near the Ochoa Ranch, a splendid, remote place in the desert looking onto distant hills. The State of Chihuahua had secured the ranch as the base of operations against the hostiles.

This was no regular military force but broke ex-soldiers, long out of uniform. A handful of Texas National Guardsmen on leave, comrades of the Guardsmen slain by Jock and the boy, formed a disciplined backbone, but they had come for money and revenge. A smattering of Rurales and an officer informally represented Mexico. The rest were worn-out bounty hunters; American and Mexican border riff raff, no better than brigands.

Joe MacIntosh, on the other hand, was a genuine relic from the frontier. When he was offered the job of scouting for Major Richard Hargan, his first reaction was to refuse; he'd done enough campaigning against the Apache as a cavalryman in the frontier days to respect them, especially when they'd been poorly treated after Geronimo's surrender in 1886. But the money was a tempting windfall for his declining years. With the frontier ending and the South West growing quiet, MacIntosh worked as a Regulator for some cattlemen in Wyoming, then he had run guns for Villa and Zapata for a while. Now he was running a fishing boat out of the little port of Anton Lizardo, south of Veracruz. He was happy there with his Mexican widow and her children and made enough to live on. But twelve thousand dollars, paid in advance, prised him loose from the domesticity of his twilight years. So, he buried his sympathy for the Chiricahua who'd been made prisoners of war in Florida, Alabama and Oklahoma, his anger at the broken promises to let them return home after two years.

No white man could find sign of Jock – it had to be Jock –and his companion. It would take an Apache to unearth Jock's meager spoor and decipher it. So Joe MacIntosh brought along two Mescalero Apaches from the reservation near the Sacramento Mountains in New Mexico; relatives by marriage, trackers, old hands, retired from the reservation police. He was amused by the curiosity and fear of the locals at the sight of two unarmed Apaches alighting from the train in Nogales, quiet and dignified in jeans and dark jackets, expression-less faces in shadow under stiff hat brims, walking awkwardly in new cowboy boots.

Out in the desert they adopted the quiet, menacing demeanor of the warrior, changing into calico shirts, breech clouts and long moccasins, their shoulder length black-grey hair bound by a bandana. MacIntosh smiled at the change in his charges, their solemn acceptance of the Colt pistols and Winchester rifles, their expert inspection of the weapons. Joe MacIntosh had insisted on them each being paid two thousand five hundred dollars, in advance. He knew they would earn their money.

While Major Richard Hargan, US Army (Retired), gentleman rancher of Van Horn, Texas, organized the main force, Joe MacIntosh and the two Mescaleros scouted the site of the massacre of the hunting party and the destruction of the posse of Texas National Guardsmen. The Mescaleros carefully read sign and had found fragments of suture, slivers of human skin, and faint traces of blood under the running board of the car; and they took note of John Injun's defiled remains. That's what said it was Jock to them.

MacIntosh and the two Mescaleros rode into Ochoa Ranch, the sun at their back, shadows leading them in. MacIntosh dismounted near the man awaiting them, removed a wide brimmed hat and wiped his brow with a red neckerchief. The two men weighed up each other. MacIntosh knew that to Hargan, he was a tramp, dressed old time in turned down long moccasins, greasy pants, and a buckskin shirt. But to be fair, to MacIntosh, Hargan was an overdressed, fleshy middle-aged dandy in starched khakis, polished brown field boots, with a campaign hat shading his face. MacIntosh's keen eye noted that insignia and badges of rank had been removed from Hargan's uniform. He disliked the way Hargan impatiently swung a swagger stick against his leg.

"Nice place you got here," he said evenly. MacIntosh reached into his saddle bag and withdrew a bottle of tequila blanco, three quar-ters full, and uncorked it. MacIntosh handed the bottle to the nearest Mescalero who took a long pull and passed it to the other Mescalero who also drank deeply. MacIntosh took a couple of long slugs, deliberately didn't wipe the neck, and offered it to Hargan, who didn't hide his distaste as he shook his head.

"The boys and me needed that," MacIntosh said, as he returned the bottle to his saddle bag. "It's Jock who's out. Leads the last of the free Apaches down in the Sierra Madre; been down there for years. Knew him back in the old days. Didn't think he'd come north again."

"Jock? Isn't that an odd name for an Apache?"

"Used to be a white man, a Scot. He was a Corpsman on the *Alabama*, before he rode with General Stand Watie in the Civil War."

"A renegade. It's time he was captured and tried, or killed. He should have been shot or deported at the end of the Civil War."

MacIntosh let that one pass and waited a long moment. He'd always quietly admired how Jock lived and what he'd achieved. When he'd drunk enough whiskey, MacIntosh wished he'd had the guts to live as Jock did. Perhaps he would have gone over himself if his lovely Mescalero wife, Her Voice Is The Sound of Falling Water, had lived. They'd only been married months, and MacIntosh had never been happier in his life, when she was killed by drunken miners near their small horse ranch. God, he had fallen in love with this girl of eighteen when he first saw her. The black hair arranged in ornate plaits framing the lovely face of Her Voice Is The Sound of Falling Water still haunted MacIntosh.

He'd brought charges, but the court discharged the miscreants. The judge gave his opinion before deliberations that the Mescalero Squaw was shot by accident and the jury said the miners were innocent. MacIntosh had prayed for justice but in his heart, he knew that no white jury in Arizona would convict their own kind for killing an Apache. He wanted to kill the miners himself, but he would have been hanged, so he buried his grief and waited, and took a job scouting for hostiles with the Army. Later, he'd put the word out among his Mescalero relatives. Eventually they sent word that his wife's killers had been blown up in a mining accident.

"Become a Chiricahua Apache when he was about sixteen. Must be in his late seventies by now, about seventy-seven or seventy-eight. Older than me. His people say he's a healer."

"His people! Who the fuck are his people? A murdering rabble; vermin! The Army should've exterminated them years ago."

MacIntosh nodded in the direction of the Mescaleros. "They're relatives of mine and speak English, Cap'n. One's my brother in law and the other's his cousin."

"Get rid of them. They stink and so do you. The sight of them makes me sick."

"Well, we ain't been in camp polishing our boots, Cap'n. You want to find Jock, you'll need them. You want to get rid of them, I may as well go, too."

Hargan had sense enough to climb down. "Brief me, Mr. MacIntosh."

"Jock never surrendered. Not in 1865 or 1886, Cap'n. A real Bronco Apache."

MacIntosh explained the unfolding of events since the attack on the hunting party. An old Apache traveling alone, minding his own business, still trying to avoid trouble. He would have returned to the Sierra Madre and brought warriors with him if he'd intended serious trouble. Jock hadn't started the journey to make war, but he and his companion were now ready to fight.

"He hasn't attacked since the wipe out of the Texas National Guard a week ago. We'd have heard about it. Jock was coming north for something, maybe religious reasons, when the hunters tried to kill him, reckoning he was easy meat. He got two of them before this other Apache – and I'm sure he's a Chiricahua – came, and I don't know why or how he got there. Probably sent by some Holy Man. But they rubbed out them hunters. And John Injun an' them Texans from the National Guard: a bunch of damned fools. They were asking for it."

MacIntosh took another slug of tequila.

"They're a tough pair. Jock's a piece of work, but I figure he won't attack if he's left alone."

"Perhaps. But religion, Mr. MacIntosh? What the hell has religion got to do with it?"

"Oh, very religious, Apaches, Cap'n. They believe in Ussen, in spite of missionaries and the government trying to knock it out of them. Jock's not a Holy Man, but he's a disciple of Ussen. Gives him special powers."

"Superstitious nonsense. And it's Major Hargan, Scout."

MacIntosh squirted a stream of tobacco juice into the dust, spattering Hargan's shiny boots. "Right, Cap'n. You're up against an old guerrilla, from out in the Nations. He won't run from you an' he'll chose where to fight you. Started with Stand Watie and perfected fighting with some of them Missouri Boys. Perfected it some more with great Apache warriors. Tell you something else; he's got a BAR and ammunition. Took it from the car. Some other supplies, and the dynamite them Texans was carrying. You ought to start worrying about it."

"I think we can deal with one old man and his helper."

"Well, I sure hope so, Cap'n. Jock hates us. Years ago, bunch of Texas scalp hunters – lowest form of mankind – murdered his wife and children. I knew Miriam, she was a good-looking black woman, daughter of a runaway slave. Apaches took her in."

Hargan stood tall, the aloof commander, staring at MacIntosh. "I can't understand why a white man would make his life among savages and take up with a black squaw."

MacIntosh looked back at the Mescalero scouts sitting quietly in the saddle, rifle butts resting there. He turned back, spat tobacco juice into the dust in the space between them.

Hargan stirred the dust with the toe of his boot, wilting under the eyes of MacIntosh and the two Apaches.

How could he convince this idiot what he was up against?

"Look, Cap'n," MacIntosh said. "Jock and that other Chiricahua have got some important people worried. They got me worried."

"Scout, it's 1927. Fifteen people are dead because of these hostiles. Our job is to get them back into Mexico, trail them to their stronghold and destroy it. I'm going to eliminate this trash, once and for all. If we could handle the Huns, we should be able to take on two Apaches. Now, do you do you know where these two Apaches are?"

"All I can tell you is that they've headed toward the San Andreas Mountains after the slaughter of the Texans and John Injun. That was more than a week ago. By now, they could be just about anywhere in New Mexico or Arizona. Hundred men might not find them, it's way too many. Make a lot of dust and noise, even if you divide them. Me and the Mescaleros' got a better chance. Say we find Jock; send him home? He ain't ever coming back here."

Jock hadn't done more than defend himself from attackers who meant to kill him. Left to himself, he would return to the Sierra Madre for whatever reason, then go home when his journey was over.

"Jesus Christ, Scout!" Hargan said. "Our job is to get them back into Mexico, trail them to their stronghold, and kill everyone in it."

"He was attacked, Cap'n. Put the lid on it now."

"Fuck you and these damned Apaches. I'm going to eliminate these vermin, once and for all. Are you on our side, or not?"

Right then, MacIntosh made up his mind to meet the letter of his agreement; he badly needed the money. But MacIntosh would never join the spirit of Hargan's command.

"I'm not on anyone's side. Me and the two Mescaleros'll track for you, and we'll defend ourselves, but we're not killing for you. We'll leave now if you like, but the Apaches'll keep their money; and you can shove mine up your backside. I told you what I think. You do what the fuckin' hell you want, Cap'n."

Hargan looked as if he wanted to shoot MacIntosh on the spot for insolence. But MacIntosh knew he had him over a barrel. Where would Hargan find another scout and trackers? Only question was, would Hargen let his anger override his sense.

For the second time in the hour, he climbed down. "All right, all right; we have a job to do. Let's get on with it. Can we pin the hostiles down?"

The Mescaleros sat quietly. MacIntosh breathed deeply. "No idea. But once, Jock told me he'd been happy in Oak Creek Canyon; had a secret place, a stronghold in the Dragoons. His wife and children were murdered somewhere in the Parjarita Wilderness, but he buried his family in this place. I don't know where the grave is. I figure he'll move between them places. Be hard to find him. Sometime, he's coming south again. The question is where."

"So, he won't go north?"

"His people are down south. He'll go back to them in time." MacIntosh pulled out a map. "Much of his happy life in the old days happened to the west, in Arizona. He'd go there and might cross the border somewhere south east of Tucson on his way back to the Sierra Madre." He described an arc, tracing his forefinger across the map, taking in Nogales to the west and Douglas to the east. "Somewhere in there. My guess is to the east; shortest route to the Sierra Madre."

"Scout, I don't think you've got reason to be afraid," Hargan said. "I'll have well in excess of a hundred men to divide into compact, mounted, well-armed patrols. And I've got a little surprise in store for these hostiles; a bi-plane, a Curtiss JN27."

"You've got a Jenny?"

Hearing MacIntosh's familiarity with the plane put a little damper on Hargan's flowing enthusiasm, but he recovered.

"The plane will be the all-seeing eyes of the force," he said. "We'll search that area; the plane sweeping a wider area along the border, ahead of the patrols."

"The Old Jenny's slow," MacIntosh said. "Jock might have a shot or two at it; bring it down."

"It's armed with a Lewis Gun in the rear cockpit. There's a gunner. I think we can deal with these two miscreants."

Hargan's confidence was flying as high as his expected plane again. All that power against one old renegade and his accomplice, a couple of old holdovers from the nineteenth century. No, there was nothing MacIntosh could say that would penetrate the man's arrogance. He'd heard of Hargan's service, going up against the Moros in the Philippines. But the man just didn't understand. Fightin' Apaches, well, it's another kind of war entirely.

Jock forgot the pain in his arthritic knees and shuffled in a small circle, puffs of dust rising from the soles of his long moccasins as he swayed and ducked, evading the missiles flying from the boy's sling. When the boy paused to reload, Jock, careful to avoid hitting him in the face, slung a well-aimed sharp stone. It hit on the torso, hard enough to hurt. Then a round stone flew out of the boy's sling and struck Jock a glancing blow on the top of the head. He went down, but not too heavily, feigning unconsciousness.

The boy, half scared at what he'd done, sprinted across the space separating them and crouched beside Jock, gently touching the bump rising on his scalp. "Jock?"

The boy stiffened when Jock pressed the cool metal against his neck and cocked the twin hammers. Jock opened one eye. "If I was a White Eyes, you'd be dead."

"What the hell is that?"

"It's a Derringer; two barrels, forty-four bullets; blow your head off this close. I keep a pair hidden in the leggings of my moccasins."

"Sorry I hit you."

"You're supposed to hit me; it's good that you did. Must be getting old."

"Are you teaching me again?"

Jock grabbed the boy's outstretched arm and got to his feet. "Yes! And you need it."

On arriving at the canyon, they'd settled the horses, feeding and watering, rubbing them down, inspecting saddles and harness, and the short deerskin boots worn by their mounts. Then they reconnoitered the canyon, going up to the rim, pinpointing the way which led over the top of the ridge to safety, were they to be discovered, and building several rock piles at strategic places where they could be sent crashing down on enemies below.

Jock glanced around. It was good to be back here after so many years, to camp again in the secret place in the San Andreas Mountains. Though Apache scouts had known of it in the old days, by 1927 its undisturbed appearance confirmed the Apaches had forgotten, and the White Eyes had never known.

They'd set up camp in a secluded canyon, carpeted in grass, decorated with mesquite and scrub oak; there was a sign of game in this quiet place. At a pretty spot, near water, they built a wickiup, hidden and not too close – water might draw in enemies searching for them.

"Up to the ridge; want to be sure everything is in place."

Jock walked stiffly on the rear slope leading out of the canyon, the Sharps cradled in his left arm, his arthritic knees slowing him down as the incline steepened. His pride made him curtly decline the stick, cut and offered by the boy. Jock found the cave he remembered from the old days, where they might make a cache of moccasins, clothing, food, weapons and ammunition. They could have lived in the cave, but Jock disliked settling anywhere he might be bottled up by an enemy, and he dreaded the rattlesnakes that made their home in such places. But it was good for depositing essential supplies.

He handed the long glasses to the boy who leaned the Winchester against his leg and swept the canyon rim, then searched the floor of the canyon below.

"No one," the boy said. "Beautiful here."

Jock nodded; he and the boy needed rest, for there had been much killing in the days since the boy had come to his aid. But there was also a need to keep their attention heightened, for they might be threatened by enemies at any time. The boy needed to unwind a little, but he must not become complacent.

The boy walked ahead, and he might have been the Jock of sixty years ago when he first visited the canyon, part of a raiding party returning from Mexico with much loot and livestock. Then, Jock had been glad to leave the canyon, caring only that his share of the horses would be enough to ask Miriam's father for her hand. He was the last man of the rearguard across the pass, and with reins in his left hand, rifle in his right, Jock excitedly kicked his horse to life, scrambling up the slope and down the other side, heading for Miriam and home.

Two horses would have been enough, but sick with worry, Jock, just seventeen, offered four to Miriam's father. He needn't have worried.

When he and the boy returned from scouting the canyon, thoughts of Miriam overwhelmed Jock as they had so often in the forty and more years since she was murdered. He felt an old done man. He worried if he could go on, doubting that he was fit for Ussen's work, so filled with longing and grief as he was. To the scalp hunter who killed her, his beloved was just a 'Nigger Squaw'. Jock would never forgive it. He'd avenged her death, but vengeance had left him empty. Miriam, such a beautiful and endearing girl had cared for him so tenderly.

Miriam's death mask came to Jock, her beauty, marred by horror and indignation at what was happening to her and their children. The bloody mess that was the top of her head. Then the hate came as he remembered the twisted bodies of his scalped, dead children. Jock chewed his bottom lip before the tears had a chance to spill over. He turned to look at the pass at the head of the canyon, wiping away the blood and tears.

The boy needed Jock's knowledge of the old Apache way to survive their ordeal. But at that moment Jock's confidence deserted him, and the boy must have seen it.

"What are you thinking about?" he said.

"My wife. It was not so far from here that we first met. I'm tired son; just an old wreck now. Don't know what I'm doing here. Why has Ussen asked this of me?"

"Done all right so far," the boy said. "What's wrong Jock? I follow you; we can do this. Let them look for us. We can beat the White Eyes who want to kill us."

Jock looked up at the boy; he might have been a warrior from the nineteenth century, standing there, tall and strong, clad in breechclout and long moccasins, the red bandana brightening his jet black hair. Jock's spirits revived.

"They have to find us first." Jock jerked his head to the back of the canyon. "But we can find them anytime. We can fight our way out."

The boy rose and picked up his bow, shouldering a quiver of arrows. "I'll hunt a while; see if I can find a rabbit or a bird."

"A rabbit would be good," Jock said, and in a sharper voice as he weighed the difficulties facing them. "Much ground to cover before we finish Ussen's work."

They were a sorry pair when General Stand Watie surrendered, and Jock ruefully examined his worn, plumed slouch hat with the CSA badge; the soiled shirt adorned with several colors of silk ribbons; the skid of grease as he rubbed forefinger and thumb on his unwashed copper hair that hung below his shoulders; the reddish unkempt fuzz that covered his face; the futile attempt at elegance, adopting the long blue silk neckerchief, knotted navy fashion learned aboard *Alabama*. Though they were not beaten as soldiers and men, the cause was lost and the romance of the Southern Cavaliers and the Missouri Boys had ended in dirt, squalor and defeat.

Jim was no better prepared than Jock for the collapse of the South. His dress was a mixture of half-leggings, grey uniform jacket, a dirty red waistcoat and a shirt that had been on his back for weeks; a long black neckerchief added a sinister touch. The black hat with a CSA badge and feathers stuck in the band, and he looked like a killer.

"What the hell are we going to do?" Jim said. "You keep wearin' that damned shirt the Yankees'll find us and think we're bushwhackers. We're Cherokee Mounted Rifles."

"Take a look at yourself. You're straight from hell."

Jim glanced down at himself and smiled. "Reckon I am."

They were proud that General Stand Watie was the last Confederate General stood down, and they wanted no Federal pardon, concerned that they'd be slaughtered if they came in to surrender. But Jock had another worry; he was a Scot and might be killed or expelled by the Yankees. In a matter of weeks, he would be sent back to Westburn.

"I still have the gold sovereigns I was paid when I left the *Alabama*," he said. "Let's go to California. Set up as horse wranglers. I've had enough of the war."

"Change our clothes?"

"Where? There's nothing here. Anyway, I'm not riding in the buff to California. The sovereigns are for the horse wrangling."

They crossed the Oklahoma Panhandle unnoticed, riding away from settlements, avoiding parties of horsemen seen from a distance, hoping that they'd left the war behind, onto the Llano Estacado and into New Mexico. Further west lay the escarpments of the Sacramento Mountains and Cathey Peak. They felt good to be heading to the high country.

"This is Apache country," Jim said. "Let's not dawdle."

But Fate wasn't content to let them pass quietly through the Sacramento Mountains. Jim, a Cherokee, and Jock, nominally a Catholic, would soon feel the tug of Ussen's power. They spurred the horses into the rippling shallow waters of a beautiful creek, a tributary of the Rio Hondo with cottonwoods on the banks. From upstream, they heard shots and women screaming.

"Colt pistol," Jim said, turning his horse back to the creek bank and riding in the direction of the shooting. Jock unholstered and checked the Hawken rifle as Jim withdrew the Henry from its holster.

Minutes later what they saw appalled them; four white men, clad in the filthy remnants of Confederate uniforms, were attacking Apache women and girls who'd been washing clothes. They'd killed a boy on guard; he was prostrate on the bank, one foot hanging in the water, and a man stood over the corpse holding the head by the hair, a knife in his right hand.

The friends didn't hesitate.

Jim shot the scalper's head off with a round from the Henry repeater. Another man was punching a girl, stopping to lift her skirt as she struggled. Jock cut him down, a bold stroke from the heavy saber severing his carotid artery, leaving his head half off. They turned to deal with the other two men, who stood, guns lowered.

"You're Rebs. We're just fooling around with these red niggers."

"Indian killers," Jim said and shot them both. "Better get out of this, Jock. There has to be a village; we'll get blamed."

"Jim wait." Jock pointed to the girl lying face down in the shallow eddies.

The Apache women were terrified, but prepared to defend themselves and one, the mother of the drowning girl pulled a knife. Jim took it from her as Jock ran to the stricken girl.

Jock dragged the girl from the water and laid her on a dry spot several yards away. She needed air so he ripped open her calico blouse, freed it from her waist and hit her a sharp slap on the stomach. Jock put his ear atop her nose. No breath. Water seeped from her buckskin skirt and her long moccasins, pooling on the ground.

"Blanket, Jim. Quick!"

He turned the girl on her face and placed the folded blanket under her stomach, raising her middle above her gaping mouth. His hands moved along her back from behind her stomach to her lungs, and he pressed strongly. Water and bile poured from her mouth. When the emissions from her body stopped, he turned her on her back and placed the blanket under it, raising her breast bone higher than the rest of her body.

Even in the midst of trying to revive her, he couldn't help noticing her looks. She was young and beautiful, about fifteen, a year younger than himself. A grey pallor shrouded her lovely ebony complexion, deadening her fine features. Jock had never seen a girl as pretty; she was more beautiful than the elegant Creole women in Galveston. Who could want to hurt her?

He turned her head to the left. "Jim, grab the tip of her tongue, hold it tight and out of her mouth. Get her arms above her head and hold her by the wrists; firm now."

The Apaches watched impassively, but Jock worried that if he could not resuscitate this sweet girl, the men and women might turn on Jim and himself, blaming them for her death. It was not clear to whom she belonged.

Jock got astride her, knees resting on the ground, placing his hands so that the fingers pointing ground-wise, fitting with the natural gaps in her lower ribs. It seemed an eternity since he'd dragged the girl from the creek, and yet there were no signs of life. But Jock refused to give up; a former Loblolly Boy and nursing factotum in the Mounted Rifles, his instincts and skills were directed to the saving of life and relieving suffering. Pivoting on his knees he threw his entire weight forward attempting to eject the contents of her stomach and chest right out of her mouth. He counted silently, "One, two, three," letting go suddenly with a vigorous push. Still she didn't respond. He realized he'd never forgive himself if she died on him.

Jock increased the pushes to about five times a minute. Still nothing. He continued until he was pushing for fifteen times a minute, attempting to replicate a pattern of natural breathing. A feeble trickle of water and half-digested food slid out of her mouth. Still she wouldn't breathe. Jock was desperate, then he remembered a treatment that might shock her back to the world. The assistant surgeon, Llewellen, had shown it to him on the *Alabama*. He gently straightened the girl, keeping her on her back.

"Light one of your damned stogies, Jim."

"What? Are you crazy? They'll kill us."

Jim glanced at the small crowd of men who'd arrived from the village, alerted by the commotion. Jock looked up calmly; the Apaches seemed to know that they'd destroyed the Confederate deserters and understood Jock was helping the girl.

"Do it Jim, for God's sake, or for sure she's drowned."

Jim handed the smoking stogie to Jock who drew on it until the tip glowed red. From the corner of his eye, he saw a burly man draw a knife and step forward. A woman laid a restraining hand on him.

"Pinch her nose Jim."

Jock drew deeply on the stogie, holding the smoke in his mouth. He held up his hand, and someone removed the stogie from his fingers. He opened the girl's mouth wide with his hands and blew the smoke into her lungs. He raised his hand and felt the rough wrap leaf of the stogie. He took another deeper drag, and the hand removed the stogie. Jock exhaled fiercely, forcing the smoke farther into her lungs.

A hacking cough, and a glob of phlegm spattered his shirt. His heart ached, watching her face contort as she retched. Gently, tenderly he turned her head to the side, and she vomited. Jock rested on his heels and wiped the sweat from his brow with the sleeve of his shirt. Jim was dragging on the stogie as if his life depended on it. Jock was raised by strong but kindly hands under his arms, it was the Apache who'd drawn his knife. A brief smile creased his stern face. He nodded approvingly.

"Thank you... save my daughter."

English. He'd said it in English.

The girl was obviously frightened and winced in pain. Her right arm was swelling, and she shivered from shock. Jock removed his neckerchief, soaked it in the creek and bathed her face with a cold compress, then he cleansed her mouth of puke and phlegm. He touched her lips with his finger.

"It's all right, it's all right," he said. "Get the laudanum, Jim; the bottle in the medical kit. Something to dry her and blankets. She's cold."

Women stripped and dried the girl, and Jock turned away. Then he fed her laudanum from a small glass. She swallowed greedily; he was glad that her eyes revealed she trusted him. He wanted her to sleep in a cool place awhile, away from people.

"I can put her arm right," Jock said.

The father wanted to know how a boy could know so much, so Jim showed him his wrist, which Jock had set out in the field and explained that Jock had worked for a Surgeon in the Confederate Navy and often treated wounded and injured Indian soldiers when they'd served in the Cherokee Mounted Rifles. The Apache grunted approvingly.

"What's her name?" Jock said.

"Miriam," her father responded.

Setting the broken forearm was straightforward. She lay on two blankets near the entrance to the wickiup to catch the light. Jock fed her more laudanum to dull the pain and gave her a thick piece of leather to bite on when the pain got bad. Jim held her shoulders and her father held her legs. She was pinned firmly, and that would make it easier for Jock to set the bone.

"Miriam, I'm going to set your arm. There will be some pain."

The girl smiled, reassured by his voice.

"Hold her steady now."

Her arm was by her side, the fingers turned up toward the front of the arm, the muscles relaxed. Gently, but with some force, he pulled the lower bone fragment away from the upper. It was a clean break and putting the bone into the natural position required only one, swift movement.

The leather bit moved, but she kept her body still and made no sound.

He stayed her with a wave of his hand in case she was tempted to move, for he didn't want the bone to move out of position and have to be reset. The splints and cloths for padding to prevent chaffing already prepared, Jock splinted her arm and bound it with the broadest of bandages left in his medical kit. It was a good set and her arm would not shorten as the bone repaired. They sat her up and supported her back and she breathed deeply a few times. Her mother wiped the sweat from her face.

Jock went to his saddle bags and removed his mother's blue linen sash; one of the few personal items that he'd taken with him to sea and kept with him when he joined the Cherokee Mounted Rifles. He made a sling, tied it round the girl's neck, and arranged it to support her arm across her torso. Blue suited her.

The splints would have to stay on for about five weeks. They would need adjusting to keep a tight fit as the swelling of her arm went down. "Keep the arm in the sling for about ten days," Jock explained to her father, "and she must exercise the arm. Then she should do very well."

Jock had time now to look around. It was a small band, but the father and mother notwithstanding, their faces were stolid, and it was hard to gauge what they were thinking.

"What now, Jim?"

Men, their wives and children barred the way and an older woman stepped forward. She waved them on and the ranks of the small crowd of warriors and their families parted; friendly looks, smiles on the faces of the women and children, and Jock and Jim were led upstream to the small village and Miriam's family wickiup. Apparently, they were honored guests.

"I am Capitano Leon," the girl's father said as he walked with them back from the stream where they had bathed, washing away weeks of filth with yucca soap before letting the rushing waters of the creek rinse their bodies. "That's the name the Mexicans gave me when I defeated them in battle. I was going to kill you both, but I saw that you gave Miriam life."

The Apache's wife had given them clean calico shirts and they walked comfortably in the new long moccasins. But Jock was embarrassed wearing the long breech clout and hoped that no one would laugh at his pallid thighs. The Apache sensed this.

"You were very dirty. It is good that you bathed. Your boots were old and had many holes; and they had a bad smell, so I burned them." He laughed. "Now you look like men, like us."

Leon explained that he was puzzled by how a Cherokee and a White Eyes were friends and found it unusual that they had killed White Eyes wearing the same uniforms to protect his family. He thanked Ussen again that Jock had saved Miriam's life. The friends explained that they killed these men because they were evil. Jock said he was not an American; he was from far away, and he did not like to be called a White Eyes.

"He saved my life in Galveston," Jim said, "then came with me and volunteered for the Cherokee Mounted Rifles."

"Thank you for telling me these things."

Capitano Leon was Mescalero, but he lived with his wife in the Chiricahua country, and the band was Chiricahua. They had come north east to visit his relatives. Soon, they were traveling back to Arizona.

He stopped and placed an arm on each of their shoulders. "Stay awhile. Travel with us. Your war is over, the old life is behind you. Learn our ways. I want to get to know you both; and I want to hear of that faraway country, Jock."

The boy returned, a small doe slung over his shoulder, and together they stripped off the hide and butchered the carcass.

Next morning, they worked quietly in the shade of the wickiup. Jock and the boy attended to the condition of their kit, repairing their wearing moccasins, each making a new pair, cleaning weapons, making replacement ammunition for the Sharps and the Confederate Cavalry Pistols. And they talked. But Jock kept the boy's mind on the dangers they'd face and set him to making a long bow.

They prayed for a good bow and then worked swiftly. The boy cut and shaped the seasoned mulberry shaft with his Bowie knife, making a symmetrical arc, giving the weapon greater drawing power. Jock made the bowstring, peeling sinew from the back of the doe and drying it. He wetted the ends of two strands and spliced them to form a single tough bow string, long enough to accommodate the curve of the finished bow. The boy strung the bow, inserting a stick in the bowstring and twisting, binding the strands of sinew as one; he chewed smooth a few bumps on the bowstring. The bow was strung loose and after complete drying the string was tightened progressively, until the final tightening. It was a powerful weapon; one end resting on the ground, the other level with the boy's shoulder.

Jock brought out a bundle of cattail reeds gathered earlier and handed about half to the boy. "I like to be prepared."

They cut the reeds to lengths of about thirty inches, fastening sharp heavy points of chipped stone and fletching them with three feathers taken from a turkey. But the boy grew impatient, engaged in this painstaking warrior's craft.

"I have a bow and I have arrows. Why are we doing this?"

"This is a stronger bow with longer arrows. I'm too old now to draw it, but you're not."

"And why do we need a longer bow?"

"Weigh it up – we have the bow and dynamite, so we have artillery. And we can shoot silently from about two hundred yards and kill with these arrows. Try thinking before you open your mouth."

Calculating the trajectory of an arrow weighted with a stick of dynamite was a tactic he'd learned from an American mercenary, who'd ridden with Villa and Zapata. For an enemy on the receiving end in the dark it felt like being shelled by a French seventy-five. Jock had the boy practice with the bow until he could land weighted arrows in an eighteen-inch circle.

Jock sent the boy to reconnoiter the canyon. If enemies were coming, he wanted to know. He jerked the remaining flesh from the carcass of the doe but thinking about Miriam kept him deep in his past.

Some men fail in the struggle with circumstances and other men fight on. Jock MacNeil was a fighter. He became a seafarer to escape a dire Westburn slum. Later he met James Gunn, retired Naval Surgeon who taught him to look after sick and injured seamen. Gunn was the one who put iron in Jock's soul.

Jock's home on the *Jane Brown* was the crew's glory hole. A boy of thirteen among hard men, dissolute men, debauchees – he refused to be brought down and with a sharp blade in his belt, kept to himself.

Jock was literate but poor, and he scrounged newspapers. His latent romantic streak blossomed, feeding on reports in the Westburn Gazette and the Irish newspapers of the fighting at Fort Sumter and the First Manasas. He scoured the pages for word of Lee and Jackson, Jeb Stuart, and Beauregard. Jock would talk to anyone who'd listen about Southern rights to secede from the Union. As boys often are, Jock was single minded, and at times fanatical, that the war for southern independence –as he described the conflict – was a struggle between David and Goliath, just like the resistance of his Highland ancestors who'd been pushed from the land during the Clearances by turncoat leaders when Catholic Jacobites were defeated by the English.

In 1862, the *Jane Brown* landed a cargo of hides from Dublin at Liverpool, and the realization of boyhood dreams, of crossing the ocean and fighting for the south, lay within Jock's grasp. Across the Mersey in Birkenhead, a ship, launched in May, was fitting out at John Laird Sons and Company. The wiseacres on the docks said that she was a confederate cruiser. It didn't take Jock long to make enquiries and approach David Herbert Llewellen, the Assistant Surgeon.

Jock respected Llewellen and he in turn liked Jock. The surgeon, an Englishman, was a tall, elegantly dressed man in his mid-twenties. In the early days, without benefit of a uniform, Llewellen seemed tall, clad in slim fitting frock coat and tight trousers fastened underneath the instep of his boots. Later, the impression of height was strengthened by his Confederate naval uniform. Llewellen's face was stiff, and his long side whiskers added years to a smooth complexion, but a smile played at the corners of his mouth suggesting an underlying kindness of character. Jock could read and write, and he counted quickly, and though Llewellen admired Jock's copperplate hand, he made him work hard before accepting his enlistment in the Confederate Navy. Jock laughed about the small lie he told; just a venial sin. Said that he was sixteen; he wanted to convince Llewellen that he was old enough to join the crew.

There was an incisive, improvising streak in David Herbert Llewellen, a talent to seize the moment and extemporize for the good of the ship. While taking Jock around the deck, a workman approached and asked for help with a nasty gash on the heel of his hand.

"Alright MacNeil. I'm going to clean the wound and you show me what you can do with the needle. Then dress the wound."

In the almost-completed sick bay where ailing and injured crewmen would be looked after, Llewellen cleaned the wound, watching as Jock inserted five sutures neatly tied; then applied the Black Ointment, a drawing salve, finally covering the wound in lint and a tidy bandage.

Jock had survived Llewellen's scrutiny.

He signed an affidavit confirming he had served aboard the schooner *Jane Brown* as Galley Boy and that he'd gained experience tending injuries. He understood that the ship would sail as a man of war for the Confederate States of America, and that articles would be signed once the ship was outside British territorial waters, where he would be signed on as Loblolly Boy. The password '290' allowed him on board. Lewellen had said he was confident that Jock would do very well, so he jumped ship and brought his kit aboard and signed on. But Jock could never refer to the vessel as the ship; for him she was always *Alabama*.

Jock was one of twenty hands on board, seamen and former Royal Navy men, many of them belonging to the Reserve. At first Jock had little to do, and being level headed he explored the ship. At midday, chewing on hardtack and cheese, Jock would leave the ship and walk to the other side of the fitting-out berth for a complete view.

Alabama was the finest ship Jock ever set eyes on, a fighting ship, a screw steamer of one thousand, one hundred tons, barque-rigged for long distance cruising. The men who'd built her said only the best materials had been used and worked by the finest craftsmen in the yard. Nine months on the stocks and the fitting out had given the South the best that art and craft could build. For Jock, she was better than any vessel to come from a Royal Navy Dockyard. Jock loved the way she lay in the water, laden with stores and bunkers, a sleek, menacing Confederate Man of War.

Jock, a solitary boy and orphan, desired to belong to her and was very happy when some of the crew, and workmen from the yard, invited him to a run ashore. Walking to the Liverpool ferry, observed by Federal spies, the men sang Dixie, and Jock MacNeil knew he was one of them.

Jock's first duty at sea was hardly naval, but he was willing to please. A party of elegant ladies and sober gentlemen came on board just before the ship, decorated with flags and bunting, left her berth, edging into the Mersey for a 'trial'. Llewellen had volunteered Jock to wait on the visitors, seeing the visit as an opportunity for Jock to shine.

Jock, on deck in smart white jacket and black trousers, conscious of his polished black shoes, and glad that his rough hands were hidden by white gloves, moved quietly among the visitors with a silver tray bearing glasses of champagne. Waiting tables at lunch in the saloon, he showed his mastery of French Service learned aboard the *Jane Brown*. The deft movement of fork and spoon in his right hand, bringing food from the serving dish to the plate impressed more than one guest. Llewellen, seated at the table, caught Jock's eye and winked approvingly.

Jock discreetly assisted the disembarkation of the guests returning to Birkenhead on a tug. The *Alabama* set a course south for a secluded bay on the island of Anglesey to embark more crew. Jock was surprised to see the new seamen had wives and girlfriends with them. While the crewmen and their women were paid an advance on their men's wages and fed and watered, two ladies of the night worked the ship.

Women were still a mystery to Jock, and an ugly rash of acne sapped his confidence. But he was maddened by tumescence, and like many boys of his age, tormented while he slept. A grotesque hag, a cruel parody of the girls he secretly longed for, haunted his dreams and fired his desire until she vanished in nocturnal emissions that left him both gratified and ashamed when he woke.

One of the tarts who'd come aboard was a match for his dream mockery of ideal women; thickening figure and sagging breasts, kohl-blacked eyes, rouged lips, and decaying teeth. Perversely, her gin-soaked breath drew him on, and he had to go with her. Perhaps Jock sought compassion, desired a caress or a warmhearted touch, but when he lay with her in the sick bay, savoring her earthy sweat and cheap perfume and ineptly exploring her soiled underclothing, he was encouraged to remove her drawers, and she forbade him from kissing her or expressing an endearment. There was at last a great surge, a thrust or two, and his deflowering was over in a few seconds.

"That'll be five shillin's. But seein' it's yer first time, I'll charge ye two and sixpence."

Llewellen had seen Jock bring the slattern on deck, attempting gallantry, handing her into the *Hercules*, slipping her a half crown.

"MacNeil," he said dryly, "you'll get the pox. Better come and see me in the morning."

The ship was hove to in the North Channel off the North coast of Ireland, holding her own in a choppy sea. Jock, glad of the oilskin jacket issued to him, stood aft and watched the fishing boat approach, and under the skillful hand of her helmsman, touch alongside. Spray fell on Jock and the wind tugged at his Tam O'Shanter just as he clamped his hand over it. A hand on his shoulder startled him.

"How are you, MacNeil?"

"Very well, Mr. Low, Sir."

Jock was surprised that Lieutenant John Low, returned from service in the *CSS Florida*, knew his name and bothered to notice him. Low's reputation preceded him aboard. An Aberdeen man who'd settled in the south and gone to a Georgia Cavalry Regiment before transferring to the Confederate Navy. Known as Fearless John Low, he'd also served on *Fingal*, an iron-hulled screw steamer.

"You sailed on the *Fingal*, Mr. Low?"

"So I did, son. A foul night when we left Westburn; worse than this evening. Well down the Firth we ran down and sunk a brig; Austrian I heard she was."

There were Scots, some of them Westburnians, that sailed on *Fingal*. Jock felt an affinity with these men who'd risked attack by the US Navy and brought her safely to Savannah.

Ahead to the northwest was Malin Head. On the port side the Irish coast and the Giant's Causeway; on the starboard side to the east, a blurred line on the horizon, Scotland and the Mull of Kintyre; deep in the Firth of Clyde was Westburn and home. Jock had a premonition that he'd never again see the town that he loved for the memory of his family and despised for its hatred of Catholics. He felt shame too, for the brother and sister he'd abandoned to the care of nuns and priests. He could not stop the sob, and his shoulders shuddered involuntarily.

The newly-minted Confederate sailor whimpered, the wee boy that he was.

Then Jock got control of himself and dried his eyes on the sleeve of his oilskin jacket. He felt Lieutenant Low's hand on his shoulder, gentler this time.

"How old are you son?"

"Sixteen, Sir," Jock said stoutly.

"Aye, right enough, sixteen going on fourteen more like it."

The Confederate Agent disembarked and was fetched onto the deck of the fishing boat. Hands flew aloft, and the ship made sail. Under Jock's feet, the hull came alive, and he grinned as Low smiled, satisfied that they were underway.

There was a palpable sense of danger on board: the war was now touching Jock directly as the ship went out into the Atlantic to evade federal warships. The *USS Tuscarora* was searching for the ship in British waters and would have sunk her had she found her. Sailing under British colors was a ruse, but the Red Duster was no protection from the guns of the US Navy.

Sailing south past Tory Island, well off the west coast of Ireland, Jock looked forward to fair weather, wondering what would change when Commander Semmes and his officers joined the ship.

Clearing Western Approaches there were days of smooth sailing. The miles rolled away in the ship's wake. Jock brimmed with happiness, the worry of the pox forgotten as he capered aloft with the younger hands and learned to avoid the Lubber's Hole, surprised to discover that he was unafraid of heights. Jock felt he'd taken an important step to becoming a Man of War's man. And he worked, getting what medical stores were aboard stowed and inventoried. His neat hand and attention to detail pleased Assistant Surgeon Llewellen, confirming it was a good decision bringing Jock MacNeil on board.

One morning after a few days at sea, Jock made a pot of coffee for Llewellen and served him. He liked it black and strong.

"Thanks, Jock." Llewellen reached across Jock in the confined space of the sick bay and brought another mug to the small table. He filled it and turned the handle towards Jock. "Join me; try black coffee; and for heaven's sake sit down."

They sipped the coffee, Jock nervously, for he was used to tea and a formal relationship with his officer.

"You're all right MacNeil. You don't have the pox, but next time take yourself in hand. I suppose that was your cherry gone?"

Jock's face crimsoned. "Yes sir, Thank you. Mr. Llewellen."

"You've made a good impression on Mr. Low. He liked the way you waited on the guests when we left the Mersey. He's seen you flying aloft with the younger hands. He thinks you're adaptable; a natural sailor. He asked me to transfer you to the deck."

Llewellen waited, letting the news sink in. "Well, Jock?"

"Like it here, sir. If it's up to me, I'd as soon be your Loblolly Boy."

He poured coffee into Jock's mug. "Then here it is, Jock."

Chapter Four

The band had camped some days at Ojo Caliente on their way south to the Chiricahua country. Jock and Jim had been with them for six weeks then, and he was liking the life, especially the chance to be around Miriam. Slowly, his love for her was attaching him to the band, and he wasn't fighting it.

Leon invited Jock and Jim to share their evening meal. Being in Miriam's company for the evening made Jock nervous, but he was glad to be near her for a few hours.

Miriam was beautiful, just fifteen, small and delicate. He adored her walk, the short elegant steps in her long moccasins, puffs of sand flying up from her small feet. He loved her ebony skin, her fine features, and the aquiline nose that gave her a haughty look. He wanted to touch her long black hair with the hint of a curl and let its softness run through his fingers. But he was ashamed that he loved the delicious swing to the buckskin skirt hugging her lovely little bottom. He couldn't reconcile what he felt about her with what he'd felt for the trollop on board the *Alabama*.

Jock and Jim sat with Leon on a soft deer hide near the entrance to the wickiup, enjoying the twilight calm. They watched a warrior take some young men to guard the horses and the camp perimeter. Leon called to his wife, and she brought him an ember from the fire. He bit the end off a thin Mexican cigar and lit it.

"I want to tell you about Miriam," he said without preamble, which Jock was learning was his way. "It was Ussen who sent her to us. We were coming back from a raid in Mexico, passing through Texas. We found her in the desert sitting by her mother's body."

Miriam's natural mother was a slave running for Mexico and freedom. She had died of thirst and exposure. It was a miracle that Miriam, then only perhaps two years old, survived.

"She was parched, burnt by the sun; blisters on her arms and legs. I held her in my arms, and I could not leave her." Leon said. "One of the older warriors had healing hands, and he looked after Miriam."

This man anointed Miriam's skin with opuntia made from the prickly pear to reduce the pain and heal her burns. Leon wrapped her in his calico shirt. She swallowed water from Leon's cupped hand and cried when it ran down her chin. She wailed loudly from hunger, and two warriors milked a goat, a part of the booty. Leon soaked his neckerchief in the warm milk, and she sucked on it. He soaked it again and fed her until she was full. But then she cried from stomach pain.

"I held her on my shoulder, and rubbed her back," Leon said.

Leon lowered his voice so that Miriam, just inside the entrance to the wickiup, helping her mother prepare the meal, would not hear him speak.

"For such a small baby she made a loud noise and a bad smell. The warriors held their noses.

"I made a cradle, a wooden frame with a hood to protect her from the sun and carried her on my back to our stronghold. She was welcome to my wife. Miriam is our daughter."

Though Jock was just past sixteen, his courage and maturity had been tested fighting for the south. Yet his only experience of women was that one brief encounter aboard *Alabama*. The love and desire he had for this girl was unbearable.

"Why did you call her Miriam?" Jock said.

"There was a medal around her neck when I found her with markings on the back. A Mexican who traded weapons and ammunition with us said that Miriam was not a White Eyes name; that it came from a faraway land called Egypt."

Jock was surprised by Leon's liquid eyes as he stubbed out the cigar in the sand. He hadn't thought the old warrior was capable of softer feelings.

"Our beloved daughter was a beautiful child," Leon said. "Miriam was our wished-for child."

Miriam helped her mother with the meal. She was dressed in a simple white cotton blouse with high round collar and a green checkered calico skirt, held in place by Jock's mother's blue linen sash which he'd given her when the splints had come off her arm. Miriam had made a broad fold and wound it tightly round her waist, lifting her small breasts. Her shining hair hung loosely on her shoulders, a fine Mexican silver rope around her neck. Her small feet, shod in new white buckskin moccasins, made no sound as she moved between the wickiup and the fire.

Jock was glad that his hands had brought this quiet girl back to life and healed her broken arm. Day by day, his attachment to her grew stronger.

They moved to the wickiup and Miriam gestured for the men to sit down, but Jock and Jim fidgeted, shifting weight from one foot to the other.

"Is something wrong?" Leon said.

"No, no," Jock said.

Then Jim brought out a flat bottle of Tennessee whiskey from in his breech clout. Jock removed a cloth from inside his shirt.

"We brought gifts." Jock held his pewter quaich at eye level. "It's a Scots drinking cup. It belonged to my grandfather. Scots use it to drink whisky."

"So we brought this Tennessee whiskey from the medicine bag," Jim said.

Jock handed the quaich to Leon, who examined the staffs and hoops engraved on it.

"It's handsome, Jock. Thank you." Leon held the cup up to Sigesh and Miriam, then held the quaich to Jim who poured whiskey into it. Leon took the barest sip, then offered the quaich to Sigesh. She tasted the liquor and wrinkled her nose. Leon smiled and handed the cup to Miriam.

Jock loved the way her long fingers and small hands formed a protective lattice around the vessel. He could not take his eyes from Miriam when she raised the quaich to her mouth and let the rim touch her full lips. Her huge eyes gazed at Jock; she took a short gulp, swallowed all of it and had a fit of coughing. She handed the quaich to Jock who drank from the exact same place as Miriam. Jim drained the quaich, then removed a cloth from his belt, wiped and dried the quaich and handed it to Leon.

"I shall treasure the cup," he said, handing the quaich to Sigesh.

Leon held an ashy ember taken from the dying fire and stuck the tip of another thin, dark leafed Mexican cigar through the ash, found the heat, and sucked hard, lighting it. Jock and Jim finished the last of the hoosh, which Jock was finding he liked. Miriam and her mother worked behind them and tidied the wickiup.

"Tell me more about how you met," Leon said. "A Cherokee and a white man, friends. It is hard to believe."

Miriam whispered to Leon and she and her mother joined the men sitting round the fire. Miriam's complexion bloomed in the soft firelight, and Jock realized that she blushed at his frequent looks.

"I was aboard *Alabama* when she sunk the Yankee *Hatteras*," he said. "We were about eighteen miles off Galveston –way to the east out in the Gulf of Mexico. I heard quick short drum rolls when our officer called beat to quarters. We cleared for action. I ran to my place in the orlop below decks."

The *Hatteras* hailed *Alabama* and Fullam, the British boarding officer shouted through a speaking trumpet, "*HMS Petrel.*" And then louder, "Confederate States steamer, *Alabama,*" and opened fire. Shot from *Alabama*'s guns smashed the hull of the *Hatteras*, opening gashes of up to six feet and set Hatteras on fire. The Federals returned fire at forty yards, but from the quarter deck of Alabama, volleys from rifles and pistols rained down on the Yankee sailors.

A quarter of an hour later *Hatteras* fired a lee gun, then another and another still. Jock heard cheering and knew that the Federals had struck. No wounded had come below, so Llewellen sent Jock on deck.

"*Hatteras* was on fire," he said. "I was on deck in time to see her sink."

Jock shuddered at the memory of the *Hatteras* disturbing the surface of the sea as the blazing hull slipped below the waves. Her boilers collapsed, and a burst of steam ruptured a sea stained by coal dust, oil and swirling debris. Jock remembered the Yankee sailors trapped inside the hull; heard Fullam's voice rising above the cheering sailors. *Alabama* suffered no serious damage- a hit on the smokestack and a man injured on the cheek.

"The Yankees didn't hurt *Alabama*. I helped injured Yankee sailors to come aboard," Jock said. "Later, the Captain sent for me."

Jock walked aft with Llewellen through the jubilant officers and crew to the Captain's quarters. The smell of gun smoke and powder wafting through the ship excited Jock, but he was surprised that Captain Semmes wanted to see him.

"This is Jock MacNeil, the Scots Loblolly Boy, sir," Llewellen said.

Jock knuckled his forehead.

"Sir."

"You know that Midshipman Hollister is seriously ill?" Semmes said. "He has the ague."

Jock respected the Captain, still amazed that a Catholic commanded *Alabama*. Llewellen nudged Jock.

"Yes, sir," Jock said.

Jock had spent the last week nursing the midshipman – at eighteen, older than himself –through a severe fever, applying poultice to a painful crop of boils. Jock was certain he would die, for neither Llewellen or the Ship's Surgeon could identify the fever or bring down his temperature. Hollister was having difficulty breathing, and he had a cough and chest pains. Llewellen believed the illness would erupt into full blown pneumonia.

"He might live if we put him ashore," Captain Semmes said.

Hollister was from a Maryland family, old friends of Semmes, and he'd brought him aboard *Alabama* in Terceira. He was the youngest officer on board and the youngest son, doted on by loving parents. Captain Semmes wanted the midshipman to live.

Jock realized that Semmes was looking for something more than obedience from him. On the crossing, he'd done no more than passed the occasional remark to Jock. Jock wouldn't have thought Semmes knew he existed. But Mr. Low must have spoken well of him, for Semmes had decided that Jock was the right man for the job.

"Mr. MacNeil," Semmes said, "I would be greatly obliged if you would take Mr. Hollister ashore. I won't have him in the care of a common sailor. You have looked after him. You are a responsible young man, among the best of the crew. Take him to Silas Merriweather, a good southern man, a retired Naval Surgeon, and friend from my service in the Union Navy. Help Mr. Hollister live. There's a fishing boat alongside, and her skipper will take you in."

It hurt having to leave *Alabama,* but Semmes solicitude had softened the blow, even if the praise added to Jock's torment.

Jock had served five months at sea on the grandest cruiser, enjoying good pay and conditions. The memory of Semmes raising the Confederate colors at Terceira; his speech standing on a canon, urging the crew to sign on to the Man of War. His own singing when the ship's band played Dixie. Jock was proud to be aboard.

Jock also loved the game of cat and mouse that Semmes played with the Federal Navy. The *Alabama* was everywhere and nowhere; a phantom ship feared by the Yankees. He was steeped in the comradeship of working the ship, bunkering, the fair-weather evenings, Jock on deck, playing his concertina, the sailors dancing a hornpipe or jig; singing a shanty. Accepted as lookout because of his keen sight; the excitement when boarders swept away to take possession of Federal ships.

Sinking USS *Hatteras* was Jock's proudest moment aboard *Alabama*. The Confederate success wiped out Yankee taunts that Rebels were only good for preying on unarmed merchantmen. Nine months aboard his beloved cruiser, and Jock had found a life.

But now that life was ending.

Llewellen nudged Jock. "Yes sir; very happy, sir."

"Thank you, Mr. MacNeil. When he is well, Hollister will help you find another Confederate ship."

Later, in the sick bay, Llewellen handed Jock a 0.36 Navy Colt revolver, snug in a shoulder holster.

"You know how to use this?" Llewellen said.

"Yes, sir," Jock said.

A silence filled the sick bay. Jock sensed he'd never meet Llewellen again and knew Llewellen felt the same.

Llewellen placed both hands on Jock's shoulders, steadying him like an older brother. "Take care ashore, Jock."

Jock meant to say something but turned away instead.

As the Bosun drove the two sailors who were lowering the sick Midshipman in a Bosun's chair into the fishing boat, Mr. Low left the quarter deck and shook Jock's hand.

"A pleasure to sail with you, Mr. MacNeil."

"Thank you sir."

Jock returned Low's salute.

Hands reached out and touched his shoulder and voices murmured, "Good luck, Jock"; "Sorry you're leavin' the ship, son. Yer a lucky healer." Jock fixed his cap securely and tugged his pea jacket closer. *Alabama* was getting underway, and hands hurried aloft, making sail. He turned aft and saluted the quarter deck and Captain Semmes returned his salute and waved farewell. Then Jock followed his kit over the side into the fishing boat.

Jock stared at the widening gap of choppy sea between *Alabama* and the fishing boat. Aboard the ship it had been good not to be despised as a Catholic. Jock watched the land and saw no welcome from the lights of Galveston.

The sleeping Hollister was lashed to a chair, barely moving in the heavy swell. Jock tugged the oilskin cover to Hollister's chin to keep him dry from the spray coming aboard. He had given his word to Semmes and he would keep it. But it was a tougher boy who turned aft watching for *Alabama*'s running lights, but they had vanished. Jock had loved Alabama, sure of the respect of his shipmates, certain that he belonged to the ship. But Captain Semmes with sugared words had sent him away.

Jock stood for'ard, as the swift-sailing fishing boat closed with the harbor, and saw figures on the dock as the boat came alongside. He stepped on to the quay and shrugged, resigning himself to a new round of life ashore.

Jock paused for a drink of water and looked around the fire. Leon was alert, drawing steadily on his cigar. Miriam sat beside her mother, eyes bright and eager. Jim rested contentedly on his elbows; he smiled at Jock, and though he knew the story well, winked encouragingly.

"I was lucky, but I didn't know it at the time," Jock said. "When I left *Alabama* she was famous. But I heard that after twenty-two months at sea she was in a sorry state; worn out, needing repairs. Discipline was slack."

Jock drank another cup of water and wiped his mouth with the back of his hand.

"The Yankee ship, *Kersarge* sunk her in 1864. I heard the *Alabama* fought well."

Jock thought about Llewellen and found it difficult to continue. Miriam caught his eye and smiled.

"My officer, Lewellen went down with the ship – drowned. He was awarded the Medal of Honor."

Capitano Leon lighted another Mexican cigar and looked expectantly at Jock.

"Eventually I got ashore with Hollister."

Jock cheered up thinking about the additions to the kit in his seabag; he was better off than when he'd joined the ship in the shabby clothes he stood in and little else. Now he had the small case of surgical instruments and medicines that Llewellen gave him, and the money belt folded around his waist under his tunic containing the sovereigns the Captain had provided. He liked the grey officer's jacket that Semmes had presented him with and had packed it neatly.

"I felt grim when I got ashore in Galveston, but I tried to put a brave face on it," Jock said.

He cut a smart figure in his dress blues and the flat cap with a ribbon he'd embroidered with CSS *Alabama*. He was chuffed with the well-polished officer's dress boots he'd gotten from the brigantine *Baron de Castine*; a prize released on bond.

Jock pressed his arm against the comforting bulge of the 0.36 Navy Colt revolver snug in its shoulder holster.

But despite his swagger and smart turn out, Jock was an empty husk, his belief in the cause fractured, his spirit in ruins.

"And you're a Scotchman," Silas Merriweather said after reading Jock's letter of introduction.

"Yes, sir!" Jock said, cap held behind his back, standing at ease in the hall of the Merriweather house.

"And you'll be a Presbyterian?" Merriweather said.

"No sir! My family is from Barra; I'm a Catholic."

"I'm a Papist myself. Many's the time I attended Mass with Captain Semmes. We'll get along fine."

Merriweather had Jock bed Hollister in a cool room. The fishing boat captain had mentioned Merriweather had turned much of his home over to the care of wounded soldiers, Yankees as well as Confederates.

"What the Hell are you doing in the Confederate Navy, son?" Merriweather asked while Jock was settling Hollister.

"I volunteered; the British seamen on board, they're all volunteers."

"What will you do now that the *Alabama*'s at sea?" Merriweather said.

"Captain Semmes asked me to stay by Mr. Hollister."

"I could use someone with your experience, Mr. MacNeil."

"Captain Semmes asked me to attend to the sick Midshipman. It's my duty, sir, to look after Mr Hollister.

Merriweather looked at the letter again and nodded approvingly. "You should go home."

"No sir! I was happy on *Alabama*. After Galveston, I'll try to find another Confederate ship."

"I like your spunk, son."

The next morning, Merriweather finished examining Hollister and concurred with Llewellen's diagnoses; the young man had pneumonia. The classic signs were there – labored, painful breathing from an infected, filled lung; fever; costive; thirst, skin, hot to the touch; flushed face; the head and limb pains; painful coughing; and an expectorant that was meager, and then profuse and bloody.

"You'll look after him," Merriweather said, "but under my supervision. I have wounded and sick here from the fighting around the city; there's little time."

"Yes, sir," Jock said.

And so, Midshipman Hollister's recovery began, first with the reduction of the crop of boils that Jock cured by use of a regular poultice. A large stubborn furuncle did not respond, and Jock drew out the root by dry cupping it with a small glass. In the vacuum created by the glass, the boil erupted in pus and blood. Jock removed white shards of root, then cleaned and dressed the gory hole. By the third week Hollister was recuperating – coughing and spitting reduced and his breathing easier – yet, Hollister remained weak and kept to his bed. Jock concentrated on relieving pain, binding the infected lung with a generous linseed poultice covered with a piece of oiled silk. He changed poultices every three hours while the pain was intense. Jock gave Hollister opiates – Silas Merriweather would have preferred Dover's Powder, but they had none. Jock had laudanum, brought from *Alabama*. and that elixir diminished the pain and coughing. Jock cooled Hollister's body by sponging him with tepid water.

"Good job, Jock," Merriweather said. "But he's still costive; let's get his bowels working."

Jock had the Midshipman eat grits and drink hot water first thing in the morning, but they had limited effect. Evacuations came only after a good dose of cream of tartar. Jock now concentrated on diet to return the Midshipman to health, walking into Galveston for eggs and milk and the makings for a nourishing broth, the food backed up by doses of whiskey. Silas Merriweather approved.

Hollister said little, giving the impression that he resented having Jock, a mere Loblolly Boy looking after him.

"You owe your life to that young Scotchman," Merriweather said. "The flannel that he bought, wear it next to your skin until you're well."

Later Hollister received orders that, when well, he was to report for duty at the Pensecola Naval Base.

By then, he had come to accept Jock. "I never thanked you properly, Jock, for bringing me ashore," he said. "You saved my life."

"Captain's duty, Mr. Hollister."

"Why don't you come with me, Jock? I'll do what I can to get you sea duty. It's what I'd like myself."

But by that point in the war, there was little chance of appointment to a blue water ship. Jock had an honorable discharge, and still felt he belonged to *Alabama*. He wanted deep sea, not shore duties in a naval base or crewing an improvised man of war.

"Very kind, Mr. Hollister. I'd like to think about it."

"Jock. There's work for us across the Gulf at Pensecola."

Jock had barely been out of the Merriweather establishment – a seat on the porch, brief visits to the outskirts of the city to buy provisions, a walk around the property – since he'd brought Hollister in and nursed him. Most of the time, he'd helped care for wounded soldiers while Hollister slept. That afternoon, smart in the cap with the *Alabama* ribbon, dress blues and pea jacket, he rode into Galveston on one of

Merriweather's horses to find out what sort of sailing work was available. But Jock, cautious in a city packed with victorious and rowdy Confederate troops, wore the shoulder holster and .36 Colt Navy revolver under his jacket.

There were signs of recent fighting, when Major General John B. Magruder retook the island for the south; scarred streets and broken houses. Citizens and soldiers greeted Jock warmly. A man invited him into his house. When the family heard his story, that he was working for Silas Merriweather, and that he was a Scot from the *Alabama*, they fed him dried fish and gave him a pot of homemade jam.

Jock quickly found that Galveston was not a major port for Confederate blue water ships; a difference from days when it was the main base for the Republic of Texas Navy. Jock knew that blockade runners sailed from the port, laden with cotton, and ships from the Caribbean and Cuba brought in weapons, munitions, and trade goods. He considered finding a berth on deck, or as steward, but Jock was savvy enough to see that the Federal Navy would run an increasingly tight blockade and knew that he risked capture sailing on a blockade runner. In the end, Jock decided not to go with Hollister, or return to Westburn.

Merriweather had asked him to stay.

"I like you Jock. You have a good heart and caring hands for the sick and the suffering; you have the beginnings of an education. Work with me. Tend the sick and the wounded. There's enough soldiers and sailors wanting the killing."

Merriweather paused.

"I'm a southern man, and I know your liking for the cause, but we're going to lose this cursed war. My son, a Lieutenant in the Navy, got killed at the Battle of Memphis. My brother was killed at Sabine Pass. Putting the southern men back together to rebuild the south, that would be noble work. Goddammit boy! In time you might become a doctor! I'll help you."

Jock didn't care for the shabby area near the port, so he turned west to the setting sun, kicking the horse into a trot for the Merriweather home. Perhaps he would take Merriweather's offer, become a doctor, settle into a life.

But fate intervened, as he rode down a side street. Jock reined in his horse at the corner to let a cart pass and saw a man collapsed on the boardwalk a few yards away.

"Stay out a' that, *Alabama*," the carter yelled, catching sight of Jock's embroidered hatband. "Just a damned drunk Injun."

Jock turned the horse and approached the man. The late afternoon had turned cool, but under his tunic Jock felt sweat trickle down his back and dampness in his arm pits. The man wasn't drunk, he was beaten senseless, and the assailants might still be nearby.

Jock had been five months at sea on a warship but had never been directly engaged in fighting. He bottled down his fear, but his hands were sweating as he unholstered the Colt.

He was an Indian all right; long black hair, a hat – discarded in the fight – with a CSA badge on the crown and feathers in the band. The round gray uniform jacket over a red waistcoat and white shirt and long black neckerchief, half leggings over uniform trousers with a yellow stripe on the outside leg. Jock gently lifted the man's head; he was about eighteen, and had been clubbed, beaten about the shoulders. The head wounds would need suturing and dressing; likely enough he'd be concussed.

He came around a little and jerked back in fright.

"Stay calm," Jock said. "I'll help you. What's your name, tell me what happened?"

"Jim; Cherokee Jim. Damned white men ambushed me. Got my money and pistol."

Jock's Scots accent apparently calmed the Cherokee. Jim's eyes were unfocused. He was groggy on his feet, couldn't stand without support. Jock helped him lie across the saddle and mounted the horse behind him.

Silas Merriweather's face was florid and angry when he saw Jock supporting the swaying Indian with long hair, blood on his face and staining his clothes. Merriweather found the mixture of Confederate uniform and colorful personal dress threatening.

"For God's sake, Jock; we have enough to do without you bringing me a drunk Indian."

"No sir! He's concussed, not drunk. He's an Indian, but he's a Confederate soldier."

Good surgeon that he was, Merriweather examined the man's head. "Well, someone did their best, but I don't think his skull is fractured."

Jock cleaned up Jim and shaved around the wounds on his head. Merriweather sutured the wounds and the bleeding stopped. Jock applied a dressing of lint folded three times, dampening it with cold water and bandaging it lightly but firmly. He would moisten the dressing throughout the night.

The Merriweather house was crowded with sick and wounded soldiers, so Jock gave Cherokee Jim his bed in the small store room where he slept and kept his kit. He got Jim undressed and laid him flat. A smile creased Jock's face; laxatives: a source of power and amusement. Tomorrow he'd have Jim swallow two tablespoonfuls of Rochelle Salts; keep him regular.

"Thank you for helping me. My head hurts."

"Rest and quiet; you'll be well in about a week. Call me if you need anything. I'll be here." Jock bunked down on the floor on a straw mattress.

With Cherokee Jim recovered and Jock stuck in Galveston, they had time to undertake additional work. Merriweather was delighted when he discovered that Jock had been an apprentice blacksmith and farrier and had him take horses to the smith's for shoeing. Jock, eager to keep his hand in, assisted the smith. Jim groomed the animals. They both enjoyed the hard work and exercise. Jock told Jim about Westburn and the seafaring which led to his joining *Alabama*. But Jock, who'd never met an Indian, wanted to hear about Jim's life.

Jim had been to school – he was both literate and numerate – and Jock had heard the story of how his people prospered, had adapted to the ways of the white man, grown successful as farmers using new techniques producing surplus crops.

"But the white man took our land, and he broke his word," Jim said.

One of the Chiefs, John Ross' father, was from Scotland and Jim knew Scots families who'd settled in the Carolinas. But despite the Cherokee efforts to reach an agreement with the white man, the Federal Government sent soldiers and forced the Cherokee off their lands and onto the Trail of Tears, settling in Oklahoma Territory. Jim's family belonged to the band of Cherokee who hid out in the Snowbird Mountains in North Carolina.

For the Cherokee, the choice between fighting for or against the Federal Government was an easy one. William Holland Thomas, a Carolinian who'd helped the Cherokee, raised Thomas' Legion to fight up in Virginia. Jim thought about joining but decided to go west to the Cherokee lands in Oklahoma Territory and enlisted with Colonel Stand Watie and the Cherokee Mounted Rifles.

"Come down to Texas from Oklahoma with an officer and some soldiers to buy horses," Jim said. "Need to get back; they'll say I deserted."

Jim wanted to know what Jock would do after he left. "Maybe you'll stay here with Doc Merriweather?"

"I might," Jock said.

But Jim had developed a strong liking for the young Scot, and he'd never expected care from a white man. The friends sat quietly. Jock still regretted his discharge from *Alabama*.

"You're for the cause. So what you going to do? Lot of fellers like me up in Oklahoma, Jock; Choctaw, Osage, Seminole; Confederate soldiers.

"I'm not a soldier, Jim. I'm a sailor."

"You can't be a Confederate sailor workin' with Doc Merriweather, Jock. You can ride, you know about horses, an' you shoot real good; an' I'm tellin' you, your doctorin' will be useful."

So Jock decided to enlist in the Confederate Army. He would once more take part in the fight of the South against the Federals. Jock's ancestors had known exile, and he was touched by Jim's story of the Cherokee exiled by Federal troops.

Jock knew of the titanic clashes of armies taking place elsewhere in the South. But the fluid, lightning war Jim described out in Oklahoma Territory, empty as the ocean, drew him in. The smaller forces engaged in a guerrilla war promised less petty discipline and greater personal responsibility.

Jock forgot about his apprehension regarding having to fight. Jim could fight and he hoped that he would not let Jim down when he met the Yankees for the first time. Jock bought a black mare and he bankrolled Jim to a Colt pistol, and holster, a carbine, and a new kit. Jock bought a Hawken rifle from a wounded ex- Confederate soldier who'd been up north in Virginia fighting and taken it from a Yankee sharpshooter. Merriweather gave Jock and Jim a slicker each and a pair of warm blankets. And he presented Jock with a saddle.

"Get rid of that sailor's cap, Jock. You'll be mounted up there. Take this; protect you from the sun." Merriweather handed Jock a cavalryman's hat. Then he removed a cloth-wrapped bundle from a drawer and opened it to reveal a heavy, curved saber. "I had this weapon when I was in the Navy. You know how to use it, Jock?"

"Yes, Sir, Mr. Merriweather. Lieutenant Beckett Howells, Marines, showed me."

"My, Jock, but you're well connected; he's the nephew of Jefferson Davies."

Merriweather told Jock to practice with the heavy blade; build up his arms and upper body. Used right, the saber would cut a man in half.

"When you're fighting and you've emptied your pistols, the saber might just save your life," Merriweather said.

The boys – Jock about fifteen, Jim eighteen – had mounted, ready to leave. Merriweather offered a hand to both.

"You boys look after yourselves. Anything happens up there, you come back here."

Jim swept off his hat in a gallant salute, his long black hair waving in the breeze, as he turned away on his pinto pony, and Jock, reining in the black mare, self-consciously doffed his new cavalry hat.

"Very kind, sir," he said.

The boys rode out of Silas Merriweather's yard and headed for the causeway linking Galveston to the Texas shore, then north for the Texas-Oklahoma border to join Colonel Stand Watie's command. When they crossed into Oklahoma, a day out from when Jock would formally enlist, Jim told him of Stand Watie, the Commanding Officer and 'a right soldier'.

At Elk Horn Tavern in Arkansas, in March of '61, Southern Cherokees captured a battery of guns and turned them on the Yankees, but, outnumbered, they had to pull back. The Yankees won, but Stand Watie covered the withdrawal of Confederate forces. Jim was sixteen at Oak Hills on August 1861 and Watie's victory meant that the south had a firm grip on Indian Territory.

"Colonel was a hero after Oak Hills," Jim said.

Battle hardened by December twenty-sixth, 1861, at Chustenahlah, Jim was in the van of the cavalry that pushed Federal Indian troops, led by Opothleyahola and Jayhawkers out of Indian Territory and into Kansas. He fought at Wilson's Creek and Cowskin Prairie.

"Met some Missouri Bushwhackers," he said. "Fearsome hard men."

Jim was proud to belong to a rough old bunch of Horse Soldiers, peerless guerilla fighters whose Rebel Yell scared many a Yankee shitless.

Jock was quiet as they approached Stand Watie's command. Jim reined in his horse and the friends sat side by side looking at the distant headquarters. Jim grabbed Jock's shoulder.

"I'm with you, Jock; there's good men over there. You'll be all right."

* * *

"Good stories, boys," Leon said." Let me walk with you to your wickiup. Another time I want to hear more about your days with Colonel Stand Watie."

Jock turned for a last look at Miriam, tiredness revealing the slightest cast in her right eye, making her so vulnerable. She waved farewell, and her smile broke Jock's heart.

They strolled through the camp, Jim content after a pleasant evening and Jock elated at being near Miriam.

"You like the young widow, Little Swan, Jim?" Leon said.

"Yes, I do."

Named Little Swan because she walked proudly, medium height, just nineteen. Her husband was killed fighting Mexicans, leaving her with a boy of two years. Her parents were also killed by Mexicans when the band traveled back from the Sierra Madre. Yet she was not poor or hungry, and didn't want for life's comforts because the band took care of its widows and orphans, the sick and old.

A week earlier, Jim had watched Little Swan struggle with a load of firewood until she fell. He'd shifted the load from where she was fighting to get up, and without thinking Jim took her arm and raised her up. With his hand, he'd carefully wiped dirt from her forehead and the sleeve of her calico blouse. She was startled by his touch and stared at him wide eyed, and he worried that he'd offended her, but by her warm smile he knew that he'd pleased her. Jim picked up the firewood and followed her to her wickiup.

Apaches allow a good deal of latitude to widows; they are freer than young unmarried women. Soon, Jim brought her game, and she made him a calico shirt and a pair of long moccasins. Jim liked when she reddened her lips. Jim said to Jock that California was faraway; he might just stay with the band.

"Though you are Cherokee, Jim, the people like you," Leon said. "Your path is hard, but easier than Jock's."

Jock knew Leon worried about his daughter. He did not want Miriam to be hurt and was anxious that in puberty she was for the first time driven by powerful emotions. Miriam had never met anyone like Jock-he'd saved her life and made her well. Even Jock could see the impression he'd made on her.

"Miriam's a quiet girl, "Leon said, "and I can tell she likes you. You like Miriam too, Jock. But, her mother worries about her."

"Yes," Jock said.

"You have hard decisions. There will always be Apaches who'll hate you for your white skin. And the White Eyes will call you renegade and hate you for Miriam's blackness."

"I can see that. I fought black soldiers at Honey Springs," Jock said. "They were brave men. They beat us that day."

The Cherokee Mounted Rifles took black soldiers prisoner. "I saw a bad thing," Jock said.

Jock and Jim guarded the prisoners and a Federal Captain punched a Sergeant in the eye. "Haul off my boots, boy," he said. "Find me some food."

Jim clubbed him with the butt of a sawed off shot gun. "Get your own boots off. Find your own food."

Jock bathed the Sergeant's eye and got the swelling down. "It'll bruise, but your eye's fine," Jock said. They shared their meager supper with the Sergeant.

"Damned Yankee White Eyes," Jock said. "Treated their own men worse than slaves. Never cared much for slavery. I fought for southern independence."

"It's hard to believe." Capitano Leon shook his head. "I will kill anyone who hurts Miriam. You understand?"

"Yes, I understand."

"Then listen, son. I see many things. Now we are strong, but the big war of the White Eyes is over. They'll come back. They are many and though we kill them and beat them in battle, more come and we are always fewer. Even so, I will not accept the reservation." He swept his arm to the horizon. "This is Apache land. I shall never surrender to the White Eyes."

A hard situation, and yet the decision was easy for him. "I'd like to stay," Jock said.

Jock slept soundly at the camp in the San Andres Mountains. Sound sleep, an indulgence that he and the boy had taken for several nights past. They were secure in their mountain stronghold and unlikely to be discovered by White Eyes. Jock knew that Americans and Mexicans would be looking for them but had no idea who might be out. They were rested, well armed and prepared to take on any enemies. Soon, he'd have to find out who was against them before heading west to where his family's remains lay.

Before dawn, she came to him, a chimera in the space above his feet. Jock recoiled from his beloved's mutilations: her face bruised and her head raw and bloody where the Texan had lifted her scalp. The White Eyes had done this to his wife and children.

Then his beloved was the chaste and beautiful girl of sixty years ago. Miriam's ebony complexion bloomed against her white buckskin wedding dress. Her beautiful face was serene, a window to her unblemished soul. And Jock felt the weight of his old wrinkled face and withering body.

"Miriam, Miriam, don't despise me. I am so old."

"My Jock," Miriam said, her voice sweeter than the scent of desert flowers. "The man that I love."

Miriam's long slender fingers, fingers he'd often held and caressed, drew him on. Jock's spirit rose with Miriam, away from the wickiup, over the ground, through the fading night. He looked back at himself snug in his blankets and felt strong. The boy was safe.

They traveled through the planes and angels between earth and heaven. Ussen's light shone from Miriam, and Jock saw Hargan's camp on the Janos Plain. And the Old Jenny, the JN27 biplane. Miriam pointed to Joe MacIntosh and the two Mescaleros. "Once they were your enemies; they are against you, and they shall attack you; but now they will not kill you."

Then she showed him Hargan. "This man is the son of him who murdered me and killed Nalin and Runs with Horses."

"Shall he kill me, kill the boy? Has he the power?"

"Nothing is promised, but you have Ussen's protection, and your power is strong."

Miriam took Jock from the Janos Plain to the west side of the San Andres Mountains, and a sylvan hollow filled with the music of running water, and they made love. Jock gave himself to Miriam, the source of happiness and fulfillment in his life. His heart was glad that still she needed him, and they knew again their young love.

"I must leave you," Miriam said.

"Shall I see you again in this life?"

"If Ussen wills it. But when it is your time, I shall be waiting for you."

"And the children?"

"The children too."

Jock could not bear the pain of Miriam leaving. "Take me with you. I am tired of life."

Miriam laid hands on his shoulders and touched old wounds, soothing lingering aches. Jock, aged, and battle scarred, had doubted his power, but from Miriam's touch came the strength and courage to go on.

"Be patient my love," she said. "Ussen desires that you give another service to our people."

Later that morning as the sun rose, Hargan's command stirred. Night sentries stood down, glad to be relieved; wranglers attended to the horse herd; patrols set out to search for the renegades. Pots and pans rang from the kitchen wagons and the voices of jostling hungry men, eager for breakfast, filled the perimeter. Ribbons of pale blue smoke from cooking fires spread above the camp.

Hargan watched it all from the flap of his command tent. He'd been in the field for about a month and had yet to catch sight of this Jock and his follower. The campaign was evolving, but too slowly, and pushing the command forward meant that he had to speak to MacIntosh. So reluctantly, Hargan walked toward the cook wagon near MacIntosh's bedroll and joined the scout for breakfast.

MacIntosh was unimpressed with his presence. "He's up there, Cap'n," he said, pointing north, over the border. "I figure he knows we're here. Hard to say when he'll come south."

"I want that pair down here, scout," Hargan said.

"Let me an' the Mescaleros cross the border and see if we kin chase them down. If I kin talk to Jock, we can settle this; and no more fuckin' killin'."

But Hargan would not, could not send men across the border to fight and reveal the troubles with the hostiles, jeopardizing his promotion. So he decided on just a small measure of risk. He'd have the Old Jenny fly both sides of the border and chase the hostiles south into the waiting mounted patrols. Failing that, the plane itself could harass the hostiles and perhaps even destroy them with grenades and strafing machine gun fire.

"But what I want is my hands on that fucking renegade," Hargan said. "When we catch him, I'll stretch his neck, I swear it."

MacIntosh cut the last of the bacon into small pieces and pushed a couple of heaped forkfuls of beans into his mouth, munching steadily. Swallowing, MacIntosh wiped up straggling beans and bacon fat with a wedge of biscuit, devouring it in two bites, his jaws working. Then he drank deeply from his coffee cup.

"'s 'at right?" MacIntosh said at last.

"Once before Jock forced himself into my life. This'll be the last time. He murdered my father and mother."

"Revenge's best taken cold, Cap'n. I reckon I'd feel the same."

He hadn't thought about it in years. He'd never actually seen what had happened to his father, and he was grateful for that. But years later, he'd hunted down the prospector who had found him and made him tell. Jock had ambushed his father's party, killed all of them, then severed his father's hamstrings and arm tendons, buried him up to his neck in the sand, rubbed him with prickly pear juice and watched while the fire ants did their work.

There were times when Hargan almost felt he understood that – his father had killed Jock's family. But he would never understand what happened next, what he had seen.

He was in the barn when, at dawn, Jock rode into his family's shabby ranch and threw pebbles at the door. He shot an arrow through the neck of the elderly hired hand who appeared. Then Hargan's mother emerged, an old coat thrown over her shift.

Jock jammed her against the wall of the house with his horse.

"Your man murdered my family," Jock said, then he cut her throat, watching silently as the blood gurgled out on to her breast.

As the death rattle started from her chest, she cursed Jock.

"Ya fuckin' Red Niggah."

It was all over before Hargan, then eight years old, had a chance to react.

"This big Apache with copper hair and a cropped, red beard pulled my sister and me out of the hay where we hid." he said quietly to MacIntosh, who seemed to be ignoring him. "He said to me, 'I am Jock, Chiricahua Apache.' I was sure he'd kill us, but he dragged us out of the barn; told us to walk to the nearest ranch. That was more than ten miles. By the time we were back with a posse, Jock had killed all the livestock and fired the property." Hargan spat again. "And now you want me to talk to him?"

"Ain't you forgettin' somethin', Cap'n? Your Ol' Man killed and scalped Jock's family for money. Murdered his wife and his children. Scalped for the bounty, one o' his Comanches killed by Jock's wife."

"My Ma hadn't anything to do with it."

MacIntosh picked at his teeth with a match, then spat out shards of bacon fat onto the sand. "True enough. But he was crazed with rage and grief."

"Well, so am I."

"Scalp hunters; lowest form of mankind," MacIntosh muttered, and raised his eyes to gaze towards the border.

"Cap'n, let's get the plane searching. We kin put out several posses. Use the map, establish grid squares and comb them. Keep moving 'til we find them. It don't matter if we catch him here or north of the border."

But Hargan didn't want to take responsibility for deploying on American soil, might never be ready for that step. In the camp, surrounded by two hundred men and the daily patrols, he felt safe from attack by the two renegades. The plane flying on the American side would surely move the hostiles into Mexico and certain destruction by Hargan's forces.

"No Scout; you get the hostiles down here after the plane finds them and then we'll kill them."

"You're the boss," MacIntosh said, "Cap'n those two Apaches git near this camp, you watch out. Be like havin' sidewinders in your pants."

"Snakes I can deal with," Hargan said.

Jock lay in his blankets and watched the dawn; in his mind's eye he saw Miriam and thought he'd been dreaming but knew that it was no dream when he felt the warmth and wetness of her on him. He'd been up for about twenty minutes, letting the boy sleep; he needed it more than an old Apache. Finally, Jock prodded the boy with the toe of his moccasin and he was awake in an instant,

"Jerky and water for breakfast," Jock said. "Pack everything; no cache here. Going to have a look at the enemy."

Jock hid about five hundred yards from Hargan's camp, unfazed by the large numbers of men in the outfit. He finished examining the camp through the long glasses, noting the pattern of patrols and the flights of the Old Jenny, but was surprised that none of the patrols crossed the border, though the Jenny did so. Jock figured that the intention was to use the plane to either destroy them north of the border or drive them into the patrols waiting in Mexico. He saw MacIntosh and one of the Mescaleros accompanying one patrol that headed west, and the other Mescalero went east with a patrol commanded by a National Guard Officer. Hargan paced through the camp, interfering and giving out unnecessary orders. Was he shy of a fight?

The camp was well set up; the kind of arrangements Jock expected from a professional soldier commanding an irregular force; fairly well ordered, rows of small, two-man tents with two larger tents at the center, and chuck wagons nearby, but no defensive ditch or perimeter wire. Earthen walls protected munitions and fuel for the JN27. It would be difficult to blow them up. The rubbish of camp life meant that Hargan had been established several days. Sloppy sentries guarded the camp. Jock noted the dominance of frontier riff raff, the scattering of Mexican soldiers and the handful of Texas National Guardsmen he and the boy might have to actually fight. Jock looked behind the façade of security and saw prisoners in a cage; men restrained by a chary leader.

He meant to shake them up, to give him and the boy the latitude they needed to travel.

Jock turned to the boy and handed him the long glasses.

"Have a good look. We're going to rattle their coop; just before sun up."

They withdrew on foot back to a range of low hills hidden by legume trees, columnar cactus and thorn scrub. They found their mounts and the pack horse, with weapons and supplies safe where they'd hidden them.

"Check your weapons," Jock said.

They cleaned and loaded rifles and side arms. Jock made the boy carefully examine the mulberry bow and the long arrows. They honed knives and Jock's saber to razor sharpness. The boy bound four sticks of dynamite to the long arrows and placed them in the quiver. The buckskin boots of their mounts were examined for wear and metal on harness and saddles muffled with soft cloths.

After sunset they ate another meal of jerky and water and settled for a few hours' sleep. Jock felt tolerably safe in this place – it seemed unlikely that his enemies would expect to find their quarry so close to the camp. Still, he drowsed, always half-awake, his brain at rest but sensitive to any changes in the surroundings. Their lives depended on this power.

In the evening, they rose and stripped to breech clout and long moccasins, rebound their long hair with bandanas, then darkened their visible parts with ash and sooty charred wood brought in a bag from the dead fire at the San Andres stronghold. Jock was glad of the dark hiding his aged, wasting body. Standing next to the boy, a near perfect example of young warrior, Jock stifled a chuckle at his own vanity. Finally, they painted their faces black with a white stripe slanting from the bridge of the nose, finishing at the edge of the ear lobes. Jock got out his buckskin bag of the sacred pollen, the *Hodentin*, and scattered a pinch to each of the four winds. They mounted and walked the horses to Hargan's camp.

A mounted guard was posted on each side of the camp perimeter, about twenty-five yards out. The horse herd was corralled behind a rough scrub fence. The last thing the man guarding the herd saw in this life was a face blacker than the night, broken by a diagonal white stripe and glaring white eye balls.

Jock caught the falling body and withdrew his saber blade. The boy quieted and hobbled the horse, for they meant to take it with them when the raid was over. Then he hung the guard's side arm and holster from the saddle horn. The night lights of the camp faintly lit up the targets.

"Two arrows into the horse herd, one on the chuck wagons and the last at the two big tents," Jock said.

Jock cupped his hand around a match, lit the fuse of the first arrow, and the boy launched it; as the missile reached the apex of its flight the second arrow followed. Two explosions came in rapid succession and the shrieks and screams of injured and dying horses rang out, as the third and fourth arrows flew towards the chuck wagons and the big tents. The surviving horse herd surged through the scrub fence, some animals galloping into the darkness of the Janos Plain, but the majority, as Jock intended, careered through the camp, neighing, terrified, crushing tents under thundering hooves and heavy bodies, running down panicked men.

In the flash of the third explosion Jock saw one of the chuck wagons overturn, its white cover bursting into flames; the second chuck wagon settled heavily on its axles. The last explosion followed on the heels of the third, collapsing the big tents in a soaring yellow inferno.

Jock drove his right fist into the open palm of his left hand. Perhaps it was too much to hope for, but he wanted Hargan dead in this conflagration. Then MacIntosh would persuade the second in command to give up and go home. Jock could complete his pilgrimage and return quietly to the rancheria in the Sierra Madre,

Jock gave a hoot of the burrowing owl and he and the boy rode along two sides of the camp perimeter and each fired half a magazine from Winchester rifles. Jock couldn't be sure, but thought they'd hit four or five of the milling men. For the raid he'd favored a repeating rifle over the accurate but slower single-shot Sharps.

Jock signed off with his signature, the cry of She Wolf. The boy in the excitement could not be quiet, and he roared out a good imitation of the Confederate war cry Jock had taught him.

They wheeled their mounts around about three quarters of a mile from the camp and looked back; flames joined the rising sun and lit the sky. The tumult of confusion and panic came to them across the Janos Plain.

It was a fine mess they'd made. Hargan could be in no doubt about whom he was up against.

Chapter Five

Hargan and MacIntosh surveyed the ruin of the camp. Smoke and charred wood stung their nostrils and the cooling, roasted horse flesh made Hargan retch. He turned aside from MacIntosh and emptied his stomach. MacIntosh waited and shook his head at the dispirited rabble wandering the wreckage of the camp.

"Like being shelled by French 75's," Hargan said.

"Arrows loaded with dynamite," MacIntosh said. "An old trick; I saw an American mercenary use it when I was workin' with Villa and Zapata. Like I told you Cap'n; these two Apaches are dangerous."

MacIntosh expected action – they had to take the initiative from Jock – but Hargan seemed stunned by the attack."Cap'n, it's bad but it could've been worse. Six dead, some supplies lost, and I reckon maybe ten deserted."

MacIntosh and the two Mescaleros had been around the camp, and behind the smoke, and desolation there was cause for cautious optimism. Most of the surviving horses were corralled, and the wranglers were already bringing in the stragglers that had run to the Janos Plain. Four men were out of action from the stampeding horses, and there were several walking wounded. But the munitions and fuel were secure. MacIntosh was sure of finding a sign to follow. There was enough food and water. And they could live off the land for a while.

"It's Jock and a boy we have to find; Mescaleros seen 'em. Tracks show both of 'em pulling two horses loaded with supplies. I reckon we kin catch them 'fore they git right up in the high country."

Hargan seemed to finally realize that his crossing the border would be overlooked by the shady politicians who'd hired him, provided he killed Jock. At any rate, that'd be better than letting them escape to the Sierra Madre, especially after last night's attack.

"All right," he said. "Put together two well-armed posses, minimum supplies, traveling fast. The plane'll spot ahead, trying to locate the hostiles. The remainder of the command will follow you."

Jock had distributed weapons and supplies between the two horses and removed the horseshoes from the animal taken from Hargan's camp, cleaned up its hooves, and replaced iron shoes with short buckskin boots. It would take time for Hargan to restore order. But it would not do to hang about; Hargan and MacIntosh would certainly come after them.

"Why didn't we destroy the plane?" the boy said.

"I want the Lewis Gun. Going to shoot the plane down out here. If it blows up, we might lose the gun.".

"Shoot down the plane? How?"

"You with the BAR and me with the Sharps."

Jock had seen an Old Jenny in action during the troubles in Mexico with Villa and Zapata. It wasn't fast and didn't fly high, maybe to about six thousand feet. But it could hang about and the slow airspeed made it the perfect aircraft for hunting the boy and himself. It also made it a fine target.

They rode steadily to a wooded place near to rough flat land at the edge of the foothills of the Chiricahua Mountains, where the high places exceeded nine thousand feet. This was the Chiricahua homeland, and Jock knew it well from the old days, a land of forest, ridges and stone spires. They unloaded the BAR, mounted it on the bipod and set it up at a high angle on a flat rock. The lighter-laden horse they kept nearby, and the remaining three animals were hidden among green stuff where the foothills stopped at the wild open face of the mountain.

At the edge of the trees, Jock lit a fire and, as it caught the newly-cut paloverde mixed with dead branches from the underbrush, a thin trickle of smoke went straight up.

"That should draw him down," Jock said.

Before long, they heard the plane. At a thousand feet they could see its outline. The aircraft was too high to strafe them, but to entice the pilot down, Jock ran into the open, looked up, shading his eyes with both palms.

The plane descended five hundred feet in a long, sweeping loop. A burst of fire from the Lewis Gun kicked up dust behind Jock as he ran for the cover of the trees and got down beside the boy behind the rocks.

The plane, now down at three hundred feet and flying at sixty miles an hour flew past the trees and the gunner fired a long burst; bullets mangled the paloverde and showered them with leaves, yellow petals and branches. Several rounds ricocheted off the rocks and flew harmlessly overhead. The fire Jock lit vanished in a rending second burst from the Lewis Gun.

The plane was at the end of its run and banked for another approach, seeming to hang in the air.

"Now."

Jock fired two shots from the Sharps into the engine, and it stuttered and died, leaving the propeller swinging in the draft. The boy fired four short bursts from the BAR, one cluster of bullets hit the engine and the rest created a pepper pot of ragged holes along the fuselage and cut away half the tailplane. Jock caught the gunner in the scope of the Sharps and shot him as the aircraft spiraled down, the pilot struggling with the controls.

The Jenny hit the ground hard, slithered across the sandy soil in a grinding run of fifty feet before tipping forward to rest on its nose, the tail up and skewed to one side. Jock waited, but the engine didn't burst into flames.

At his signal, the boy ran towards the plane, a war painted fiend, stripped down to breech clout and long moccasins, a Winchester at high port. Jock shuffled behind him on his arthritic knees. The terrified, shocked pilot stopped struggling to get out of the cockpit and brought out a Mauser Machine pistol, but fouled the butt on the cockpit edge as he pointed the barrel at the boy. Jock pulled the .45 Colt automatic from its shoulder holster and at ten feet shot him in the head. When they reached the plane, he put another bullet into the pilot's temple.

"Watch what you're doing," Jock said. "He would have killed you."

"I was close to him."

"Take no more chances."

They detached the Lewis Gun from the rear cockpit edge and gathered four round pan magazines, each containing ninety-seven rounds of 30.06 ammunition. The boy held a heavy bag with both hands. "Ten grenades," he said.

They loaded loot onto the pack horse, and the boy moved about nervously. He slung the BAR across his shoulders, eager to be away and up the mountain, before the posse came.

"Wait," Jock said. "We might be dealing with idiots."

An officer of the Texas National Guard led the posse to the plane crash. He and his men came in on a headlong rush, determined to rescue the pilot and the gunner.

Jock watched them from behind the rocks, galloping carelessly towards the plane. They were dealing with idiots. He touched the boy's shoulder.

"Shoot. Kill them all."

The boy fired withering bursts from the BAR and cut down six men and their mounts. Two horses screamed from their wounds and two wounded men struggled beneath their stricken mounts. Jock and the boy moved swiftly. Jock shot the two survivors in the head with the Colt .45 automatic and cut the horses' throats.

He shook his head. He'd left the rancheria in the Sierra Madre just for a pilgrimage to visit the resting place of Miriam and the children.

He knew that Ussen had work for him, but he had not looked for trouble. Then the White Eyes and the Mexicans had attacked him, and now events must take their course. If war was what they'd sought, they had what they desired.

"Get the rifle ammunition, we can use it for the BAR and the Lewis Gun," Jock said.

He pulled the pin on a grenade, moved back a safe distance and threw it into the plane. The explosion set fire to the fuel tank, incinerating the Old Jenny.

An hour later, Hargan's posse appeared with MacIntosh and the Mescaleros, one of them having ridden to find them and explain that the National Guard Lieutenant leading his posse had ignored his call for caution.

"Jesus Christ, Cap'n!" MacIntosh said. "It's another fuckin' massacre. That officer was a damned fool."

MacIntosh scanned the mountain with his binoculars, and above the tree line he saw the hostiles toiling up the hill, each of them pulling a pack horse.

"There they are, 'bout an hour ahead, mebbe a little more. We kin catch 'em."

"Bury our dead first," Hargan said.

"What! Let 'em get away? You want more blood on your hands, Cap'n? Main party can take care of the dead."

They were through the paloverde and chaparral about two thousand five hundred feet from the pass that would take them over the far side of the ridge. Jock was confident that no one outside his band knew of the route. Then they would descend and escape, riding across a rocky plateau with good cover to their destination, several days away yet. He and the boy were at five and half thousand feet, but they were slowing down with them riding, each pulling a horse laden with kit, rifles, side arms, and ammunition. The bigger horse was tiring under the additional twenty-eight-pound weight of the Lewis Gun, its heavy round magazines and the bag of grenades looted from the plane. The smaller horse was protesting at the twenty pounds load of the BAR. Ahead was a steep rocky waste, and they dismounted to lead the horses towards the pass at eight thousand feet and their escape route.

The boy was unaffected by the altitude, but it was starting to tell on Jock. His labored breathing and nausea slowed him. Jock stopped and retched, vomited again and once more until his stomach was empty. He cursed old age. In his younger days when he'd gotten to know these mountains and learned the secret pathways, he might have run up the last part and pulled the laden horse, too. Ten years ago, he'd have managed a steady pace to the top.

The boy turned, worried. "Jock are you all right?"

"Yes, yes. Keep going. Got to get to the top soon."

They had splashed through the freezing, swift-flowing mountain streams to break their sign and make it difficult for pursuers.

"My feet are cold," the boy said, and shivered, looking down at his worn, sodden moccasins.

Jock grunted. His feet were frozen, his moccasins tattered and sopping, and he felt fever coming on as they labored on and up over rocky ground and sharp stones. The boy was in the same condition. As they led the horses ever higher, Jock slowed again. "Get your blanket around your shoulders. Keep warm and keep going."

Jock's larynx was burning, and his throat glued solid. It was difficult to swallow, and with a choked nose, he was gasping through his mouth. The boy was close on his heels. Jock paused and blasted air through his nose in a useless attempt to clear it. His ears popped, and he spat a thick green-yellow mucus, soiling the ground. His nose choked again. Jock shook his head. The boy was hawking and spitting green phlegm onto the ground as well. They were leaving a clear trail of bloody foot prints and foul catarrh, but they couldn't swallow this filth.

He looked back and through the long glasses saw Hargan, MacIntosh and one of the Mescaleros clear the tree line. Behind them came another dozen riders; a mixture of Federales, Texas National Guard, and the best of the riff raff. They rode confidently. Shooting down the plane and ambushing its rescuers had made Hargan act decisively. Jock and the boy were in sight and the bloody, snotty trail they left no longer mattered.

He considered ditching the heavy load of weapons – he could do it and still leave them well armed and moving faster than the pursuit. But he wouldn't discard the armory so easily. Intuitively, he was certain that before he went back south and home, if such was Ussen's wish, they would be glad of it. Jock had the initiative and could bring the posse to action when he chose.

Of course, if Hargan's men reached the pass first, they'd kill Jock and the boy.

"Jock!" The boy halted the horses he was leading and pointed to a steep ridge that emerged at the back of the pass. A second posse was coming up a rough narrow path. They would slip from view behind the ridge and emerge near the top of the pass. In an hour, perhaps an hour and half, the initiative would slip from Jock's grasp. Silently he cursed the fever, the altitude, his bloody feet, and he railed against old age.

He examined this new threat through the long glasses. The Mescalero was riding out front ahead of a portly officer of the Texas National Guard. The remaining ten riders were evenly divided between border riff raff and National Guard. And they could ride, expertly negotiating the rocky way. But Jock knew that to reach the pass they'd have to dismount, and he was sure that these men would not move fast leading horses over rocky ground and at altitude. Jock allowed himself a grim smile; of course, he knew of this steep approach to the pass, but he'd counted on the pursuers not knowing; certainly not Hargan, and good as he was, not even MacIntosh. One of the Mescaleros must have known.

They were in trouble. Jock felt terrible and the boy was sick too. But they had to go through pain and conquer fever. They must reach the pass first.

"Look, son. If we don't make the pass first, they'll kill us."

Jock stopped and sucked air in through his mouth and felt calm. They had been moving steadily upward. He searched the last several hundred feet to the pass through the long glasses. It was a dreadful rock-strewn slope. The approach to the east side of the ridge was steep and littered with big rocks where the boy could get above the second posse. Jock handed the boy the Sharps and explained again the firing mechanism; the falling block arrangement, the precise aiming afforded by the double triggers.

"Sight your target. Ease off the first trigger. Squeeze the second trigger when you have the target in the scope. Long-range now; Sharp's good at more than a thousand yards. Kill an officer, wound men, cripple horses. Get up there now, you have to slow them. Meet me at the pass."

The boy found the strength and was on the pass, scrambling up a rock face to reach the higher ground. Minutes later, Jock heard the distinctive boom of the Sharps and smiled.

Somehow, Jock kicked his body on, hauled, coaxed, cajoled the four horses, roped together, and took them over the pass, out of sight of the posse. He hobbled the horses. Hargan and MacIntosh were closer now. The crack of the Sharps and then another. Jock was so tired now and took a few moments of rest on the far side of the pass.

"Where's the boy," he muttered.

Then the boy was by his side. "I shot the officer and one of the men, wounded another one. A horse fell off the path. I heard it screaming. They took cover, slowed down."

Jock would never surrender, and he wasn't going to let the boy be killed by the last of frontier scum and riff raff up here in this desolate wasteland. Old knowledge returned and there was a growing confidence that he could retain the initiative. "There's another path," Jock said.

A rocky shelf, here and there little more than three feet wide. A fall of a thousand feet on the left side. Untrodden in forty years. He'd escaped along it, years ago. A mounted warrior toppled by an attack of vertigo, killed on the rocks below. If they couldn't get the horses and the weapons over, they'd push them off. They would carry their personal arms and walk off the mountain.

Jock led the boy to the edge of this terrifying escape route, and he was afraid.

"Can't go there. Can't take the horses across," the boy said, looking at the break of four, maybe five feet in the path.

"Believe in Ussen, son. Shake off the hands of Catholic Priests and the Indian School." Jock placed a firm and reassuring hand on the boy's shoulder. "Come on, son."

Miriam's visit had rewarded Jock with blessings and greater power. He knelt facing the sun and sang a prayer to Ussen. His god was listening and gave Jock the power of miraculous deeds. Jock willed the illumination of the narrow ledge and towering rock face with heavenly light, brighter than the sun, a piercing beam of holiness that no White Eyes could bear to look on.

Two shots hit the rock face above their heads. Hargan, MacIntosh and the two Mescaleros were riding down the far side of the pass and the posses' spilled over the edge behind them.

"Look hard, son. Give your heart to Ussen," Jock said.

And in the center of the light they saw Miriam, smiling, ghostly, chaste in her white buckskin dress and she beckoned them with open arms.

Jock handed the reins to the boy, and protected by Jock's power and Miriam's holiness, he walked the horses along the path and stepped onto a bridge of light to cross the gap. Jock led his horses across the bridge of light and Miriam smiled as her purifying light bathed her beloved.

"What the fuck is going on?" Hargan said. "Those two bastards are walking on air."

"I told you, Cap'n," MacIntosh said. "Jock's a disciple of Ussen. It's a fuckin' miracle."

Across the bridge of light Jock handed the reins to the boy and placed two sticks of dynamite firmly in a crack at head height on the rock face, leaving a couple of inches proud.

They moved forward out of the light to a turn in the path hiding them from their pursuers. Jock got down to the prone position and took aim with the Sharps at the dynamite sticks embedded in the rock face.

The two Mescaleros rode to the gap in the path, confident that if Jock and the boy crossed, then they too could find a way. Behind them, half a dozen of Hargan's best men followed.

Miriam's ghost, a wraith threatening death, barred the Mescaleros. They felt guilty and spooked, knowing that White Eyes had mutilated and killed her, and ran their horses back, scattering the horsemen behind. They regrouped, but less assured, rode to the gap.

Jock hit the dynamite with a round from the Sharps. An explosion, followed almost immediately by a second detonation, and a section of the rock face slowly disintegrated, the avalanche carrying away about fifteen feet of the path, killing shrieking men and screaming horses.

The carnage stunned the posses' and they fled in disorder, past Hargan and MacIntosh, joining the two Mescaleros a safe distance back. MacIntosh directed Hargan's gaze to Jock, silhouetted in the dust, defiantly shaking the Sharps.

Hargan withdrew his Winchester from the saddle holster, firing two rounds at Jock and hitting the rocks above his head; he fired twice more, but failed to hit him.

"Cap'n," MacIntosh said, "that old man is holy. He's protected by Ussen."

The sparse clatter of rocks disturbed by hooves broke the eerie silence, the horses picking their way along the rocky path, taking Jock and the boy down the mountain.

Hargan turned to MacIntosh. "What now, Scout?"

"After we rest, tonight we'll go to the secret place where my family lies," Jock said. "There's no time now for the Gila or Oak Creek Canyon." They were off the mountain, having made a brisk descent. Though weak from cold and fever they'd kept good order, not losing mounts, arms, or equipment. They had two, maybe three days in hand. With the demolition of the path, Jock had shaken and demoralized Hargan's posses', obliging them to retreat to the plain and count their dead and wounded. They would regroup in time and keep coming after him and the boy until the deciding engagement.

MacIntosh would assume that he'd go west, supposing that MacIntosh had worked out that they were headed to the place where Jock's family were massacred. So Jock headed forty miles north west to the foothills of Mount Glen, passing the Cochise stronghold on the way. They were careful to leave little trace of their passing, keeping back from towns and places where people lived, making detours and wiping out tracks, keeping to hard rocky surfaces where possible.

Raised temperatures left them feverish, and with their sinuses infected it was impossible to breathe properly and hard to swallow over painful sore throats. Fighting nausea, they kept swallowing the viscid green phlegm that ran down the back of the throat. The boy gagged.

"Don't spit and don't vomit," Jock said. "Leave no sign the Mescaleros or MacIntosh might find."

They fought the sickness and rode hard until reaching an old Apache hideout before dusk. The boy drooped from fever and exhaustion, and Jock felt grim.

"Look to the horses. Hide them in the small arroyo. Grass and water there. Leave the weapons and supplies here."

While the boy rubbed the horses down, let them drink, and hobbled them in tolerable grazing, Jock scraped out a shallow pit in the sandy soil with a sharp stick and a flat, spade-shaped rock. He made a stack of small boulders and laid in dried brush and dead wood that wouldn't smoke. He cut short cotton wood poles, a few inches taller than himself and gathered more brush, building a low temporary wickiup around the shallow fire pit.

The boy moved weapons and supplies near the wickiup. Jock nursed the fire to a fine blaze, heating the boulders until they suffused the wickiup with a comforting heat. They chewed on jerky and drank water. Jock gave the boy the cottony part of brown foot root that the Chiricahua called *me-tci-da-il-tco*.

"Rub this on your feet. They're a bloody mess, and so are mine," Jock said as he nursed his bruised and battered feet. "We'll repair the moccasins later; wear a new pair tomorrow."

"I'm sweating, Jock."

"Me too. The heat is good. Wrap on another blanket. Take deep breaths now."

Jock fed the fire with silver sage, called *chin-dei-ze* by the People. Jock and the boy inhaled strongly, the smoke easing their aching sinuses. Stripped to breech clouts, they endured the sweat streaming from their bodies. Each breath was easier and deeper as the silver sage took effect.

"Here's the last dose of medicine." Jock raised a pot from the fire and poured tea made from osha root, the *ha-chi-di.*

The boy held his nose. "What a smell!"

"Drink it to cure your coughing. Rub some on your forehead to get rid of headaches. But never take it before a hunt. The stink'll scare the game away. Feeling better?"

"Yes."

"Sleep now. Up before dawn."

The boy fell into untroubled slumber, and Jock grinned, his mouth a ruin of empty spaces and worn teeth. The boy had fought ruthlessly and well, yet, sleeping, his face had the innocence of youth.

The smell of hot coffee invaded Jock's deep, dreamless sleep, and a gentle hand on his shoulder brought him awake. The boy smiled, his face fresh as young paloverde leaves.

"I woke first," the boy said.

Jock was irritable at having slept on. It was on the tip of his tongue to say something rude to the boy, but he couldn't resist the rich coffee smell. He took the cup from the boy, swallowed a good mouthful of the hot coffee and rubbed sleep from his eyes with his free hand.

"Must be getting old, sleeping like that."

The cup of coffee finished, Jock was fresh and alert. The wickiup was empty and the fire glowed dully. The boy grinned. "The weapons and the supplies are on the pack horses. Your horse is ready."

Jock saw that the boy wore a new pair of moccasins. Silently, he handed Jock a new pair. Jock grunted as he took them. "You'll be taking over."

Jock was far from ready for another hard day in the saddle. The initial freshness he felt after the coffee waned, replaced by lethargy and the pain of sore joints as cold and fever took a renewed hold of him. The boy saw the change, and the thick beads of sweat standing out on Jock's forehead. He risked sharp words but kept close by him; and just as well, for Jock collapsed when he tried to mount. The boy caught him.

"Get me to the horse," Jock said.

The boy steered Jock to the horse and handed him the reins, placing his left hand on the saddle horn, but Jock couldn't lift his leg high enough and fell back, leaning on the boy, his breath coming in rapid, shallow bursts.

"I'm sick, son, I'm sick."

The boy swallowed fear. Jock might joke about his taking over, but he was not yet ready to make the decisions on which their life depended.

Yet what had Jock said? He should let go of the White Eyes' god and trust to Ussen.

Jock was too weak to walk, and the boy picked him up, surprised at his lightness, and laid him down in the wickiup beside the dead fire.

"We have to be away from here no later than first light tomorrow," Jock said.

A tall order. The boy got the damp sweaty shirt off Jock and removed his moccasins, leaving only his breech clout. The boy was surprised at Jock's thinness. But he knew Jock's toughness from their weeks together and dismissed the thought that Jock was an emaciated wreck. Wrapping Jock in two blankets, his hands touched the scars of old wounds, bullet holes, faint proud tissue from the cuts and thrusts of sharp knives.

"My dues from an active life," Jock said, a faint smile creasing his fevered face. "Make the horses safe and get a defensive position ready, use the Lewis Gun, and…"

"It's all right, Jock. I'll deal with it. I know what to do."

And the boy was surprised to find that he did. He started the fire using dried wood that would not smoke. He made tea from the osha root and propped Jock up so that he could drink it. He hobbled the horses, kept them loaded and out of sight, ready to escape. Then he built a firing position from rocks for the Lewis Gun and the spare magazines, siting it to the front of the wickiup so that he might keep watch and attend to Jock. If the White Eyes came, then the boy would kill many of them.

Mid-morning. The sun warming the hideout. Jock cold and feverish, drifting in and out of sleep. "Help me," Jock said.

The boy took Jock into the arroyo to relieve himself. Jock's arthritic knees could not bear his weight, and he clung to the boy as he half-carried him back to the wickiup.

"Knees hurt and now damned piles," Jock muttered. "Bring me the medicine bag."

Settled again in his blankets, but with no lessening of the cold and fever, he rummaged irritably in the medicine bag.

"Can I help?" the boy said.

"No!"

Jock removed a handful of dried sagebrush root from the medicine bag. "Heat some water, then go outside. Pound the *i-ia-ai*. Make powder."

Jock bathed his tender parts, and when the boy returned he mixed the powder with water until he had a medicinal gruel.

"Get out," Jock said.

The boy expected a quiet vigil while Jock rested. A sharp chesty cough broke the silence as Jock cleared his throat and spat a gob of phlegm into in the heart of the fire. The boy removed the damp inner blanket, and Jock pointed to a long-faded scar running up the right side of his ribs. "An Apache did that to me, back in 1865. I was about sixteen."

The boy wrapped Jock in a dry blanket and tucked the outer blanket in at the edges. "All right, all right," Jock said, pushing the boy's hands back. "Look son, thanks for taking care of me. There was no need that I spoke rough."

The boy inclined his head acknowledging the apology, sensing that Jock wanted to talk. "What happened?" the boy said, pointing at Jock's ribs.

"Well, it was after the raid on miners near Santa Rita," Jock said.

Leon had told the warriors to keep their children from approaching a group of White Eyes' mining near Santa Rita, but one day a friendly, curious boy of fourteen hung around their camp. They were hard rough men. The miners accused the boy of theft and though the youth had stolen nothing, they flogged him until his back was collage of bloody, torn flesh and ribbons of skin. Healing would leave the youth's back covered by a spider's web of life long scars.

Capitano Leon waited, calming, checking the hot-blooded young bucks in the band. A few days later Jock saw the raiding party assemble, and he was cut that he hadn't been asked to join.

"These men who burrow in the ground," Leon said, "they are your people, Jock. You don't have to come."

"They are White Eyes and I'm part of this," Jock said, his face white and angry. "But I guess I'd best be leaving then."

Leon and Jim broke ranks and stayed Jock's horse. They were both proud of him. And Jock was chuffed when he saw the warm acceptance in their faces, the nods, and murmurs of approval from the warriors. Jock had put the world of the White Eyes behind him. He was free of Westburn and though proud of service on his beloved *Alabama*, and his time in the Cherokee Mounted Rifles, those years were behind him too. Jock had crossed the Rubicon to join the Chiricahua.

"Jim was in from the start, being Cherokee," he told the boy. "But I was glad when they let me join the raid."

Jock had learned a good deal about the arts of guerrilla war fighting with Stand Watie – to ambush, not to be shy in the charge, and hand-to-hand fighting – but Capitano Leon's warriors belonged to a higher order of fighters.

"Jim and me, we fell short of being Chiricahua," Jock said. "We took risks when we hit the camp."

The band attacked the camp from the east, charging out of the sunrise, galloping through rough tents, horses leaping over low fires. They rounded up the ten miners and had the injured boy identify his tormentors. A warrior pushed two men at rifle point to the front. One of them whimpered and cowered in fear of his life. The other, a tall man in dirty white combinations and rough mule-eared boots, with tangled red hair and a matted beard was unbowed. "Fuckin' savages," he said.

The miner turned his attention to Jim wearing the remnants of his Confederate uniform jacket above breech clout and long moccasins. The miner spat at Jim, the gob of mucus splattering on the fore legs of his mount.

"Fuckin' reb injun. No better than a goddamned nigger. An' you!" He turned to Jock, prominent in his Confederate Naval Officer's jacket but otherwise clad Chiricahua fashion. "Piece o' white Southern trash gone renegade; worse than a fuckin' nigger."

"I'm a Scot," Jock told him, "and yes, I fought for the south."

Capitano Leon looked at the father of the injured boy and jerked his head towards the now-tearful miner. The father walked his horse and, as he came level with the miner, he drew his knife and with one swift motion of his arm cut the miner's throat, leaving him prostrate and twitching, gurgling his own blood.

The execution shook the defiant miner, and beneath the matted hair and dirt his face was grey and sweaty. He struggled, and the warrior restraining him struck a blow to his kidneys with the butt of his rifle, pulling him upright.

Leon waved Jim and Jock to his front. "I don't know this word, 'Nigger'; what does it mean?"

"It's a foul word for a black man," Jock said.

"He would call Miriam, Nigger?"

"Probably," Jock said.

"Definitely," Jim said.

"I shall kill him," Leon said.

"I'll fight him," Jock said.

"No. This White Eyes does not deserve a fight, but you can kill him."

A brief trot, and Jock's horse was beside the miner. "Turn him loose," he said to the warrior holding the man. In a clean movement Jock unsheathed the saber attached to his saddle, a powerful downward back handed stroke, the blade shining in the morning sun and the miner's head fell to the ground, a fountain of blood shooting out of the stumped neck. The body crumpled at the knees and lay twitching in its own blood.

Capitan Leon nodded, and the line of warriors formed a half circle and fired into the huddled miners. They shot seven and left the survivor standing, eyes shut, face contorted in terror, head bowed, clutching his shoulders. Gun smoke and the smell of spent ammunition drifted above the heap of corpses.

Silence.

The man opened his eyes.

"You came here, and you made holes in the ground for the yellow iron, and you did not ask permission," Capitano Leon said, "but we brought food and welcomed you. You hurt the boy terribly. This is Apache land. Tell your people what happened in this place. Go! Do not return."

The Chiricahua looted the camp and then burned it. They blocked the entrance to the mine. Jock looked back at the carnage and destruction, turned his horse, and followed Leon and the warriors.

Later that night when the camp was quiet, the friends walked to the creek and sat on the bank.

"Never thought I'd hear that word nigger out here," Jock said.

"Me neither," Jim said.

Nigger; Jock hated it when he heard southerners use it. "Davie White, first black man I met. A steward on the *Alabama*. A bit older than me, but we were good friends."

David White was the slave of a Delaware man. Semmes took him on board the *Alabama* from the Yankee merchant ship, *Tonawanda*.

"Captain Semmes set him free, and he enlisted. He was for the south," Jock said. "Everyone liked him. He said he was better off in the Confederate Navy. He was never called nigger. I heard he went down with the ship."

"I crossed over that day," Jock told the boy. "I started on the path to become one of the people. It was the right thing to do. The miners, common riff raff, would've murdered someone, attacked a woman. That miner deserved my sword. Miners destroy the land. They'd do anything to get their hands on gold."

"And that?" The boy pointed again to the old scar tissue running up the right side of Jock's ribs.

That had come some days later. Jock wasn't exactly basking in glory at the killing of the miner, but he was glad of the increased respect of the warriors which followed the killing.

A party of Mescaleros came to the camp to visit relatives. Normally, such a visit was an occasion for celebration. An hour into the visit a warrior, about twenty, saw the warm looks that Miriam and Jock exchanged. A war club hung by a thong from his wrist and there was a large sheathed Bowie knife on his belt. He stuck his face into Jock's face.

"You are a White Eyes," he said. "You do not belong among us. Go now, or maybe I shall kill you."

Jock turned his back and sheathed the saber he'd been honing and cleaning.

The Mescalero spat at Capitano Leon's feet. "Why do you let the White Eyes stay?"

Then he spun Jock by the shoulder and spat a mouthful of phlegm in Jock's face. Jock grabbed the long black hair and delivered a Westburn Kiss, a head butt, an old trick he'd learnt while serving on the schooner *Jane Brown*.

The Mescalero raised his hands, covering his bleeding mouth and broken nose.

Jock punched him left and right to the heart and stomach and he fell on his knees. "Leave, you damned fool," Jock said and turned.

"Jock!" Jim shouted, and Jock staggered from the thud of the Mescalero's war club hitting his shoulder. The pain was excruciating, and he was afraid that he might lose the power of his left arm, but he kept a tight grip of the saber. Jock turned and grappled with him, spots of blood landing on his face as the Mescalero breathed heavily through his mouth. Jock managed to trip him and leapt back. Feeling returned to his left arm as he unsheathed the saber, throwing the metal scabbard to one side. The Mescalero rose, the Bowie knife in his left hand and the war club, a wicked long instrument, in his right. Jock saw Miriam bury her face in her mother's shoulder. The entire village and the Mescaleros were watching. Leon raised his right arm and made a snatching gesture, 'Kill him', and Jock was fighting for his life.

Jock wielded the saber in both hands, blocking and parrying the swinging war club, but he lost count of the cuts from the Bowie Knife after the fourth. His arms were nicked, two slicing cuts to his chest and his shirt in tatters. His arms and legs stung painfully.

Jock closed in, pinned the arm wielding the war club to the Mescalero's side, and twice smashed the guard of the saber into his face, hitting the injured nose and bruising the jaw. But he'd left his right side exposed, and the Mescalero drove the Bowie Knife at Jock's stomach, missed and cut across Jock's ribs.

They were both butcher-red for Jock had cut the Mescalero's arms and torso as he blocked and parried thrusts from the Bowie Knife and the shattering blows of the war club. Jock drove his knee into the Mescalero's groin, sending him staggering back.

"Draw him on and confuse him," Jock muttered.

The grave faces of Leon and his wife passed in front of Jock, then Miriam's solemn stare, Jim's anxious look, the silent warriors and women of the band. Jock had to kill the Mescalero.

Jock dropped to a half crouch, torso turned, a narrow target. Left arm bent and on guard, sword hand level with his cheek, the blade pointing down, inside edge of the weapon resting on his forearm, the perfectly honed edge uppermost. He made a short attacking leap forward and as the Mescalero came on to meet him, he gave the Rebel Yell. The Mescalero's stride faltered, and Jock swerved left. As the Mescalero passed, Jock swung the saber down with both hands and opened a deep gash in the Mescalero's back.

Jock held the saber across his middle and waited. The Mescalero was still game, a slow turn facing Jock, the strength of his arms leaking from the gory back wound. The Mescalero rushed. The war club raised, left hand at mid torso, the Bowie knife probing the air.

The war club found space as Jock, crouching, turned under the Mescalero's knife hand. The Bowie knife sliced along his scalp as he raised his left arm, driving the saber, cutting edge uppermost, through the Mescalero's ribs and into the lung.

He let the weight of the Mescalero's body slip down on the blade until stopped by his arm pit. A bloody foam stained the Mescalero's lips. Jock tilted the dying man to the right, placed a foot under his arm pit below the blade and withdrew the saber.

The Mescalero fell to the ground and quietly bled to death. The shamed Mescaleros took the body and left.

Jock stayed upright, sinking the point of the saber into the sandy soil. Capitano Leon supported Jock by his left elbow. He removed the saber from his right hand and handed it to Jim.

"I didn't want to hurt any of the people," Jock said, "but I had to kill that man."

"We are honored by your bravery," Leon said. "Come, you are wounded."

"My first experience of Apache medicine and it worked," Jock said to the boy.

The healer would have nothing to do with anything from Jock's medicine bag. He dressed the wounds and bruises with arrow-leafed balsam root, bandaging Jock up. Jock had neglected God since leaving Scotland, but he felt the power of the healer's prayers to Ussen as he treated the wounds.

"I felt a holy force that filled me. I rested for a day or two and Leon got me up, and the pain left my body."

Miriam came and he was glad to see her, but she did not return after the third visit. The old woman took good care of him. Jim and Leon were with him often, and several warriors cemented their acquaintance.

One day Leon took Jock for a short walk. Jock's wounds were tender, but they'd closed. They went armed. Leon carried a bow and a quiver full of arrows. Jock's breath quickened as he kept up with Leon and the Hawken rifle grew heavy cradled in his right arm as they toiled up a hill behind the camp.

"Beautiful," Leon said, sweeping his arm south west across Apacheria to the forested hillside that ran to the edge of the desert and Mexico faraway.

"Like the sea," Jock said.

"I asked Miriam not to see you for a while," Leon said. "I know you wanted to see her, and she wanted to come, for she worried about you."

"I don't understand," Jock said. "Have I offended? If I have, I'm sorry."

Leon laid a reassuring hand on Jock's shoulder and smiled. "No. You are an honest young man, and well liked. You are almost one of us; and Jim, too. But there is something that you have to understand about Miriam. She is not yet a woman."

Miriam was ready to complete the sacred ceremony of White Painted Woman, marking the onset of her menses and her passage from girlhood to womanhood, the time for marriage and bearing children. Leon welcomed the attraction between his daughter and Jock, could not fail to notice it, but he was a watchful father and understood that she was in the turmoil of first love.

"Miriam is a good girl; pure, dutiful, well mannered, and honest. Some of the young men of the band think of Miriam as a wife. There has been interest from the young men of the Chiricahua down in the Sierra Madre. But I do not think that is what she wants, and I shall not have her unhappy. Be patient, Jock."

They sat a while in silence for Jock didn't know what to say. He loved Miriam. Though he'd had shocking experiences fighting in the Civil War, he was just a youth looking forward to his seventeenth birthday. Marriage and a family lay far ahead.

"You are a young man and there is much that you have to do," Leon said. "But Ussen sent you here, maybe. I believe that you and Jim want to stay with us."

"Yes, we do."

"Then neither of you can afford to wait. You must undertake the novitiate and become warriors."

While Jock talked the boy made more tea with the Osha root and handed Jock a cupful. "How do you feel now?" the boy said.

"Soon be able to ride," Jock replied. "The pain is going."

"So you stayed?" the boy said.

"I had much to learn."

Jock and Jim were in fine shape, but they fell short of the toughness and endurance expected of Chiricahua warriors. First, they learnt to run. Not just a few hundred yards or even a mile or two, but twelve miles. Then the distance required of a war party raiding on foot – fifty miles and more, in a steady shuffling trot with brief stops for rest. The young men prepared by running to the tops of mountains holding a mouthful water without swallowing or spitting until they returned to the starting point. It took Jock several attempts to pass this test. And he was surprised at the distance Miriam ran without swallowing or spilling a drop of water from her mouth.

Miriam, able to shoot arrow after arrow on target, trained him with the bow. She used a girl's bow, not the powerful weapon requiring the drawing power of a grown man, but in close quarter fighting Miriam's shooting was deadly. She was delighted to be close to Jock, teaching him the ways of the band.

Jock shot badly, despite patient coaching from Miriam and encouraging remarks from Jim and Leon. After a frustrating morning, with his arrows missing altogether, or just hitting the edge of the target, Miriam removed the bow from his hand and lifted the quiver of arrows from his shoulder. Miriam had had enough of his idle ways. She handed him a sling. Sweat ran down Jock's spine.

"Do you know how to use that?" Miriam said.

"No. Guns I had in the Army, not toys."

"Go over there and try to hit me with a stone."

Jock walked back about sixty yards from Miriam and slung a stone at her. He missed. He loaded the sling and sent another missile across. His eye was sure and the stone might have clipped Miriam, but she skipped safely aside. Then Miriam loaded her own sling. A missile shot past Jock's head, and he recoiled instinctively. Before he could recover, he was hit on the chest.

"Aahh!"

Another missile hit his left elbow and his cry died in his throat. He bent over, shielding his throbbing joint. Jock came erect and a stone hit him on the crown of the head. Miriam swam in front of his eyes, his knees buckle, and he collapsed.

Miriam was sprinkling water on his head, and her anxious face was the first thing he saw when he came to. Gradually his vision cleared, but his head ached, and he raised his right hand to explore the bump.

"Shoot well with the sling," Leon said, smiling. "Then you can master the bow."

Knocked out by the girl he loved, Jock regretted his laziness, and wanted to earn Miriam's respect.

Leon took Jim by the arm and walked with him to the target to gather the arrows.

"Are you ready now to shoot with the sling?" Miriam asked.

"Yes. I'm sorry." Jock raised himself on one knee.

Miriam's long, sensitive fingers hesitantly caressed the bump rising on Jock's head.

"Does it hurt?"

"A little," Jock said, glad of her touch. "Don't stop, not yet."

He looked up and she smiled, and though he didn't need it, he took Miriam's hand and got to his feet.

Jock mastered the sling, moved onto the bow, and Miriam was pleased with him.

The war leaders were hard on the novices, but they watched Jock's shooting in silent admiration. With the Hawken rifle he was the best shot among the novices, so Leon matched him with the best shot among the warriors. Jock beat him. Then they made Jock shoot with a Henry repeating rifle. Jock beat him again.

Jock's skill with the saber was also widely admired in the band, but the sword wasn't an Apache weapon, and no one wanted to take him on, not even in a practice fight. Instead they tried him out with the knife Still carrying the scars from the Mescalero's Bowie knife, Jock had reckoned that at some point in the novitiate there would be knife fighting. A natural with the Bowie knife, Jim had taught Jock what he knew.

The first fight was a draw, so they fought again. His opponent was about nineteen – usually friendly but needled at not beating Jock. He fought hard and landed a couple of low painful blows with his knee, then he nicked Jock's knife arm, leaving a cut that bled freely. Jock ignored the smirk on the warrior's face. At the next pass, Jock grabbed his opponent's knife hand at the wrist with his left hand, forcing his arm up, creating enough space to expose the ribs. Jock reversed his knife and drove the hilt into the ribs.

The move and the pain was unexpected and his opponent staggered back. Jock tripped him by the heel and he landed on his back. Jock stuck his blade in the sand, a half inch from the man's side and stood back. Generously extending his hand, the Apache, a gracious loser, grabbed it and got to his feet.

"There's no novitiate now," the boy said, "not on the reservation."

"Ah, but I think Silver taught you well," Jock said.

"Yes; he took me to quiet places that only old people know. I was ready when I came south to find you."

"Yes, and you've learnt more since you came with me. Still, the novitiate is the right thing for a young warrior. I volunteered. I learnt not to take myself too seriously."

Jock had fought longer than some of the younger warriors in the band. He'd fought clear of a horse shot from under him. Twice he'd survived hand-to-hand fighting and could fight from ambush. He rode well. That experience said Jock was a soldier. Leon needed for Jock to become a warrior. He knew that Jock had it in him to succeed.

Chapter Six

"How do you feel now?" the boy said.

"Better," Jock said. "My power is strong again." He could feel that his fever and arthritis had retreated. Best yet, his piles had shrunk. They would leave at first light.

"Sleep a little more," the boy said. "I'll keep watch."

Jock was weary, but not so fatigued that he needed to sleep. He wanted to talk. Jock remembered how good he felt all those years ago, made stronger and confident by the Chiricahua, when he'd come into his manhood and claimed Miriam's hand.

Jock gestured with his arm. "I became a warrior in these parts, back in 1867."

"Was it hard? Were you afraid?"

"I was prepared, and I was tested, but no, I wasn't afraid when I went out. Remember, I'd been with the Cherokee in the Civil War."

"Tell me about it?"

Jock counted off on his fingers. "I went to the Sacred Mountain to find my power, and Leon took me to the sweat lodge and then on the four raids of the novitiate."

The Chiricahua lived and fought in small bands. Guerrilla warfare was second nature to them, and they knew whether a raiding party should be three or thirty, or a hundred warriors. Out raiding, or if the rancheria was threatened, they would scatter in several directions, confusing enemies, arranging to meet at secret places. Perhaps their greatest strength though, was that they were part of the land of Apacheria; they held its secrets in their bones, as no Mexican or White Eyes ever could.

Enemies frequently mistook the small numbers of Apaches for weakness. But on first contact, they learned otherwise, receiving lessons from the schools of hard knocks and sudden death.

"We were few, and fought in small war parties," Jock said. "If we'd fought big battles with all our strength, we might have been defeated and wiped out maybe."

They'd brought a small doe back from the hunt to the rancheria, and the crone who looked after Jock had swiftly removed the skin and hung the carcass. Leon offered their help, knowing that she was frail, but she chased them away, cackling that men were not fit for women's work. They left her talking to herself and went to the creek to wash away blood and dirt. When they'd dried their faces, arms and torsos, Leon turned to Jock.

"You must find your power, Jock. It is time to give yourself to Ussen."

"I am ready?"

"Yes."

Young Chiricahua men and women seek their power with four days fasting and praying on the Sacred Mountain. It came to the seeker through a medium – an animal, a plant, a piece of quartz, the cone of an evergreen.

"I shall take you now to the medicine man, *Ha-tan-e-ged-eh*. He talks to Ussen. In his medicine bag, there is an Army sword. He wants to meet you, Jock, the man from faraway, a fighter and friend of the Cherokee who is becoming one of us. I told him about your skill with the sword. Show him your saber."

Ha-tan-e-ged-eh waved them to sit down beside him outside the door of his wickiup. Jock handed him the long, curved, beautifully made saber. He made a few practice swings and nodded approvingly.

The medicine man apparently cared nothing for appearances. He wore a greasy leather cap with four eagle feathers spread at the front.

His worn buckskin shirt covered the top of his off-white breech clout. He smiled at Jock's puzzled expression but when he spoke, Jock felt the holiness in his rich, deep voice. "I walk in the mountains; for my power."

Jock was calm, and the power of *Ha-tan-e-ged-eh*'s eyes held him. "This sword is your weapon, but it is not your power," *Ha-tan-e-ged-eh* said. "You must go to the Sacred Mountain, the Home of the Mountain Spirits that connect us to Ussen. You are ready; maybe you shall find it there."

He reached into the bag containing his sword and exposed the hilt with a worn gold tassel attached. Then he withdrew an amulet, a thin tanned strip of buckskin, partly bound with gold thread from the tassel.

The medicine man fastened the buckskin strip on Jock's upper arm, just below the shoulder. There was a moment of pain and shock – remembering the collapse of his family and the guilt of his childish confessions and penance; the lingering terror of priestly rebukes threatening eternal damnation which haunted him for days afterwards. But as the strip of buckskin tightened onto his arm, there was no more terror, no guilt. Jock was at peace.

"Wear it on the Sacred Mountain." *Ha-tan-e-ged-eh*'s face creased in a thin smile, and he handed Jock a small buckskin pouch, its opening rucked by a rawhide drawstring. "For your power, if you find it."

Jock climbed the Sacred Mountain, clad in breech clout and new long moccasins; spending four days without food or water, praying to Ussen for the sign that his voice was heard and that he accepted Jock. After two days of prayer and fasting, Jock, seeking Holiness in greater mortification of his flesh, cut his arms and chest with a sharp stone. His wounds turned crusty, the blood drying on his body. Stoically, patiently, he prayed for the sign as hunger, thirst and fatigue threatened his spirit. And then, on the fourth day She Wolf, guardian of her young, came out of the sunrise.

Jock had chosen a secret place, a small plateau high on the Sacred Mountain. Behind him, a short demanding scramble away, was the summit. Below him was the forest and far beyond it the great sweep of the South Western desert. Jock sat, legs crossed, arms resting on his knees. His head hung low on his chest as tiredness wore him down, and he didn't see She Wolf draw close. His eyes flickered open, and Jock saw the white forepaws. He looked up into her piercing, seductive eyes. She was beautiful, but he was afraid, and the wolf knowing this reached out, nuzzled his hand and his fear vanished.

"I am your power; touch me, share my wisdom and my strength," She Wolf said. "It shall be many years, but you shall be a great warrior and give heart to the people."

Jock had heard about She Wolf from *Ha-tan-e-ged-eh*. At their first meeting he'd said that her power gave stamina and heart for the long journey. Jock raised his arms to She Wolf and recited the warrior's song, *Let me be strong; let me be strong like the wolf.*

She Wolf moved closer, and tentatively Jock touched the purity of her glorious white coat. Warmth came, and he buried his hands deep in her fur where it was flecked with red matching the color of his own hair. Her smell enveloped him. She came closer still and gently licked the wounds he'd made on his arms and chest; the dried blood vanished, and he felt the lacerations closing. Her penetrating golden eyes beguiled Jock, and he felt love come from her, as her tongue washed the scars of old wounds; and the deep ache that was in them went and his body and spirit were made whole.

She Wolf raised her right foreleg, and Jock took it. There was a shiver, then She Wolf withdrew her paw, and her right dewclaw lay in Jock's hand. He secreted the dewclaw in the small buckskin bag given to him by *Ha-tan-e-ged-eh*, which he would wear around his neck, under his shirt for the rest of his life. She Wolf and her dewclaw: they were his medicine and his power.

Jock's eyes locked on She Wolf's shining eyes as she extended her forelegs and slowly withdrew. She stopped and raised her head exposing the pure white fur of her throat, and his heart filled when her long howl shattered the morning quiet. Jock raised his arms and from deep within came his own long wolf-howl of farewell. She Wolf turned and ran; Jock's eyes followed her until she vanished into the rising sun.

Jock stood – he'd found his power, his ordeal over. With a clear head, and an open heart, he ran down the rocky slopes of the Sacred Mountain.

Leon brought Jock and Jim to the built at the edge of the village, near spring water one afternoon. The following day they would go out on their first raid.

"The lodge is good," Leon said. "It will cleanse and heal your body and make your soul pure. To go to the sweat lodge brings good fortune."

"But She Wolf healed me, gave me power," Jock said.

Jim remained silent.

Leon smiled indulgently, for Jock had done well on the Sacred Mountain. He was approving of the scars Jock had inflicted on his body in the search for the holiness necessary to receive his power; and it was good that She Wolf had come to Jock. Jock's heart was almost Chiricahua, but he was a young man and had yet to learn to talk less and listen more.

They walked together, and novices. "Jock, it is good that we do this before a raid," Leon said. "The Creator, a power that is neither a man nor a woman made the world in four days. It is hard for us to understand this mystery, but it is in our faith, and we believe it."

This mystery didn't seem at all far-fetched to Jock after his time on the Sacred Mountain. When he was growing up in Westburn, he'd heard about several mysteries from priests when he attended school; that God made the world in six days and rested on the seventh; that the Saints of old still watched over him, and the Holy Spirit guided the Church. Jock believed that when he went to confession the priest had the power to forgive his sins. He believed in the miracle of transubstantiation as the bread and wine became the body and blood of the savior, Jesus Christ. Jock expected to feel Holy when the Host passed his lips. He never did.

"This human world is a shadow and false image," Leon said. "The reality is hidden in the world of the creator and his power."

Jock and Jim remained silent.

"The sweat lodge comes from Child of the Water. It is sacred; the knowledge is handed down to a few men."

"Child of the Water?" Jock repeated.

"Yes," Leon said. "He is very holy, and has power."

The Chiricahua believed that the first people on earth were White Painted Woman and her brother, Killer of Enemies. The brother was there to hunt and provide food, but when he killed game, Owl Man Giant stole it, so White Painted Woman and Killer of Enemies starved. One day, Life Giver, a spirit, came in a thunderstorm. His lightning entered White Painted Woman. Nine months later the baby was born, and White Painted Woman called him Child of the Water. Child grew into a great warrior and in a savage fight, slew Owl Man Giant.

"White Painted Woman reared her son to destroy evil creatures and to make the earth fit for man," Leon said. "It was White Painted Woman, Killer of Enemies and Child of the Water that created this present world. Child of the Water does Ussen's work."

Leon swung his arm in the four directions. "It is Child of the Water who made the good things of the world for man. He made arrows with zig zag markings to slay the Owl Man Giant. That is why we mark our arrows in this way; for power. Child of the Water guides us in all things."

Leon lifted the buckskin pouch out from beneath Jock's shirt, "*Ha-tan-e-ged-eh* made this for your time on the Sacred Mountain. It is perfect and very holy; he follows the way of Child of the Water. *Ha-tan-e-ged-eh* did a great thing for you, Jock. Open your heart to the power."

The building of the lodge was supervised by an old man, a custodian of knowledge. He directed some younger men in its construction, encouraging their work with prayer and song. They built the lodge like a regular wickiup, but smaller at four and a half feet high and six feet in diameter. The oak frame was tied at the top and a cladding of brush and skins secured to the frame. There was no smoke hole. The door faced east to celebrate and honour the gifts - the dawn, the sun, and the new day. Just inside the door and to one side, the helpers dug a shallow pit for the hot rocks.

One by one the seven members of the war party arrived. Jock and Jim stood apart, waiting with Leon. Everyone was clad in a loin cloth.

"Now we are rubbed down to prepare for the ritual," Leon said. "Choose from pounded pinon needles or ground juniper."

"Why pinon or juniper?' Jock asked.

"Pinon soothes cuts and sores," Leon said. "Juniper cleanses the air and stops infections. But they are both good for the body."

Jock followed Leon and was treated with juniper. Jim preferred pinon needles. Leon pointed to bunches of sage at the door. "Bind this around your head. Sage purifies and consecrates us."

Four large rocks on forked sticks were brought from the fire and placed in the shallow pit dug inside the door of the lodge. The old man brought water, and each man drank from a cup in which four pieces of mesquite bean had been placed.

"You will itch when you sweat. It is forbidden to scratch with the fingers," Leon handed them a stick made from the branch of a fruit-bearing tree. "Scratch with this."

The men sat in a circle, leaving an open space to the east, and the old man sprinkled water on the hot rocks. Gradually, the small space was filled with a thick steamy vapor, and the warriors took it in turn to sprinkle water on the rocks.

At the entrance another man was adjusting the door, stopping the heat from escaping. The old man with the power was with them leading the prayers and singing of special songs for the lodge and praising the earth and the sky.

Jock lost the sense of time passing, he might have been in the sweat lodge twenty minutes or several hours. He hadn't strived for the beyond, content to sweat out the impurities from his body. But knowledge came anyway and Ussen lifted and blessed Jock, delivering him to a trance. Love pierced Jock's breast and he understood that he would belong to Miriam and she to him. He wanted to know more but wasn't ready. Ussen returned Jock to his body deeply contented and reaching for the known – the sweat lodge, the place where he could find Miriam, and Jim, and the wisdom of Leon.

When the old man finished praying and singing, Jock followed Leon and the warriors out into the twilight and to the brook. Jock was drained physically by visions, ecstatic praying and singing in suffocating heat. Plunging into the brook water brought him back to the world.

"We have submitted to Ussen; we are ready," Leon said.

Afraid of looking foolish, he held the special cap prepared by the Shaman for novices at arm's length. "What's this?"

"For your protection," Leon said. "Listen and learn. The men know you can fight; that you are not a coward and it was good when they saw you defend our honor against the Mescalero. But now they are watching to see if you are obedient and can become a warrior. It is time for you to show what you can do."

Jock was attempting a difficult thing, becoming Chiricahua; to belong was an honor seldom given. Fail and Leon would turn him away. He'd lose his friendship with Jim, already married to Little Swan. But what Jock couldn't bear was never seeing Miriam again.

"Remember, Jock. The novitiate is where you learn to become a warrior," Leon said. "Some things you will understand at once, but you may not see the point of other things for a time."

Novices worked under constraints. Jock understood the importance of telling the truth, and that it was rude to laugh at another person's expense, for he was honest and polite. It was hard at his age to maintain purity of mind, but there was little opportunity to corrupt the body. The threatened consequence of gluttony in middle age for greed during the novitiate did not disturb him; serving in the Cherokee Mounted Rifles had taught him when to curb his appetite. Chiricahua men plucked out facial hair with tweezers, but Jock had grown a close-trimmed wispy red beard. Nevertheless, he followed the other novices and used the scratching stick to avoid a hairy face.

"You'll attend to the warriors when out raiding; help them bed down, look after their horses." Leon grinned. "You'll wake up tired, maybe, and take some water through the drinking tube, and you'll kindle the fire, make breakfast. But you may eat only selected food."

If he did not observe instructions, Jock would have bad luck with horses, another threatened consequence. He knew horses at least as well as any warrior in the band, but he did not protest and would obey. When he was in the Confederate Army he'd put up with hunger and thirst, eaten what had come his way, hot or cold, and drank when he could. He could chew on tough meat – cuts from the neck of deer, cattle, and sheep – nor did it trouble him to be forbidden entrails, or meat from the head.

"Whether we are mounted or raiding on foot, do not gaze at the sky," Leon said. "If you do, heavy rain will come."

"You tell me many things."

"Yes. I know that your time as a soldier has toughened you. You are not a simple beginner, but you have much to learn in a short time." Leon bit the end from a dark-leafed Mexican cigar and lit it with an ember from the fire. "The Chiricahua men and women make the children. But the men go to war and often their life is short. So women are more valuable than men. Women give life to the people. The love between man and woman is a sacred thing."

Miriam passed, carrying firewood. She was lovely, dressed in a pale blue calico blouse and fine buckskin skirt. Her long moccasins looked new. But what drew Jock's eye was the deep blue of the linen sash that he'd given her, bound high on her waist and accentuating the points of her small breasts. He'd seen her wearing the sash in this fashion once before and was happy to see her wearing it again.

But when she placed her load outside the wickiup, her mother hauled her inside and he heard the older woman's raised voice. Several minutes later, Miriam re-appeared dressed in her working garments.

Her eyes were red and tears stained her face. Jock regretted her embarrassment. He was so happy that she seemed to have dressed to please him.

Leon saw the happiness on Jock's face and smiled. "Miriam made her skirt and blouse; she was wearing new moccasins, but her mother does not want to see her clothes ruined. Miriam is young and there is time coming for her to dress up. It's good that she has to wait and learn patience."

Modest, sweet-spoken Miriam. Jock had never heard her utter a coarse word or indulge in displays of affection. It was not the Chiricahua way. When he dreamt about her, he wanted to tell her that he'd never known anyone like her; wanted to say how lovely he found her. But he feared he'd be trapped in the conventions of elliptic asides and obscure hints that shaped conversations between Chiricahua men and women.

Among married couples, conversation was free from crudity. Leon and his wife had an affectionate relationship, but it was not expressed publicly beyond quiet smiles of respect that they exchanged and their considerate remarks.

But sometimes marriages broke down and couples divorced. If a man found his wife in adultery, he might cut off the tip of her nose. Jock had seen one or two women with this disfigurement. The Chiricahua recognized the shift in social standing when a couple parted or a husband died, allowing divorcees and widows a measure of latitude in their relations with men.

"Sometimes it is hard to please women," Leon said. "Before I found Miriam, I wanted to help with the heavy work, but this upset my wife. I pleased her by not helping."

Jock knew that Leon was a good husband, protected his family, hunted, provided food. He was responsible for a couple of widows and their families and for some of the aged in the band. Leon was an example to other men.

"Some pretty girls in the rancheria, Jock?"

"Yes."

A striking woman in her early thirties passed, a boy and girl in tow. Though dressed for work her buckskin skirt and calico blouse were clean and tidy, attire chosen to draw attention. The lips reddened with berry juice highlighted her light skin and drew the eyes to her rather sweet, oval face; and her dainty moccasins decorated with beads and ornate stitching flattered her small feet, features admired by the Chiricahua men. She greeted Leon respectfully and smiled at Jock.

"Good looking woman; a beauty. But her head is easily turned. Once she went with a man from another band when he flattered her. Her husband was deeply hurt; he refused to cut the point off her nose, but he fought and killed the man. That did not make her very happy; and she has much to say – her tongue is a sharp stone."

"You know my wife, Sigesh, Jock?"

"Yes."

"She has a sweet nature and a loving heart, though her tongue can be wicked if I irritate her. But no man can turn her head; and if he tried, I would kill him."

Jock liked Sigesh. He did not find her at all plain; more comely, he would have said. She had the warmest smile, which lit up her face. Sigesh's beauty lay within, kept safe for Leon.

"We have no children of our own now. We had a son, but he was sickly and died very young. Sigesh was heartbroken." Leon breathed deeply, mastering the grief that welled up with the memory of his son's death. "I think maybe Ussen kept us without children so that I found Miriam and we could be a family. Sigesh was so happy when I brought Miriam home."

Jock was surprised. Guarded though it was, what Leon said had taken great effort. In matters of the heart he was not talkative. Rather, he showed his affection for his wife and his daughter in a kind word or a wave of the hand. Once when his wife was unwell with a cold, Miriam had cooked a rabbit. Leon sent her first to feed her mother. When they were done and he thought that Jock was not looking, Leon had touched her forehead, and she'd smiled and bowed her head.

"Miriam is not a classic Chiricahua beauty, Jock."

Leon was too polite to mention what men did not like, but Jock knew anyway, having listened to warriors criticize women with big feet, or ample lips, a large nose, the long face with dark skin.

"No."

"But you like her?"

"Yes."

"So do some of the other young men."

Jock was embarrassed by Leon's teasing. But suddenly, what he liked about Miriam was clear and it wasn't her looks. Rather it was Miriam's quiet loveliness that had grown on Jock. She was more endearing now than when they'd first met more than a year previously. Miriam was not tall, just an inch or two above five feet, her carriage, the noble stride of her slender neck, the proud, dignified way she held her head, suggested deep reservoirs of spirit and inner strength. Her looks drew his eyes; her strong nose and prominent cheekbones, the dark eyes that he wanted to gaze into for long moments. Her Girl-Boy face; the fleeting androgyny, but her long black hair with a hint of a curl heightened her femininity. Her face was endearing when she pulled back her hair; but when it hung loosely below her shoulders, she was adorable. Miriam's was a delicate beauty, the looks of her Benin forebears, the fair nature that came from her Chiricahua upbringing. Jock loved her.

Meetings between unmarried young men and women were frowned on. But Jock, lacking experience with women – apart from his one sordid encounter aboard *Alabama* – was puzzled by the frequent 'accidental' meetings of boys and girls. He'd met Miriam a couple of times in the outer environs of the rancheria, surprised to see her there, but too shy, too cautious to do more than greet her formally. One day they met though, and he could not avoid a lingering conversation.

Jock had gone to the creek to bathe and attend to his toilet. He'd stopped shaving and was trimming his soft wispy beard using a mirror propped on a low branch of a cottonwood, and a combination of open razor, comb, and sharp scissors.

The first he knew that Miriam was present was when he saw her face in the mirror beside his own. Her hair was gathered loosely in a single plait, turned over her right shoulder. Her deep black complexion shining, eyes wide with surprise; she was altogether lovely.

"I don't shave, but I like to keep my beard neat," Jock said to her reflection.

"Chiricahua men pluck out the hair on their face with tweezers," Miriam responded.

"I know."

He smiled at her likeness, and she smiled back. There was no guile in Miriam. Her heart had led her to Jock, and her right hand appeared in the mirror as she tenderly touched his beard with her long slender fingers, letting them linger on his cheek. Jock moved his face against Miriam's fingers and was glad when she increased her touch, and then she returned her fingers to his beard.

"It's lovely and soft."

"Your face in the mirror, Miriam. That's what you see when you look in still water?"

"Yes."

Jock turned and handed her the mirror, sad that her reflection had vanished but glad that he was looking directly at his beloved.

"For you; a present. Don't worry. I have another."

They paused, eyes locked.

"Every day look in the mirror, see how lovely you are."

"Oh, thank you, thank you," she said, blushing at his daring as she tucked the mirror inside her calico blouse. Then she gathered her laundry firmly under her arm. "I'd better go."

Jock caught Miriam lightly but firmly by the shoulder. He was determined to tell her that he loved her, but only managed, "Not yet. Please."

Miriam looked around. "We will be seen."

Jock looked down into the beautiful eyes of this appealing girl and was glad of this 'accident'. Miriam returned his gaze. He wanted to hold her, but was checked by respect for her, so gently, he cupped his right hand under her chin and she did not draw back. The Chiricahua did not kiss, but he kissed Miriam. He closed his eyes but saw her puzzled expression when he opened them.

"What are you doing?"

"Where I come from, men and women kiss when they care for each other. Again?"

"Yes."

Her taste was on Jock's lips and in his mouth once again. Miriam touched his lips with her fingers. "I must go."

Before departure there was thorough preparation for the raid. "Sit by my side, Jock, and you too, Jim, and we shall get ready. We attack on foot."

"On foot?" Jim said.

"Yes. Horses need care and that slows us. We run swiftly, travel far, arrive silently. In the raid we shall take horses, mules for the loot and run the cattle and sheep to the stronghold. We shall not fight unless we must. Bring a spare pair of moccasins, soles and buckskin. We shall run a long way."

"How far?" Jim asked.

"Seventy miles, maybe."

Jock and Jim exchanged a worried look.

"I know that you can do that." Leon handed them a small pack containing dried corn, cakes made from the prickly pear and nutritious berries. "Mix this food with water. It is good while we are on the move, but if we find a stray mule or cow, we'll butcher it. Do not worry; you'll get used to the taste of raw meat."

They worked on checking weapons, finishing their preparation.

"Do not let the Mexicans take you," Leon said.

In Chihuahua City, the Mexicans displayed the dried ears of Apaches killed in battle or taken prisoner. Sometimes they put the heads of the people on the top of poles. Leon smiled. "The Mexicans pay many pesos for Apache scalps, so take care Jim. But Jock, you do not have to worry, maybe. With the red hair, your scalp is worth little."

Jock took part in the war dance now that his novitiate was complete. This was no death song, just words for the way forward. The fifth raid, Jock's first as a warrior. He understood that he was expected to fight in the front rank. Jock felt he had more to prove than Jim. He was younger than Jim, and though the Chiricahua did not refer to it, Jock was conscious of his whiteness. He was anxious to belong to the Chiricahua.

Each warrior sipped water that would not be swallowed. The precious liquid remained in the mouth for several hours, moistening the tongue until finally they swallowed it to ease their thirst. In the first light they ran for the mountains.

Fleeter than light infantry, swifter than cavalry, ten men went out clad in breech clouts and long moccasins. Jock was allowed a shirt to protect his fair skin from the sun, and they were carrying spare footwear and rawhide soles, a little food, water bags, arms, and ammunition. Shuffling along in single file, they might seem a party of shambling cripples to a fool, but the short rapid strides ate distance.

Clearing the stronghold, two warriors moved out ahead, the eyes of the raiders. If they spotted enemies one warrior remained watching, the other would return to inform the main party.

They kept to the mountains, running all day and through the night, stopping for short rests and another mouthful of water. A mile or so from their destination they stopped. Leon separated from the band and sat facing east. Jock's keen ears heard him singing quietly. Then he returned.

"The wind will come," Leon said.

Just before dawn they came down from the mountain to the plain and deployed around the prosperous Mexican ranch with its well-constructed buildings. Some years before, the band had raided here and come away with rich takings of cattle and sheep, horses, blankets and weapons. Now Leon was back, ready for another battle in the long war with the Mexicans. He'd fill his larder, replenish the band's herds of horses, cattle and sheep, take weapons and ammunition. The interval between the last raid and the present was calculated to lull the ranch owner and his people to permit the accumulation of goods and animals useful to the Chiricahua.

Jock heard the wind whisper and then shriek. Sand blown to fury stung him. With a pale sun behind they came out of the tempest and attacked. They left a badly damaged main building and smoking ruins of outbuildings. Warriors herded about two hundred head of cattle, sheep, and horses. Mules were laden with guns, ammunition, clothing, and blankets. The dead had been stripped of all useful clothing and weapons. Jock had fought well, had done his share, killing and wounding vaqueros who'd defended their employer's property and their own small holdings. A dozen men had been killed, but Jock was shocked by the slaughter of women and children. He held a horse by the reins, standing alongside Leon who tightened and adjusted the saddle for the journey back to the stronghold as a file of warriors, rifle butts resting on the edge of saddles, rode past.

Leon sensed his discomfort. "Mexicans are our enemies," he said. "Years ago, they tried to make us slaves in their mines, to work and dig underground. When we met in them friendship, they made us drunk and killed many Chiricahua; they killed our women and children. If they could, the Mexicans would wipe out the Apaches."

The last warrior in the column turned and waved to Leon and nodded to Jock. "That one, El Tigre, the Mexicans call him. He was born Mexican. We took him when he was about three years old and raised him Chiricahua. Now he is thirty, maybe, and one of us."

"He never wanted to go back?"

"No. He had a chance once – in adolescence, there was an exchange of prisoners. He chose to stay."

Out in the Territory, fighting the Yankees had often been savage, but Jock had fought as part of a company or regiment, up against soldiers. Though Jock had heard about the brutality of Missouri Bushwhackers and Kansas Jay Hawkers, he had not seen it firsthand. Despite what Leon said, his exposure to the ferocity of the raid left him empty.

Leon studied Jock's face. "Listen to me, Jock," Leon said. "Mexicans killed my mother, and I have lost many friends because of them. You came among us, and did a good thing saving our women from bad White Eyes; had Ussen not sent you Miriam would be dead. I'm glad you stayed with us, but we did not ask you to stay."

Jock saw three terrified children, two boys, and one girl, all under five and weeping, mounted behind warriors.

"They shall be Chiricahua, belong to families," Leon said, "to replace children killed by Mexicans."

"Like me?" Jock said.

"No Jock. We shall raise them Chiricahua. You have chosen and we accepted you, but this is a hard life. It is not for you, maybe."

Two hours later and the raiders were making a swift passage, riding steadily towards the stronghold. Two warriors riding ahead, scouting, five warriors running the livestock and the mules carrying the loot. Jock was in the rearguard with Leon and Jim. In little more than a day, they would be home.

Leon turned his horse round. Behind them, a dust cloud suggested a strong pursuit. The landowner whose estate they'd plundered meant to catch up, take back his property, avenge the killing of his people.

"I'll ride ahead, warn the men," Leon said. "Tell them to hurry for the secret rendezvous."

Jock watched the Mexicans through the Dollard and Aitchinson telescope taken from a dead Yankee officer back in Oklahoma. Big party, maybe fifty well-armed men riding hard. He handed Leon the telescope.

"Hmm," Leon said. "Good long glass," he added, studying the Mexicans. Jock reckoned Leon would not want to scatter the raiding party and risk losing the animals and booty taken in the raid. He put the glass down. "This Hawken rifle with the small long glass; maybe heavy. I wondered why you ran with it. It shoots far?"

Jock held the rifle up, inviting Leon's admiration, weighing it in his hand, demonstrating its balance.

"It's a strong rifle; accurate, double set triggers, long barrel. A sharp shooter's gun. I can hit them from half a mile."

Jim had come equally well armed. A Spencer repeating carbine and a pair of Dragoon pistols were holstered at his waist, along with a Bowie knife. He had a bandolier of ammunition for the Spencer slung across his chest. With the seven rounds in the magazine of the Spencer, he had nineteen shots before reloading; and the Spencer could be rearmed quickly.

"Deal with these Mexicans?" Leon said.

"We can do that." Jock managed to mask his doubt. Jim as well.

"When it's over, you can find your way to the rendezvous?"

"Yes," Jock said.

"If we return to the stronghold without you, Miriam and Little Swan shall be worried. Take this." Leon handed Jock a Colt Dragoon pistol.

Jock stuck the weapon in the bandolier around his waist, a partner for the holstered Colt on his right side.

A quick sawing with his heavy knife, and Leon shortened the barrels of a shotgun taken in the raid. He smoothed the edges of the barrels with a hard, rough stone. "You know how to use it?"

"Yes." The sawn-off shotgun and not the saber was the preferred close-quarter weapon in the Cherokee Mounted Rifles. Jock slung a bandolier of shotgun shells slanting around his torso, making a saltire with the cartridge belt for the Hawken rifle With the breech loading, single shot Hawken rifle, two Colt pistols, and a loaded sawn off shotgun slung across his back he had fifteen shots before reloading. Not perhaps an ideal weight for a warrior on foot, but Jock now felt he was up to it and was unfazed by additional arms.

"Remember, my power is the weather," Leon said. "Wait for the storm."

"But how can we see in a storm?"

"Do not worry, Jock. Your power is coming. I feel it. You shall see enemies and guide Jim."

With Jock and Jim's mounts in tow, Leon headed east leaving the tracks of three horses away from the route taken by the warriors heading for the secret rendezvous, tempting pursuers to divide and come after him, fooling them to believing that all the Chiricahua were ahead and none in their rear. Eventually, Leon would shake off any pursuit and turn north.

They agreed a plan of attack. Jock and Jim set off in a rapid shuffle-run over rocky ground where they would leave no tracks, weapons resting lightly, taking a wide loop from the false trail that they'd made with Leon. On the bare rocky terrain where cover was an insuperable problem for Mexicans or Americans, the meager scrub and tumble-weed provided refuge and a place of ambush for the two friends. Without thinking, drawing on what they'd learned, they separated thirty yards and lay prone, a clump of brush held in front of their faces. At a distance they were all but invisible to the pursuers.

The Mexicans came up at a good pace and were hazy in a dust cloud of their own making. Jock and Jim waited until the tempest filled the atmosphere. The riders in the van of the coloumn slowed down for they could not see. Horsemen in the rear of the coloumn collided with them. But Jock's eyes cut through the haze and dust and saw the body of milling animals and men.

He fired the Hawken rifle into the heaving mass. To his right he heard the crack of the Spencer. Through the sharp jingling harnesses, and snorting beasts, they heard a man's scream. Jock, with Jim some yards behind, ran in a low crouch a dozen yards into the gloom to-wards the rear of the column. Jock knelt on one knee, reloaded the Hawken rifle and fired again. Almost simultaneously the Spencer cracked once, twice, creating the impression of an ambushing war party.

Five men were down.

The Mexicans shot wildly, wounding or killing their own. Calmly, Jock reloaded the Hawken Rifle, unslung the shotgun and slung the rifle. Jim was beside him, methodically feeding three rounds into the tube magazine of the Spencer. They made a gap of maybe twenty feet between them and ran towards the disintegrating column. Ten feet out, Jock fired the shotgun and Jim, working the Spencer sent four rounds into the packed horses and men. Shrieks of pain cut through the roaring wind. Jock's heart raced then thudded, drumming heavily in his ears. Effort, fear and excitement pumped sweat, soaking his dusty shirt, but as Leon had taught him, Jock took deep, calming breaths, slipping two shells into the shotgun. He wondered how Jim was feeling. He heard the report of the Spencer several feet behind him and a man and horse crashed to the ground. Jock fired again, and a wounded man screamed. Jim was beside him and slung the carbine just as Jock slung the shotgun. Colt pistols in both hands, they charged into the remnants of the column, thumbing the hammers, blazing away eight rounds each. Two rounds left in their pistols, they holstered one, grabbed the reins of two shocked horses standing in the melee, and sprung into the saddle. A ball clipped Jock's ear lobe, sticky blood running onto his shirt, and he heard Jim's voice cut through the din of battle.

"Jock! Are you hit?"

"A graze. Go!"

They drove their mounts into the wreck of the Mexicans, steering horses with their knees, arms pumping up and down, aiming, swinging here and there, metal biting flesh, pistol whipping their way through the column. Triumphantly, Jock called on his medicine and raised his voice in the long howl of She Wolf as Jim's Rebel Yell rang in his ears.

Jock's head cleared as they reloaded their weapons. He'd been in close quarter engagements out in the Territory, but this was the first time he'd fought with Jim against overwhelming odds, and he understood that this was the courage expected of Chiricahua warriors. He dismissed cutting the horse's throat. It annoyed him, letting a fine mare go, and the beautiful saddle with the big horn. Jim felt the same. Reluctantly they shattered the holstered rifles against a rock, for they were already carrying heavy arms. They whacked the horses on the flanks sending them running east, the hooves leaving sign should the Mexicans decide to follow. Jock doubted they would, confident that they had no appetite left to fight.

He passed Jim his leather water flask. Jim took a mouthful and passed it back. Jock took a sip of water and slung the flask. The water would stay in their mouths for several hours; like the born Chiricahua they could survive in this wilderness without water for forty-eight hours.

They nodded and a savage grin creased their faces. Jock was proud that they'd cut up the Mexican column and survived. Their fighting skills in guerrilla warfare were near perfect and their powers of endurance matched the mounted warriors ahead of them. They were going where no Mexican could follow, traveling by dead reckoning, Leon's directions clear in their heads, making the long run across the mountains, crossing the plain that night, and climbing again to the rendezvous. Jim was in front, Jock a few yards behind. They loped up the rocky slope, jumping across gaps in the ridge, gaining height until they reached the plateau where they'd start the distance eating shuffle-run.

That night the band celebrated the return of the warriors from the raid. They feasted on mescal, venison, wild potatoes and flatbread made from Dropseed grass seeds. Tiswin was passed about, but not too much, for Leon knew the dangers and excesses that followed drunkenness among the people.

Several warriors spoke of their exploits, but Leon was called by a veteran warrior to speak of Jock and Jim's rearguard action, and he did so handsomely, to the point that Jim, a quiet man and Jock, naturally reticent, squirmed with embarrassment. Leon waited until the band was silent.

"You belong with us," he said. "You are Chiricahua."

There were cheers and shouts of approval. Little Swan came to Jim's side and smiled proudly at her husband. Jock searched the assembly for Miriam. He caught sight of her in the background. A young girl still, not yet a woman, Miriam could not fully attend the celebrations. She smiled and raised her hand acknowledging him and Jock's heart soared.

The next afternoon, Jock sat with Jim outside his wickiup, cleaning and maintaining weapons. They saw an older woman approach with Leon.

"This is She Whose Hands Heal," Leon said. "She asks for your help."

"I am honored," Jock said.

Hanging back was a distraught, pretty young woman, newly married.

"This is Gentle Wind," She Whose Hands Heal said, "and she is sick with worry."

"It is my husband," she said through her tears. "It is his face."

"Please," Jock said, beckoning her. "I'm sure I can help."

Jock knew of course that four warriors suffered wounds in the raid, but none were life threatening. In the celebratory mood that took hold of the village when the warriors returned from the raid, worries about wounds vanished. Jock hadn't offered to help, thinking that it was polite to wait until he was asked, concerned that his intervention might be resented by the band's established healers.

Jock got out the Confederate medical kit. He had no laudanum left so there was little he could do to relieve pain, but that was not an overwhelming concern, for warriors prided themselves in their tolerance of pain.

"Jim, can you bring the tequila?" Jock said.

A handsome warrior of twenty had been slashed across the face in hand-to-hand fighting during the raid. The cut ran diagonally from the top of his right ear to his jawline and had begun to heal. Here and there where the blade had struck, the wound had ragged edges and these would heal leaving proud flesh.

"Make a small fire, Jim," Jock said. He looked at the warrior. "This is going to hurt." He offered him the leather pad to bite on when the pain became intense, but the warrior shook his head, dismissing concerns about his suffering. "Bite on this; I insist on it. And do not move," Jock placed the leather-bound stick between the warrior's teeth.

"I can make the scar neat and when it heals it will not be easily seen," he said. "But you must keep still while I treat you. If you leave nature to heal the wound the scar will make you ugly."

Behind him, he heard the young woman sobbing.

Jock sterilized a scalpel in the pot of boiling water. Gently he removed the forming scab, and cleaned the wound with a swab soaked in tequila. The young warrior's breath whistled in Jock's ears as the liquor stung the wound. Then a film of sweat gathered on his brow when Jock trimmed ragged flesh and skin at the edge of the wound. The bit moved as his teeth anchored further into the leather binding.

Jock selected the finest curved needle and silk suture for the job. The warrior sat impassively as Jock stitched, jaw muscles corded, his teeth grinding deeper into the leather pad, beads of sweat erupting and running down his face; twenty-eight times the needle penetrated the warrior's flesh, the sutures drawn tight.

Jock dabbed the warrior's face dry with a clean cloth. They were both drained, but Jock was pleased with the result – fourteen neat stitches, and he knew from experience that the wound would heal in a fine line. Though it would never vanish, in time the scar would fade. He asked She Whose Hands Heal to prepare a dressing of opunita and helped her bind it over the wound.

"In a day or two, we'll remove the dressing," Jock said. "In a week, I'll remove the stitches. You shall look very well. Don't worry."

The young man reached out and took hold of Jock's shoulder. "Thank you."

His beautiful wife nodded and smiled through her tears.

Chapter Seven

Jock and the boy rode west around Tucson and came to the Tucson Mountains. A haze hung over Tucson and the sprawl of the city surprised Jock; it had been a long time since he'd come this far north. They were nearer the White Eyes civilization and settlements than he cared to be, but he reckoned no one would expect to find two Apache warriors so near a city. Moreover, he was sure that Hargan would not deploy this far north.

They sat quietly in the saddle, and the sound of a car carried across the desert. Jock searched for it with the long glasses and spotted a Model T Ford truck, heading away from them towards Tucson. He put the binoculars back in the case and secured it to the saddle horn.

"All this was Apache Land. Tucson was a small place, and the White Eyes and Mexicans living there were terrified of us." Jock swept his arm around. "We raided here well into the eighteen nineties."

Some years before, Jock had sent a couple of warriors north to cache ammunition and supplies in a cave below Wasson Peak. That's where he was headed now.

He explained it to the boy. "You never know when you might need supplies or ammunition. Rounds for the Sharps; hard to find now. Cave's up there."

They dismounted and hobbled the horses. Jock withdrew the saber from its scabbard attached to the saddle.

"You need the sword?" the boy said.

"Maybe."

The cave wasn't deep, just an extended hole with barely enough room to stand. Jock made a small torch of dried branches and it cast a flickering light into the shallow cave. They crouched and entered, Jock in the lead. In the unsteady light, Jock saw the tarpaulin weighed down with rocks, covering the hump of the cache.

"Just the ammunition," Jock said.

The snake-rattles echoed off the ceiling and walls of the cave. A mass of ophidians came from behind the cache and slithered towards them, angry that their shelter from the heat of the day had been invaded.

"Diamond Backs," Jock said. Hissing, spitting, aggressive serpents, four and a half to seven feet long with thick, well-fed bodies closed in. Agitated rattling echoed in Jock's head; his right hand soaked the binding of the saber handle and sweat trickled down his back and ran into the cleft of his ass. Jock glanced at the Boy. Sweat popped out over his forehead and flowed down his face. Silently, Jock appealed to She Wolf and touched the buckskin bag containing her dew claw hanging around his neck.

The fury of the serpents was contagious and spread from the thickest bodied aggressors to the quieter reptiles, drawing them into a writhing, threatening, compacted aggregation. Jock's power was strong. He held the saber at half arm's length away from his chest and made a slow protective arc, back and forth, and the Diamond Backs did not penetrate the defensive sweep of the saber.

"Go. Go, cursed serpents; leave," Jock said over and over, and the hissing rattling mass divided, creeping, wriggling around them and fled the cave.

Jock turned away from the boy, vomiting up the contents of his stomach. "I hate snakes."

One large Diamond Back, its middle disproportionately thickened from gorging on rodents the previous night had slept through the crisis. Now it was angry, disturbed by the boy moving the tarpaulin to reach the ammunition stored under it. In the flickering light from the torch the serpent lunged, mouth closed, the head a flying missile shooting ahead of the thick body, upper and lower jaws opening on a cavern of fangs. The serpent struck, and recoiled, curling back to attack again.

The boy jerked involuntarily towards the snake, and the Diamond Back struck a second time, fangs sinking into the flesh of his right leg above the top of the long moccasin.

Jock severed the snake's head with a powerful saber chop, the blade sweeping an inch or two from the boy's leg.

Laying the torch down, Jock lifted the decapitated, twitching body on the edge of the sword, holding the weapon with two hands and hurled the creature out of the cave.

"Quick! Outside," Jock said.

The boy hobbled into the open and Jock followed, carrying the ammunition. He lifted the corpse of the snake on the blade of the saber, and heaving its inert weight with both arms, threw it out of sight among rocks. It was difficult to gauge how much venom had been injected. Jock looked at the boy's face.

"Twice, twice it bit me."

"The second time hardly counts," Jock said. "Most of the venom's used on the first strike. You're going to be sick, but you won't die; I won't let you."

Jock had the old Confederate medical kit out and applied a bandage tourniquet just above the four holes made by the Diamond Back's fangs, arresting the circulation of the venom in the blood stream. He poured Tequila over the scalpel to sterilize it, then he did the same for the wounds. He held the leg firm and made a longitudinal cut a couple of inches above each fang mark towards the heart. The boy recoiled, blood oozing out of the incisions.

"How are you feeling?"

"I feel dizzy; my lips tingle."

The boy turned his head from Jock and vomited up the residue of his stomach. He had the dry heaves and painful retching, but his breathing was normal. Jock felt 1 the pulse at his neck, and it beat steadily.

"I'm going to suck out the venom."

"But you'll be poisoned."

"Nonsense!"

Jock seated him on a rock to get the heart above the bite. There was no danger to Jock of taking the venom into his mouth so long as his lips, tongue and mouth were free from scratches. Neither did swallowing the stuff present any danger. He didn't relish it, but sucking out the poison would help save the boy's life.

Jock sucked and spat out venom and blood for several minutes, then helped the boy to his feet.

"Slowly, now. Let's get away from here."

Jock stowed the ammunition on the smaller pack horse and helped the boy to mount. They rode slowly but did not go far, stopping at a spring in a sheltered spot. It was a hot day, and the night would be warm. They would camp out. Jock had the boy lie down and covered him with a blanket, then laid their two lariats around the edge of the camp to keep the snakes out. He made a small fire. The wood smoked pale, then burned. Then he heated a bell-shaped glass from the Confederate medical kit. He smiled to calm the boy as he eased the tourniquet.

"Stronger suction. A doctor taught me this when I was in the Confederate Army."

He held a cloth around the base of the hot glass and applied it to the wound. As the glass cooled the air inside it sucked out more blood and venom. Jock kept up the cupping for fifteen minutes, the boy sweating and twitching all the while. Jock steadied him firmly with both hands.

"Keep calm, son."

Jock loosened the tourniquet and cut more flesh and skin around the wound to avoid retention of venom, then tightened the tourniquet again. The fire caught and soon yellow coals formed. He eased the tourniquet again. If any poison remained, better to releases minute amounts into the boy's system over time.

Jock went back to the fire, wishing for a small bellows that would make the fire white hot. But he did his best, feeding dry wood, puffing hard into the flames until the center was pale yellow. He had the handle of the cautery cloth bound as he dipped it into the heart of the fire. Jock felt the handle heat up through the cloth and was glad to see the tip of the cautery turn from red to bright red and finally a pale-yellow matching the heat of the fire.

Working quickly, Jock inserted the point of the cautery into the lesions, then smoothed the injured flesh around the wound. Jock breathed through his mouth to avoid the rank smell of burning flesh. The boy lay still, biting on the leather-bound stick that Jock had placed in his mouth, face calm, sweating, enduring the pain. Jock dried his face with a clean cloth. The cautery left a burn mark that would heal to a smooth scar. He prepared a dressing of opunita and bound it over the wound.

Jock looked at the boy's anxious face and took him by the shoulder. "You did well. Maybe some fever, but you're going to be all right. We'll stay here until you feel better. Anyway, I want to think about our next move. We still have the initiative."

Later Jock laid his hand on the boy's forehead. He was burning hot and sweat streamed down his body. Jock removed the calico shirt and dried him, wrung out the cloth and dried him again.

"I'm cold," the boy said.

Jock felt the rising shiver, the violent quivering of the boy's abdominal muscles and his quickening pulse. He began to ramble, not making any sense. His pulse slowed. Jock covered him with his own blanket.

"Drink the tequila; swallow. Take more. Need to get you warm."

The alcohol warmed the Boy, and his pulse grew stronger. Jock sat by the boy all night, waking him from time to time and feeding him tequila.

Later, as the sun cracked the dark horizon, traces of venom in the the boy's system made his temperature soar. Jock heated water until it was tepid and applied a damp cloth to the boy's forehead. Then Jock gently applied the cloth to the boy's torso giving him blessed relief, bringing down his temperature. He dried the boy off with a dry cloth.

"Sleep now."

"What about Hargan?" the boy asked.

"He'll be hanging about around the border; won't look for us this far north. But he'll be coming." An explosive laugh burst from Jock. "Imagine the hue and cry in Tucson if Hargan's riders appeared and it got out that they were hunting hostile Apaches. And it's just you and me."

The fire reduced to dull glowing embers. The retreating night was warm and there was still light from the moon and a fading starry sky. Jock retched at the thought of food and spat sour bile into the fire.

Hargan brought the two posses' back to the base on the Janos Plain. He'd sent an officer of the Texas National Guard and four guardsmen to the Ochoa Ranch by Samalyuca, to bring in more supplies. The officer was also authorized to engage any late recruits and bring them to the base.

MacIntosh was chafing at the inactivity. "Cap'n, let me and the Mescaleros and a couple of good men go after Jock. See what we can do."

"No. There's been enough trouble in the US. I hope it can be kept quiet."

"I'll chase him south across the border."

"No. We'll continue patrols between Douglas and Nogales. He'll come south eventually."

"Yeah, eventually. Fuck knows what he'll get up to in Arizona."

"You think they'll attack Americans and American property?"

"That's what he did in Texas when they came after him. Look Cap'n, you can never tell with Apaches."

MacIntosh knew that Hargan was a worried man, but he really didn't think that Jock would make trouble in Arizona. He was sick of Hargan's dithering. The wasted pursuit after the attack on the camp, the shooting down of the Old Jenny, the loss of men. Jock and the boy had hit Hargan hard and he was still reeling.

Jesus Christ! All that damage by an old man and a boy. Hargan hadn't grasped, didn't understand how dangerous Apaches were. The old soldier that was so much a part of MacIntosh respected and admired Jock's skill and daring, but the frontier fighter knew he was damned dangerous.

What really grated on MacIntosh was the hole Jock had driven into Hargan's confidence. A professional soldier, a West Point man, reduced to flapping and wasting time. The two Mescaleros agreed with MacIntosh – Hargan had shifted from contempt for Jock and the boy to a palpable fear, and it wasn't pretty to look at.

"Cap'n, we're fuckin' about."

Hargan stared past MacIntosh, then rode out front to get away from him.

The Mescaleros joined MacIntosh. "He's afraid of Jock," one said, and the other nodded.

The Guards Officer had brought forty new recruits, rough men, on fresh mounts, two wagons, one packed with ammunition, and the other with food and supplies. Hargan looked smart again in a starched uniform, but not being on official Guard business was without badges of rank or insignia. His polished field boots reflected dazzling points of light, the brim of his campaign hat shading his eyes, swagger stick looped to his wrist and swinging at his side. There was a hint of his old confidence when he invited MacIntosh to breakfast.

"How was the food?" he asked. "Better than jerky and stale biscuits, eh?"

"Good." MacIntosh was content with a bellyful of venison, fresh biscuits and potatoes.

"Can you find the hostiles, Scout?"

"I think I know where he's heading. If me and the Mescaleros don't find them, no one can."

MacIntosh knew Jock back in the old days; figured he would go to where his family was murdered. He knew the location of the massacre and was sure he could find it again after all these years. MacIntosh didn't know where Jock had buried his wife and children, no one did.

However, he was sure of picking up Jock's trail and would take it from there.

"Just you and the two Mescaleros. Pass the border quietly and hunt him down here. I'll have patrols out. I'll kill that old man and the boy myself."

"Hmm," MacIntosh said.

He'd been expecting Hargan's bombast once he got back to camp, had foreseen his change of mind. So the previous evening, MacIntosh and the Mescaleros had checked saddles, weapons and ammunition, picked the best of the horse herd, discarded their stinking clothes and worn moccasins. They washed in the creek and felt better eating supper in clean clothes and new long moccasins.

"I'll leave in an hour. One of the Mescaleros'll bring word when we have Jock on the move."

"You will kill Jock and boy?" the Mescalero said. They were free from the camp and heading west for the border. MacIntosh was sure they'd pick up Jock's trail in the Parjarita Wilderness. But, MacIntosh knew that if he were unlucky or careless, it would be Jock and the boy on their trail.

"Not me. Cap'n wants to do that himself. We chase him down here or we bring him in."

"Same thing. Parjarita or here, we kill Jock. But maybe he'll kill us."

The two Mescaelros snorted; their brutal laughter cut across the sound of creaking saddles and jingling harness.

"Yeah maybe." A tight smile creased MacIntosh's face. It was a good question. MacIntosh and the Mescaleros had known Jock in the old days. They respected him, but MacIntosh liked and esteemed Jock well enough to offer him a way back to white society when the Apaches were having a hard time of it. He'd gone to Leon's camp to offer Jock a job as Sergeant of Scouts. Jock refused.

"No thanks. I heard about the miners killed your wife. That was bad. But your family took care of them, made things right."

"Thanks, Jock. Think about the offer. This life can't last much longer."

"I've thought all I need to."

MacIntosh knew the story of Jock and Jim killing ex Confederate soldiers they'd caught molesting Chiricahua women, Jock saving Miriam's life, setting her broken arm and Leon giving Jock and Jim life when they were fugitives and had few personal belongings, apart from their weapons and filthy, patched Confederate uniforms.

"I'll always be a renegade to the White Eyes," Jock had said. "I go among them and would have to kill the first man who called Miriam, 'Nigger Squaw;' or our children 'High Yaller Breeds'. Here we are all Chiricahua."

"Just tryin' to help, Jock."

"I understand, MacIntosh, but I'll never turn my back on Jim, my friend, and Leon. He gave us life."

It was the reply MacIntosh expected. He hoped that, were he in Jock's place, he'd have given the same answer.

It never occurred to MacIntosh when he was offered this job with Hargan's force that he would be hunting Jock. He'd assumed that Jock was dead and that it was some other Chiricahua survivor that he was up against. Now he knew, and he did not care for what lay ahead of him and the Mescaleros. Oh, sure, he'd have killed Jock back in the old days when he was in the Army. It was different then with the Army at war with the Chiricahua.

But an old man making a sentimental journey? Why couldn't they just have left him alone? But the hunters had attacked Jock and that fuckin' murderer, John Injun, had gone after him and Jock had had to defended himself. It had gotten out of hand.

MacIntosh didn't want to kill Jock and the boy or hand them over to Hargan, who would execute them and defile their bodies, keeping Jock and the boy from entering the Happy Place.

The Happy Place – the Chiricachua hereafter. Jock must long for it, this beautiful land, a subterranean paradise, an underworld of green country, well-watered, the creeks lined with cottonwoods. Miriam waited for Jock there.

MacIntosh's throat swelled throat and the tears came. He wanted the Happy Place where Her Voice Is The Sound of Falling Water waited. He hawked and spat.

"Fuck this!" he said. "Gettin' soft, an' thinkin' like a Chiricahua."

At sun up Jock made a shade for the boy and he rested all that day. By late morning, the boy was improving. They chewed on jerky and drank water sparingly, and Jock watched for enemies. He knew that more hard fighting would come and trusted Ussen to protect them and to send Miriam to guide them. Jock was sure of his power from She Wolf. He relished this quiet interlude, these moments of precious calm, but was never one to waste time.

"You know about pemmican," Jock said. "Can you make it?"

"I've heard of it, but I can't make it."

"You ready to learn?"

"All right."

Jock laid out jerked deer from the supply of jerky. Then he placed a handful of acorn nuts on a flat rock.

"Shell these."

"I didn't know you had them. Where did you get them?"

"Picked them up here and there. The desert and the mountains, son, it's our larder. Keep your eyes open."

With a sharp, thin branch, Jock pierced the haunch of a rabbit he'd killed and skinned while the boy slept. He hung it over the fire, gathered the fat and juices in a cup and laid it aside to cool. While the boy pounded the nuts on a flat rock with the hilt of his Bowie knife, reducing the kernels to a fine powder, Jock tested the blade of his Bowie knife for sharpness, chopping and pounding the jerky until it was ground. He mixed the fat and the meat, added the ground nuts, shaping them into balls. He tossed one to the boy and popped one into his mouth.

"Pemmican, a ready meal. Lasts a long time. Good food for a journey."

"Tastes good."

Pemmican. The taste of it took him back to the old days. Miriam used to add a little sage to the mix. Her pemmican tasted so good.

He'd shared a dish of pemmican with Miriam when they married. The richness of the wedding feast contrasted sharply with their simple camp. The breeze lifted and the fire flared, casting shadows on the rocks.

"Are you all right, Jock?" the boy said.

Jock had removed himself to a faraway place, deep in the well of memory. He must remember. The boy grew anxious when he saw his old warrior grow misty eyed.

"We rode on white horses to a quiet place. Sigesh had built a small wickiup, the door hung with silver bells that rang when Miriam brushed against them; and in the night we heard the bells when the wind came through the trees."

The boy poked the fire with a stick to hide his embarrassment at the emotion in Jock's voice. Jock slurped loudly from his coffee cup.

In the south west the fighting between the Apaches and the White Eyes was a series of vicious guerrilla wars. Leon's band was small. He kept back from the Americans, shunned contact begun by the enemy, and by carefully planning movements between the United States and Mexico, struck where he chose. Always he sought to retain the initiative. He chose where to raid with great care and if he had to fight, it was usually an ambush, a swift, brief volley of guns and arrows, then vanish into a desert or mountain fastness.

"It was a hard life, son. Game was scarce, and the whites were everywhere, so we raided and we fought," Jock said. "Cavalry chasing us, skirmishing; but we often went hungry. We called ourselves *Indeh*, the dead; and the Americans *Indah*, the alive. It wore us down."

The band was so hard pressed that many women joined their menfolk in fighting the Americans. Miriam fought alongside Jock, leaving the children in the care of her mother.

"My wife fought hard. Several times the fighting was close, and she was deadly with her small bow; could put four or five arrows in flight simultaneously."

It was a rough wooing, a harsh wearing down. A ruthless, punishing regime that ate away the will of the fiercest Apaches, causing Leon to change his mind about life on the reservation.

"Leon decided to go in and submit to the White Eyes," Jock said. "He was heart sick at the suffering of the women and children."

And it was a ragged, hungry band of about hundred that Leon led to San Carlos. But they were proud and kept their arms, electing to go to a remote, quiet part of the reservation.

The slice of land, this sliver of misery where the band camped did not raise the spirits, and after a few weeks a widespread mood of depression swept through the small encampment. The people felt bottled up and constrained. It was a hard life there, too. Some of the band died from influenza, a White Eyes sickness.

Leon found it was easier to enter the reservation than to leave it. The Army wanted Leon's band where they could be watched. Breaking out to freedom meant being hunted down by soldiers and maybe civilian posses'.

Jock too was sick at heart with the reservation, the restraints on the free life of the band untrammeled by the world of the Americans. The White Eyes notion of how the Apache should live on handouts and rations aged Leon, a man Jock loved: leader, warrior, and the father of his beloved Miriam.

After three months, Leon, Jock, and the warriors planned a breakout. Everyone stocked what little food they could from the meager rations, jerking meat from the occasional deer killed on the hunt, the women making pemmican. Pairs of warriors slipped out and went down to Mexico and stole or traded for ammunition, bringing some of it to the reservation and caching the rest in secret places unknown to the Americans.

"There was a lot of excitement as we got ready to break out of San Carlos," Jock said. "The Holy Man at Cibecue, *Noch-ay-del-klinne* had the people worked up, promising a return to the old ways; and Nana was raiding. He came to our camp."

"Nana? the boy said. "My father told me about him at Fort Sill."

"That was back in eighteen-eighty-one. I wished then I'd fought with him."

Nana, a leader of the Warm Springs Apaches, came with four men. He wanted warriors for the raid. His face was forbidding under a hat with a narrow, upturned brim, the old-fashioned Mexican jacket, soiled white calico shirt, long off-white breech clout and grubby white trousers said that he'd been out for some time. His long moccasins reached his knees, and he carried a long stick, curved at the top. There was a Colt revolver tucked into his belt. Nana meant to avenge Victorio, who'd been killed by Mexican cavalry at Tres Castillos, his band massacred; the surviving women and children made prisoners.

"Nana was old, but he was tough," Jock said. "Traded insults with Leon."

Leon beckoned, and the warriors dismounted. Nana sat on a stool by Leon's fire. Sigesh brought food and Miriam came from the wickiup to help her mother.

"Mescalero warriors coming, maybe twenty-five," Nana said. "You will join me?"

"I must go to Cibecue. I want to hear what the holy man *Noch-ay-del-klinne* has to say."

"No good shall come of it."

Nana had visited *Noch-ay-del-klinne*. He went with him to the Mesa of Wisdom and saw him summon the ghosts of Cochise, Mangas Coloradas and Victorio from the Happy Place. The dead chiefs wreathed in mist emerged from the ground, just up to their knees.

"He says the dead chiefs and the dead Apaches will come back. I have seen the chiefs and they do not want to come here. They said, make peace for the White Eyes are everywhere. But I fight. Already, we have killed many and defeated the black soldiers." Nana hawked and spat into the fire as saliva flooded his mouth. "Your black daughter is beautiful. Why is she married to this White Eyes?"

"Jock is no White Eyes; he is from a faraway land that you have never heard of – Scotland. He has become one of us. He is Chiricahua."

Leon laid his hand on the butt of the Colt revolver holstered at his side. Nana's warriors stiffened, and one stood. Nana waved him back to his place. A slit of a smile cut his face, exposing stained teeth.

"Toothache; it's making me irritable."

Jock fetched the battered Confederate medical kit. "I can help you."

His direct approach surprised Nana and calmed him. Jock had him open his mouth. Two warriors held his shoulders and a third tilted his head back. In one clean movement Jock extracted the infected tooth with Chevalier forceps throwing the black fang into the fire. A large fragment of root remained and before Nana could object, Jock cut the gum with a scalpel and extracted it.

"Spit."

He cleaned the tooth socket with a swab soaked in tequila before Nana rinsed his mouth with water. Throughout this painful episode the old man had made no sound. Jock wiped the sweat from his face with a clean cloth.

"Thank you," Nana said. "Jock fights well maybe; and he could help any wounded, but take him to Cibecue. There's something waiting for him up there. I feel it. Then leave the reservation for the Blue Mountains."

"He will understand the words of *Noch-ay-del-klinne*, maybe," Leon said.

Leon gave Nana four good warriors. They would find the band in the Sierra Madre when the raid was over.

Jock was disappointed that Leon had kept him from Nana's raid, but Leon and Nana knew what was best for him, and for the band.

"Jock. I know you wanted to go out with Nana. Come with me to Cibecue," Leon said. "Listen to *Noch-ay-del-klinne*, for I hear he tried the ways of the Americans and went to the White Eyes Church, like the one you belonged to in Scotland."

Noch-ay-del-klinne had attended the White Man's school at Santa Fe, acquiring knowledge of Catholicism. He enlisted with General George Crook as an Army Scout. Then he went with other Apaches to see the White Eyes' *Nan Tan* Grant in Washington. The President gave him a silver medal. *Noch-ay-del-klinne* became disenchanted with the ways of the White Eyes, withdrawing to the mountains to fast and meditate on the story of the Redeemer and the Resurrection. Some Apaches thought he was merely a healer, a herb doctor. But to many he was a Holy Man of great power.

Noch-ay-del-klinne's power came from the love for his people. He suffered for them and with them as their world changed forever. He searched for earthly salvation, to return the Apaches to the days before the White Eyes spread across the land, praying for their redemption. *Noch-ay-del-klinne* would give new life to the chiefs recently killed, resurrect the dead Apaches and drive the White Eyes away.

When they arrived at Cibecue and made camp Leon took Jock with him and called on *Noch-ay-del-klinne*.

"You are welcome," *Noch-ay-del-klinne* said. "I knew that you would come; and that you would bring this man, Jock."

Holiness emanated from this slightly built man of less than middle height. *Noch-ay-del-klinne* was free of the barbs and warts that infested the demented Irishmen standing between Jock and God when he was growing up. His soul was wakened by *Noch-ay-del-klinne*, and he was bathed in the holy power flowing from him.

The rhythm of the drums and the singing drew them to the meeting place. Jock, knowing that Miriam too sought power to protect him, Nalin and Runs with Horses, guided her to the dancers. They faced inwards forming the spokes of a wheel, with *Noch-ay-del-klinne* in the center, sprinkling the sacred *hoddentin* in the four directions. The sound of the drums increased; the singing fervid; a holy ensemble filling the night; and by the light of the fires and torches the people danced and swayed ecstatically; grace lifting them to a higher plane.

"That night, son, I felt strange," Jock said. "Like the time She Wolf came to me. My face shook with pins and needles, and power like lightning shot down my arms and my chest filled to bursting. I collapsed in a trance. Leon dragged me to the wickiup."

The next morning *Noch-ay-del-klinne* invited Jock and Leon to walk with him on the banks of Cibecue Creek. They strolled along the pleasant valley by the cottonwoods growing by the water, skirting the patchwork of small corn fields and peach orchards cultivated by the Apaches. They stopped at a quiet spot on the banks of the creek.

"Last night She Wolf came, but you did not see her." *Noch-ay-del-klinne* said. "What you felt in your body was her power. I called her and she came and marked you."

He opened Jock's blue calico shirt exposing the deep claw marks on his chest. "There is no pain?"

"None."

"I want our land to be free from the White Eyes. Then we shall have peace." *Noch-ay-del-klinne* said. "But if my power does not work, there will be harder times for us. She Wolf has given you more power. You might need it." He handed Jock a dew claw. "This was on your chest. She Wolf left it. Keep it with the other one in your medicine bag."

"You liked him?" the boy said.

"Very much, Jock said. "He was a kind and gentle man, a mystic. But people heard what they wanted in his words. Some said it was a message for peace; others wanted to fight on."

Noch-ay-del-klinne promised miracles, terrifying the White Eyes, scaring the Army that he might unite all the Apaches and make the scouts desert. Nana was still out, eluding and defeating civilian and military pursuit, terrorizing Arizona and New Mexico. Frightened Indian Agents worried that *Noch-ay-del-klinne*'s preaching would lead to more war. And *Noch-ay-del-klinne* made impossible promises. Jock, despite his deepening spirituality, and fondness for the man did not forget Nana's warning and doubted that the dead Apaches would return.

The Army invited *Noch-ay-del-klinne* to the fort, meaning to keep him in captivity, but he refused to come in. He wanted to resurrect the dead chiefs and all the dead Apaches, telling his followers they could not return while the White Eyes were present.

Jock sat beside him on Navajo blankets outside his lodge. *Noch-ay-del-klinne* handed him his Peace Medal given by President Grant in Washington. Jock read the inscription on the back: 'On Earth Peace, Good Will Towards Men.'

Jock intuited that *Noch-ay-del-klinne* knew that the words on the medal meant nothing, that White Eyes would lie and offer friendship. *Noch-ay-del-klinne* dressed in his finest garments, a deerskin medicine cap hugged his head, adorned at the front with two eagle feathers, and gleaming copper studs fixed to the headband, black hair flowing over his shoulders. The Medicine Shirt of finest deerskin protected him from the guns of the Army. The adornments of red and blue curved symbols, the small Maltese Crosses reminded Jock of vestments worn by priests celebrating the Mass. The pristine white breech clout and the long deerskin moccasins added elegance. A serene *Noch-ay-del-klinne* turned to Jock and smiled.

"The White Eyes cannot harm me. My power and the Medicine Shirt protect me."

But Jock worried when he saw the dust cloud made by the column of soldiers and Apache scouts approaching Cibecue, and he feared for the Holy Man's safety. A line of thirty troopers wheeled in front of *Noch-ay-del-klinne*'s lodge. The officer, speaking through his interpreter insisted that they were friends, but if warriors came to rescue the Holy Man, or if he tried to escape, they would kill him. The threats sent a current of rage through the Apaches gathering near the Holy Man's lodge. Leon nodded and levered a round into his Winchester, Jock cradled the loaded Sharps, and Miriam strung her small bow.

Noch-ay-del-klinne said that he would go with the soldiers when he'd finished eating. He sat on a rock with his wife and child, and she implored him to escape to the hills.

"The White Eyes are going to kill you," she said.

"I have done nothing wrong. The White Eyes will not kill me. The people should not fight."

Many soldiers and scouts waited for *Noch-ay-del-klinne* to leave. And there were more soldiers ahead. Finally, a sergeant pulled him roughly to his feet, making him start. Apache voices protested, growing louder when it became evident the Holy Man was a prisoner. Jock, Miriam and Leon were in the vanguard of the furious warriors who followed *Noch-ay-del-klinne* and his escorts, crossing the ford on Cibecue Creek.

The soldiers were oblivious to danger. An officer approached, waving his arms, "*Ucashay, ucashay*," he said, telling them to go away.

When the soldiers imprisoned *Noch-ay-del-klinne* behind a wall of pack saddles and equipment, the Apaches were sure they meant to kill him. Scouts mutinied, firing on the soldiers who shot back. The Apaches attacked, and Jock and Leon were among the first to rub out some soldiers. They closed in and glimpsed *Noch-ay-del-klinne* taking cover from the intense firing. Miriam working her small bow sent five arrows flying, wounding two soldiers and killing a scout.

The Holy Man crawled from his prison to reach the safety of his followers. Jock shot at the soldiers, but missed, and his rate of fire was slow with the single shot Sharps. A sergeant and a soldier with a bugle over his shoulder, ducking and weaving, caught up with Noch-ay-del-klinne. The sergeant shot him as his wife embraced him. But he did not die, for his power and the Medicine Shirt protected him.

Noch-ay-del klinne's son galloped into the Army camp to save his father and mother, but the soldiers shot him down. Leon gave covering fire from his Winchester but had no better luck than Jock in hitting soldiers. Another soldier sprinted across the open ground and shot *Noch-ay-del-klinne* again in the head, but still he did not die. His wife tried to pull a rifle from the saddle of a trooper, but soldiers killed her with their guns. A soldier carrying an axe came and split the Holy Man's head open, and finally he died, his power vanquished; the protection of the Medicine Shirt ruptured.

Jock lowered the Sharps.

The Apaches surged forward, and Leon led Jock, Miriam and his few warriors into fierce skirmishes with the Army. There were hundreds of warriors at Cibecue, and they fought hard, but in small bands without cohesion. Had they followed a leader they might have rubbed out all the White Eyes.

Afterwards, Leon led his people from Cibecue, and they rode in silence for San Carlos; Miriam wept at what she'd seen, worried about being on the run again, terrified for the lives of the children. Her tears saddened Jock.

At Cibecue, hope went out of Jock, and Miriam; Leon too. They became stoic, determined to obstruct the grain of the white man's progress. Bad times were coming, many Apaches would give up. The word of the White Eyes was worthless; a man could not deal with them. They talked and then imposed their will, destroying anyone resisting. Jock saw how low they could sink when they killed *Noch-ay-del-klinne*. He knew that he could never live among the White Eyes. A few Apaches would fight on, the incorrigibles and Jock would be one of them, proud to be hostile and a renegade. He tried not to think about how long the band could survive.

Hours later they rode into the reservation at San Carlos, and they saw that the band was ready and glad to be leaving.

Jock was silent for a long moment overcome by sad memories. He turned to the boy. "I never found God when I was a Catholic. Priests got in the way, but meeting *Noch-ay-del-klinne* changed me. He touched my heart and gave me the power to lead and never surrender."

"But your power has worked," the boy said. "*Noch-ay-del-klinne* taught you to be strong and not to trust the White Eyes. Your power let you see things and call on the spirits. It's nineteen twenty-seven, and your families are safe in the stronghold in the Blue Mountains. And we have hurt those who mean to kill us."

"It hasn't been without a cost."

The few days Leon was at Cibecue with *Noch-aye-del-klinne* the Government agent in charge of the reservation, name of Reyes, had grown worse and the band's frustrations simmered. When Leon came back, the discontent had boiled over.

Reyes, responsible for the welfare of the Apaches in that part of San Carlos had watered the beef, rigged the scales for short measure, and tried to sell rot gut whiskey. Grown cocky at the unkempt appearance of the band, the long breech clouts and stained shirts of the men, the worn garments of the women, he insulted, then struck Sigesh, Leon's wife when she went to Reyes and demanded full rations.

"I shall kill him," Leon said.

Jock, viewing Miriam's vexation at her mother's bruised, swollen face said, "No! Leave it to me. You need to lead us from this cursed place."

Leon, the women and children, and most of the warriors had left the reservation before dawn, striking for the border, and the Sierra Madre. At sun up Jock and four warriors went to the agency. Jock smashed in the door of Reyes' sleeping quarters.

"You have cheated us, and you struck Sigesh."

"Fuck off. You'll get the rations I issue, and the hell with that damned squaw."

Jock pistol whipped Reyes, leaving his face a bloody mess.

"Fuckin' renegade," Reyes spat out through blood and broken teeth. "You and your Nigger woman and yer high yaller brats. I'll have you arrested for this."

Jock gave him a second ferocious pistol-whipping, the barrel of the Confederate Cavalry pistol fracturing a cheek bone and breaking his nose.

"You steal our food and blankets and sell it to other White Eyes. Our children go hungry, and you try to make the warriors drunk. You deserve a slow death, but I shall be merciful."

Jock cocked his pistol and shot Reyes in the head, splattering blood and brains over the pillow.

He gave the low howl of She Wolf, and the four warriors came up. They rounded up twenty head of cattle and some mules. Jock smashed off the padlock securing the agency store, and they took all the dry goods, the guns, and ammunition they could load on the mules. Jock and a warrior each took an axe and shattered the casks of rot gut whiskey.

Leon and the remainder of the band were traveling fast and by now would be well out of San Carlos, picking up cached ammunition on the way to the border. Jock's small band moved the cattle and the mules quickly, avoiding the Cavalry pursuit that would inevitably follow, heading to a prearranged meeting place across the border. They would join Leon and the rest of the band and head for safety of the Sierra Madre.

Leon never again considered the reservation, and neither did Jock.

The boy was recovered from the bite of the Diamond Back rattler. By evening, he was well enough to ride. They would travel, starting before dawn on the second day.

Jock dipped the biscuit in the last of the juices from the roasted rabbit. For the moment they had eluded their pursuers, and he was content. Jock drank deeply from his cup of coffee, washing down the last of the biscuit.

The next encounter with Hargan's command might come near where he'd buried his wife and children. MacIntosh knew where the murder had taken place; and in the old days, so did many Apaches and White Eyes, but there could be few of them alive now. Jock smiled; only he and Jim knew where they were buried.

"Have you been to the Sacred Mountain?" Jock said.

"No," the boy replied. "On the reservation, the White Eyes did not like the old ways."

"You're learning the way of the warrior with me."

"Jock." He was wakened by the sound of her sweet voice, and he was glad when her cool ghostly lips touched his cheek. She was undefiled, wearing her white buckskin wedding dress and the long white bridal moccasins. Jock reached out for his wife. "Miriam," he said.

Miriam's ghost took Jock back to their wedding night. She was painfully shy of disrobing in his presence, so Jock left the marriage wickiup, and as he went out the entrance his shoulders brushed the hanging silver bells setting them ringing, the sweet chimes prolonged by the breeze.

Jock had waited so long for his love, and in his eagerness, he returned too soon for he saw her naked. Her complexion glowed in the firelight and bashfully, Miriam turned her head away hiding her profile with her long black hair. Jock had never seen any woman unclothed let alone a Chiricahua maiden. Miriam in her near nakedness was unbearably beautiful. And so desirable, wearing only her long white bridal moccasins.

His heart was so full of love for her and he searched for the words to tell her, but a lingering modesty from his Catholic youth, stronger now that he'd become Chiricahua, tied his tongue. He managed a hoarse whisper, "Oh, Miriam." Jock held her shoulders so that he might see her face, neither of them able to resist the desire for the sweetest of lingering kisses.

"Let me help," Jock laid her on the white deerskin covering their marriage bed, and he removed her long moccasins. He glanced at her silken black bush, wanting to touch her; and she, sensing this, waited until he'd folded her moccasins, took his hand and laid it there. And he understood that Miriam had the power of life and when she embraced him, he gave himself to her hands and knew that her love would make him stronger. Miriam's contentment with him was complete, and she turned into him. In the faint light of the fire, he kissed her cheek, and felt the warmth of her blushing desire.

"Be still Jock. I come from Ussen to protect you. Waken the boy."

Miriam's sharp words brought Jock back to the present.

The boy sensed that she was Jock's wife and had come to them from the Happy Place, and that she had been sent by Ussen.

"You are Miriam?" the boy said.

"Yes. Are you afraid of me?"

"No. I am glad that you opened my eyes and I can see you. You are so beautiful."

Jock grinned, his mouth a wreck of yellow, worn teeth and dark spaces. Since he left the rancheria, Miriam appeared when Jock needed her, reversing the cycle of visits separated by long absences in the years after her death. And he was glad that when she came, she was as beautiful as he remembered her in life. And she had made love to him, reviving all the passion of their marriage, bringing the promise that she waited for him when his time came to go to the Happy Place.

"Sit with us," she said. "You are good protecting my husband. Now you are on the warrior's path. I want to take both of you faraway. Shall you come with us?"

"I will."

Miriam's ghost did not need protection from the night air, but she accepted the blanket that Jock lifted from his own shoulders and wrapped around her. She passed her hand over the dying embers of the fire, and it glowed again. Jock and the boy warmed their hands close to the flames.

"Have you found your medicine and your power?"

"Not yet" the boy said. "There has been little time to go to the Sacred Mountain."

Miriam watched over the events threatening to overwhelm Jock and the boy. In a matter of days, the boy coped with graver dangers than many warriors had experienced in years.

"Silver prepared you, and you have learnt much from Jock. Now you are made a warrior. Your name shall be He Who Fights Well."

Miriam unfastened the silver necklace, a finger-thick braided rope of Mexican silver that was hers in life and handed it to the boy. "Take it."

His outstretched hand trembled, suspecting that the silver necklace was intangible and would pass through his fingers. The boy closed his fingers on the middle of the herring bone pattern and the ends of the silver rope flexed resiliently.

"Always wear it round your neck; for your power."

Chapter Eight

Miriam transported Jock and the boy along the celestial path above the Parjarita Wilderness. She pointed to MacIntosh and the two Mescaleros riding from the south, heading northwest.

"They are going to the place where the scalp hunters attacked," she said. "They think they can pick up your trail and find you there. You must go to where my bones lie."

MacIntosh and the Mescaleros found the site of the murder, but they never found any signs of Jock. After two days of searching, MacIntosh gave up and returned to the camp on the Janos Plain.

"You and that pair of savages!" Hargan said. "Can't do your fuckin' job."

MacIntosh was weary and frustrated, and he'd never seen the Mescaleros so worn-out. Jock had just vanished into the Parjarita Wilderness, and the three of them were getting old and he didn't need Hargan's shit right now.

MacIntosh eased the Colt in the holster, and spat a thick gob of mucus at Hargan's feet. "Cap'n get yourself back to Samalayuca. Hump a whore. Better still, why don't you just fuck yourself right here, this minute?"

Hargan flexed the swagger stick in both hands and with a jerk of his head beckoned a Guard Officer who unfastened the flap of his pistol holster. "You're under arrest. I'll have you in irons."

Behind him, MacIntosh heard the snap of the Mescaleros levering rounds into their Winchesters.

"Yeah?" MacIntosh had his Colt out and pointed at Hargan before the Guard Officer could clear his holster. "This ain't the fuckin' Army. Make a move, you son of a bitch, an' we'll kill you an' any other damned fool as sticks his nose in."

A shaken Hargan drummed the swagger stick against the gleaming shaft of his right boot.

"Listen, Cap'n. You're goin' nowhere without me an' my relatives. We'll catch Jock down here when he makes his run for the Sierra Madre."

Hargan's head jerked up and down, once. He hesitated, turned on his heel, and strode back to his quarters, the swagger stick cutting the air as it swung in time to his step. The laughter of the Mescaleros followed him all the way to his tent.

With Miriam's words fresh in his mind, Jock and the boy rode hard to where the bones of Jock's family lay. Forty years since he'd been there, but Jock could've found it blindfolded.

Jock sat by the rise in the ground. He'd buried Miriam and the twins together in an arroyo hidden by Cholla cactus but where the sun shone in the morning. The rocks he'd piled on the grave had settled, but only a few had rolled off. Their bones remained safe from scavenging coyotes and javelina.

"You all right, Jock?" the boy asked.

Must be bad to show on his face like that. Jock's life surged in front of his eyes and the happiness, and the horrors of Apacheria overwhelmed him. His melancholy was at odds with the warm sunlight filtering through the Cholla cactus and desert scrub. He picked a rock fallen from the grave, weighed its round smoothness, and hurled it into the distance.

"This Hargan's the link in the chain," Jock said. "We waited five years for the children. Hargan's father killed Miriam, Nalin, Runs With

Horses, and murdered my people. I killed the father but let Hargan live. He was just a wee boy."

Jock, Jim, Leon and the warriors of the hunting party had come back that day in eighteen eighty-four to scenes of horror: dead bodies lay scattered throughout the camp. Jim and two warriors searched the surrounding wilderness for survivors and brought in the women, Little Swan and Sigesh among them, and some children and a few old men.

Indignation was Miriam's death mask. Her buckskin skirt was pulled above her hips, exposing her bloody thighs. Jock drew the skirt down her legs. He laid fingers on the bullet wound below her heart. The twins lay face down, torn flesh and dried blood on the crown of their heads. It broke Jock's heart to see the mutilated bodies of his son, Runs With Horses, so like himself, and his beautiful, loving daughter, Nalin who had his blue eyes. She was small and neat like her mother. They were the best of them both.

It was Sigesh who told him that Miriam had lingered to try to protect her children. Jock found the man whose throat she'd cut, carved out his genitals and threw them in the fire.

The slaughter devastated the band. The families prepared the bodies for burial, wailing women shattering the wilderness. The people had to get away from this place, but burying loved ones had to be done right. The families would inter their dead that day.

A measure of life went out of Leon and Sigesh, and out of Jock too. Some families painted the faces of the dead red to make them look better, but Jock did not want his wife or the children crossing to the Happy Place with painted faces.

They bathed their bodies, gently with love and grief. Sigesh wept quietly and then her grief erupted in shrieks, and she ripped her clothes and cut her hair to the ears. As grief became unbearable Leon wept until his shoulders heaved. Jock took his Bowie knife and hacked off his own red locks to the ears. He made cuts to his arms and bled for his wife and children and was glad the pain hid his tears. As the funeral processions passed through the camp, the people cried out for the dead.

Jock and Leon dug a grave in an arroyo, well away from the rancheria in a sunny place hidden by Cholla cactus. They lined the grave with brush and rocks. Jock dressed his children in their best garments and wrapped them in the family's finest blankets. They helped Sigesh, nearly too heartbroken to function, dress Miriam in her wedding garments and wrapped her in the buckskin robe that Jock had given her for a wedding gift.

They sat Miriam on her favorite pinto and held her up. They lifted his son onto his chestnut pony; his daughter onto her dear black mare. And as a sign of mourning, Sigesh cut off the manes and tails of the horses. Jim and Little Swan and their children held them in place as they walked slowly and solemnly to the burial place.

Jock laid Miriam and his children with their heads facing west to sundown. Leon placed Miriam's small bow and arrows beside her and Sigesh arranged baskets and cooking pots by her daughter's side. The boy's sling, his bow and arrows and the daughter's favorite dress and a doll from her childhood went in. They covered their loved ones with brush and branches, then a smooth layer of dirt and leaves. The grave was secured with a covering of rocks until there was a small mound that would keep out coyotes, javelina and other animals. And they were sure that their souls made their way to the underworld guided by family ghosts.

After the funeral, Leon, Sigesh and Jock destroyed the remaining possessions of Miriam and the children: saddles, pots, baskets, and clothing. It was the custom, to show that they did not value property above their loved ones. And it meant that the departed could take these things with them to the underworld and would not arrive there poor. Later Leon, Sigesh, and Jock purified themselves and washed their hair.

Jock's grief and sorrow would diminish as time passed, but it would never fully leave him. It was the Chiricahua way to avoid using the name of the deceased, but Jock could not refer to her as 'She who once belonged to me', or 'The one who used to be my wife'. She would always be Miriam, and he whispered her name every day for the rest of his life.

The bereaved warriors gathered around Leon, clamoring to hunt down and kill the murderers.

"We must save the band, and get away from this place," Leon said. "Go to the Blue Mountains maybe. Jock can kill these murderers."

Jock was empty and without feeling. His will alone directed him to avenging the deaths of his family and the people of the band. He traveled light; calico shirt, breech clout and long moccasins. A powerful stallion and a McLellan saddle. Water and jerky, a blanket roll behind. He was heavily armed: a bow and a quiver of arrows fastened to his blanket at the back of the saddle. A Colt pistol and ammunition strapped to his waist. A bandolier of rounds crossed his torso for the Sharps, in its saddle holster, and another for the L.C. Smith ten-gauge shot gun slung from the saddle horn.

He tracked the scalp hunters, and on the second day got ahead at nightfall and set an ambush, hiding himself among rocks about two hundred and fifty yards from their camp. At sunrise, as they stirred. Jock killed the surviving Comanche with a shot to the head from the Sharps. The scalp hunters wasted bullets in a wild volley and rode off. Jock shot the horse from under the last man, pinning him down. The rest of the gang kept running.

Jock reloaded the Sharps and fired, shattering an elbow of the prostrate man.

Jock took his time for it would not be hard to follow the trail left by the scalp hunters. He shot the Texan in the face with the shotgun, defiling him; and he chopped up the face of the Comanche with the Bowie knife. Carrion would soon reduce the remains to bones and shards of flesh. He had a look with the long glasses and saw the three surviving scalp hunters and the pack mules silhouetted on the skyline, riding hard.

Jock followed the trail at a steady lope and soon had them in sight as they crossed a long stretch of open ground. Closer now, he examined them again through the long glasses. They were well armed with pistols and Winchester rifles, but their horses were stumbling and exhausted. One man seemed to be the leader.

Jock pulled parallel to them, watching them through the long glasses. He saw ashen faces.

The leader fired three rounds at Jock, but he was out of range. Then, after some arguing, the three riders charged him, well-spaced, shooting as the range closed.

Jock guided his mount to the prone position in a hollow. He lay low behind the saddle, presenting a minimum target, the Sharps ready.

They closed fast, firing rapidly.

He shot one out of the saddle, reloaded, aimed and shot the other man, leaving the leader to the last. By then, Jock was well within range, a couple of rounds spurted sand and dust and a shot ricocheted off the saddle horn.

Jock hauled the Colt from its holster and fired twice, killing the horse with a round in the head, the second shot wounding Hargan in the chest as he went down.

Jock let the surviving horses run on. He cut the mules' throats, buried the scalps and took what ammunition he could carry and destroyed everything else.

"I made this Texan suffer before I killed him. I cut his heart out," Jock said to the boy. "Then I went to his ranch, and I killed the hired hand, cut his wife's throat, and burnt the place to the ground. But I could not kill his children. I feared I would become like him if I did, so I let his son and daughter live."

For two years Jock took the Bronco Warrior's path, spreading terror across Arizona and New Mexico, raiding into Texas, crisscrossing the border to Sonora and Chihuahua, going after Mexicans. He killed many White Eyes and Mexicans, and some Comanche; there was blood on his hands. Revenge did not assuage the grief of losing Miriam and his children.

One night, desolate in a lonely camp, unable to light a small comforting fire that might attract the Army patrol looking for him, Jock prayed to She Wolf, and she came and guided him home.

Jock found Jim and the remnants of Capitano Leon's band in a secluded place in the Parjarita Wilderness.

Jock shrugged off his grief when he learned that *Ha-tan-e-ged-eh* was dead, killed in an ambush by Mexican cavalry. Americans had attacked several times, killing warriors and their families. It shocked him when he heard from Jim that of the handful of old people surviving, many, thoroughly dispirited, had surrendered and went onto the reservation. It was the time of *Indeh* again; they were the living dead.

Jock felt a shattering stab of pain in his breast when he heard that Sigesh and Leon were dead, and he wept silently. Brought low by heartbreak, Sigesh had succumbed to influenza carried to the rancheria by Americans trading guns and ammunition.

The American cavalry killed Leon in a pointless action. A Leon unburdened by grief would have ambushed the patrol, harassing the band, but melancholy caused him to lead a rear guard of three warriors in a full-on attack. A black trooper shot Leon out of the saddle close to Janos, just north of the border.

"He wanted to die," Jim said.

The friends sat quietly. Jock had spent too long away. The struggle for revenge had left him an empty shell, hard, and cruel, without compassion. Had he come back earlier he would have cared for Sigesh and kept her alive, or shared Leon's burdens after Sigesh's death and kept him from an untimely end.

"Leon and Sigesh needed you here, Jock," Jim said.

Jock gave the barest nod of acknowledgement. For several days after he arrived Jock, powerless and depressed, could do nothing. Had the Apache Scouts and the Cavalry found them it would have been over. But Ussen kept them safe.

One morning, the fourth after his return, the Apaches came into the rancheria. They arrived in ones and twos: old, young, middle aged; a clutch of Mescaleros who'd run from the reservation. A Chiricahua who'd served as an Army Scout brought his family, not wanting to be a prisoner of war with the Chiricahua sent to Florida when Geronimo surrendered.

These lone Apaches, guided by Ussen to the remnants of Capitano Leon's band, had walked and run barefoot over many miles. The few on horses were shod in torn buckskin boots. Rags and dirt covered their bodies. They were the living dead, the *Indeh*.

"They've come to you," Jim said.

Jock looked at these shabby survivors, rooted to the soil, numb from exhaustion, old people prostrate with fatigue, others holding sleeping children in their arms. A new mother helped by her distressed husband removing the cradle from her back.

"Why, Jim? I'm just a white man who thought he could be a Chiricahua. I should've stayed in Westburn."

Jim cuffed Jock hard with the back of his hand.

Jock was unseated and fell over. The blow hurt his swelling cheek, but it was Jim's rage that cut deeply.

"Never say that again. They are your people."

Jock doubted that he could lead the remnants of Capitano Leon's band and the stragglers joining them. He was thirty-eight. His family was dead and his life ruined. He wanted to hide, to find time to heal.

Jim grabbed Jock by the shoulder and pulled him upright, then hauled him to his feet. "Stand up, Jock! You are Chiricahua. Leon gave us life; and Sigesh and he gave you Miriam. She Wolf said that it would be many years, and now it's your time."

Jock saw the people – his people – clad in dirty rags, worn down by running from the Americans. The new arrivals needed help and direction. Sadness, regret and guilt kept him quiet a moment longer. So much evil, and the band reduced; dear friends and loved ones lost. He resolved that later, he'd go to a quiet place and ask She Wolf to guide him.

"All right Jim. We won't let it end here."

They were the last free Chiricahua. They would never surrender but now was not the time to fight. They prayed to Ussen for guidance on the way south to the Blue Mountains. Hope and a longing for the old paradise enveloped Jock.

"I swear, we shall go deep in the Sierra Madre, to the secret places in the Blue Mountains and find what we have lost in Arizona and New Mexico."

They would be a small band, and Jock would keep them strong and free. It could never be like the old days, but it was what they could have.

The band prepared for the run to the Sierra Madre. The men hunted with the bow, and the women made jerky and pemmican; and from the deer skins they made moccasins. The warriors made bows and arrows for all the men and women able to fight. The men had guns, but many of the guns were old and uncertain. What they needed most were horses, new guns, and ammunition.

One day, an exhausted old woman, a late arrival in the winter, her bare feet tattered and bloody from walking on sharp stones arrived at the camp, bringing bad news, and an opportunity. She had avoided death, escaping during the confusion of an attack on open ground by a party of hunters from Tucson. They shot and scalped her grandson.

"Come, mother," Jock said, lifting her in his arms. He laid the old woman on a blanket under the brush arbor. A woman gave her water and Jock brought out the old Confederate medical kit. Gently he washed her ruined feet with hot water and Yucca soap. Then with a probe and tweezers, he removed grit and dirt from her wounds. He bathed her feet again, for there was no alcohol to sterilize the cuts. Jock applied opunita and bound her feet, not too tightly, with what clean cloths he could find.

She took his hand, pressing it to her withered breasts. "Thank you, thank you."

"My duty. Rest a while; stay in my wickiup. Tomorrow you shall have new moccasins. Soon you'll be well."

Later, when the old woman was made comfortable, Jock and Jim went to see her. "Tell us about the White Eyes," Jock said.

"The one that killed my grandson had a black beard. He was the leader. They were drinking whiskey."

"How many?" Jim said.

"Ten, on good horses. Four mules carrying supplies. Many guns; much ammunition. Please bring my grandson's body back."

Jock promised that he would recover the body. He sent a mounted warrior to find the White Eyes. Then he organized a war party; Jim, himself, and four warriors, armed with an assortment of guns, all carrying a bow and arrows. The warriors, keen to avenge the murder of the young boy were also galvanized by the chance to obtain new weapons, good horses, and supplies.

Two nights later, the war party watched the Americans for an hour and there was no sound. The man on watch was half-asleep. He died quietly with an arrow in his heart. Horses tethered on one side, and the sleeping men arranged around the fire. One man got up and relieved himself noisily at the edge of the camp. A warrior cut his throat. Jock sent another warrior to guard the tethered horses, to keep them from breaking loose during the attack.

The raiders came out of the east, light-footed, jogging silently towards the sleeping figures, the rising sun at their backs, blinding any White Eyes who might waken. The warriors caught a whiff of stale breath tainted by whiskey as they reached the sleeping men. It was over in a couple of minutes. The Apaches knifed seven men to death and brought the hung-over and querulous leader to Jock. He struggled with the two warriors holding his arms.

"One thing worse than bein' born Apache, and that's becomin' one. You're that fuckin' renegade, calls himself Jock."

Jock landed a punch that wrecked the man's mouth and nose. "Why did you attack the old woman and kill her grandson?"

"One less fuckin' Apache," he said, spitting blood and teeth.

"I'll give you time to think about what you did," Jock said.

A warrior stripped the white man, hauled off his boots and he cowered naked. Jock watched as two warriors hung him by his heels from a scrub oak, hands bound behind his back. They made a slow burning fire beneath his head that would eventually roast his brains. While he died, he looked on the naked corpses littering the camp site.

The war party vanished. Soldiers looked for them but didn't find them. On the way back to the rancheria, they searched for the old woman's grandson and found a boy's decomposing body. The coyotes or the javelina had fed on him and he had no face left.

"His grandmother must not see him like that," Jock said.

A warrior wrapped the body in a blanket and laid it to rest in a shallow grave that Jim and another warrior had scraped out of the hard ground. They covered the boy's remains with rocks to keep scavengers out.

The rancheria wasn't much, but it was a safe hideout. Many Apaches could not have found it, would have ridden or walked past the wickiups well hidden among deep thickets of desert scrub and Cholla cactus. But it was temporary. They had always to be ready to run if the soldiers came.

The pregnant woman, a young widow of twenty had arrived alone a few days before, after Americans killed her husband.

"It is her time," the old woman said, vigorous again, her ruined feet almost healed. "I must look after her."

"All right," Jock said.

"It won't be a boy," the old woman said. "The baby has been quiet inside the mother."

The perspiring mother-to-be swallowed salt and four tiny, lightly-colored leaves of arrow yucca to ease the birth. The old woman knew her business. Jock turned to the young widow. "Do not worry. I'll protect you and your baby."

She was a pretty girl, unfortunate, widowed so young. But her looks would attract some of the young men, and one would marry her. Until that happened, she was Jock's ward.

In the run of life men absented themselves from a birth. But these were not normal times and Jock stayed to help the old woman. The midwife heated water to boil the pounded root of antelope sage. The young widow squatted, legs apart, in front of an oak post set up by Jock and Jim where she could steady herself. Her two assistants were at her side ready to hold her arms, should she need help. The midwife bathed her quim in the hot mixture and massaged her stomach downwards. "The baby will come soon."

Jock turned his head away when her waters broke. A few minutes later he dared look again and saw the baby resting on the mother's stomach.

The old woman cut the umbilical cord with a small sharp knife, knotted it, and tied it with a string made from yucca leaf. She dashed cold water on the baby's body and sprinkled a few drops on its face; and it cried, not loudly, but a sweet mewing and they knew she would grow up strong.

The midwife bathed the new baby in tepid water to which she had added feather plume to keep the baby from crying, then she gently rubbed a mixture of grease and red ochre on the baby's body to prevent soreness of the skin. They laid the baby on a soft deerskin robe – an old one, but whole – and wrapped her up carefully.

"I do this," the old woman said, taking the baby and holding her small bag of sacred yellow pollen, the *hoddentin.* "But since you came back from the Bronco Warrior's path you have brought good luck and Ussen's blessing; please."

And Jock took her pouch and starting with the east, threw the *hoddentin* to the four directions. He took the robe and the baby to the four directions in the same order.

"Name her?"

"Yes."

A crisp winter morning; the sun lightening the drabness of the rancheria: the dwellings leaked rain, and it had rained much before the baby was born. Now drying clothing and blankets steamed in the sun.

Jock held her proud and high for all the village to see. "This is our little baby!" Jock said. "Our little baby, Girl Who brings Light!"

Jock's heart was full when they cried out, "Yii, Yii."

"Hope has come again," he said.

Despite the joy of the band, Jock was sad remembering the birth of his own children, and how much he loved Miriam when he saw her holding them, how tired she was, but so proud of the babies.

They had wanted children and as the waiting stretched out from months to years, they grew desperate. He hurt remembering how low Miriam had been when her monthly troubles came and blaming herself, and he blaming himself, and the coolness which kept them apart for many months.

Jock couldn't speak about it to anyone and rage gripped him when he imagined a malicious man or woman had cursed them. Perhaps a relative of the Mescalero warrior Jock had killed hired someone with the power to make Miriam, or himself, sterile. A concoction of herbs might have been secretly fed to them. Or rock crystal ground to a fine powder and put in a drink.

One day *Ha-tan-e-ged-eh* came to see him. "I have looked to my power, and no one has acted against you. You must have faith. Ussen will bless you with a family. But you must help him. Go with your wife."

And Jock and Miriam were close again. A midwife brought honey to encourage pregnancy. Later, she held a ceremony. She fed Miriam eggs and the testicles of a rabbit over several days. Then she threw the *hoddentin* to the four directions. The midwife prayed and blew smoke in the four directions.

"It will be twins," the midwife said. "A boy and a girl." And Jock was glad and held Miriam. The waiting made Nalin and Runs With Horses all the more precious.

Despite his sadness, Jock was proud of this young mother, a girl grieving for her husband. She had come through the wilderness to find the band and bless them with her sweet child. She was so pretty, and he glanced at her as he held the baby aloft and saw her affection for him as she smiled through her tiredness. Fleetingly, he desired her, and wanted a life with her.

But it would not do. She deserved a younger man near her in age to be her lover, companion, her husband throughout her life. Not someone almost twice her age, weighed down with responsibilities.

Ussen had called him to leadership, and there was so much to do. It would take all his energy and intelligence, everything that he had learnt in the long war with the White Eyes, leading and tempering these men, women, and children for their new life. As his heart ached for this sweet girl smiling at him, Jock found an untapped reservoir of strength. The memory of his beloved wife and children, their full, happy life together was enough, and he was thankful for the good years. He would not let go of Miriam, Nalin, and Runs With Horses; his love for his wife and family would be always with him as he gave himself to Ussen's work.

The assistants attended to the mother, ready to bind her with a cord.

"Use this." Jock handed the midwife Miriam's blue linen sash.

The mother smiled. "Thank you,"

"It was my wife's; you should have it now. Wear it until you feel strong."

And it was a good omen that the new baby was a girl, promising new life to the band. The midwife moved swiftly and wrapped the afterbirth and the umbilical cord in the piece of robe that the mother had knelt on. They would not incinerate or bury these tissues, and let wild animals eat them and bring harm to the child. The old woman blessed the bundle and took it to a nearby fruit tree, for life comes there each year and they desired the renewal of life in this child. She held the bundle to the tree and prayed.

"May this baby live and grow," the midwife said. "May she see you bear fruit many times."

Then Jock placed the bundle high in the tree to keep it safe. From inside his breech clout he withdrew a fragment of the precious blue stone about the size of a half-dollar coin. The stone, a gift from Ussen strengthened the spirit and guided man in the path of life.

"Thank you, Mother. Make a cradle. Let the blue stone guide you in our new life. May you see ahead for us and bring more children into the world."

When they came back, not an hour from the birth, the mother was up looking after the baby. It mattered to Jock that Girl Who Brings Light was born in the hidden refuge; her coming was a blessing on the Last Hundred and the place where they came into being.

Everyone in the band knew that Geronimo had surrendered to General Miles, and that for the White Eyes the Apache Wars were over. Jock and the band had not given up though. Hidden in the Parjarita Wilderness, Jock waited until winter and in December 1886 led the band south east, crossing the border near Sasabe, making their escape to the Sierra Madre and the Blue Mountains.

About halfway to the Blue Mountains down in Mexico, Jock and three warriors riding ahead of the band encountered a lone shepherd mounted on a mule and his flock of three hundred sheep. It was the second good omen.

A trio of intelligent black and white collies, strong working dogs, ran to the shepherd, snarling through bared teeth, but were cowed by the sight and smell of the Apaches, and a warrior laughed when he saw the tails between their legs. Jock stopped him killing them with arrows.

Jock rode close to the shepherd and took the reins from his hand. "Don't be afraid. We're not going to kill you." Jock pointed to the flock. "Yours?"

"A few. Not all. They belong to the village."

"You know who I am?"

"You are Jock the Chiricahua. I have heard of you."

Jock had taken many dollars and pesos from the Tucson hunters. Apaches normally ignored money, but he thought that in this changed world the silver might be useful. "I want one hundred of your sheep. I'll pay in dollars." Jock drew three hundred dollars from his saddle bags and gave them to the shepherd.

"They are worth more."

"Maybe. But as well as the money, I'll protect your village. But, if you tell the soldiers I was here, I'll send warriors to kill you and destroy the village."

"How can you do that?"

"My men are everywhere and see many things."

The band needed friends. This was the first step in establishing a loose network of Mexican villages that Jock would protect in exchange for information and trade. The peasants were safer under Jock's protection than from anything offered by government troops, who molested the women and took what they wanted.

He offered his hand; hesitantly the peasant took it. Jock pressed a few silver pesos on him. "Be our friend?"

"Yes."

"Good. If bandits come, or soldiers make trouble, send up smoke, and I shall come. Leave crossed sticks in the ground by the water tank."

The band rested after meeting the shepherd, and a lanky boy of fourteen fed his horse. The boy was naked but for the bandana holding back his long black hair, breech clout, and long moccasins. Jock hailed him. "Do something for me?"

The youth was awkward in front of Jock and just managed to nod his head.

"Good. I need you to organize the sheep."

Jock gave him a few words of guidance, and the youth along with several boys and girls rounded up the sheep, forming them into an elongated phalanx about twenty feet across the front. The young people matched pairs of the strongest sheep, lashing them together by their horns and positioned along the sides of the phalanx, a living fence preventing the flock from straying while on the move. The youths and young girls spaced at regular intervals ran alongside, maintaining the swiftness of the flock.

Ahead, a handful of the fleetest runners led the way and set the pace. In the rear the remaining fifty or so members, some on foot, all the old and infirm on horses, urged the sheep on. Younger children were in the care of the older women.

A mile ahead two scouts rode watching for enemies, and left and right, mounted warriors protected the flanks. Jock and three warriors formed the rearguard.

The twenty-five warriors and seventy-five women, children, and old people were proud, confident and alert. The people gave thanks to Ussen that the children felt safer, and with each passing mile the soft shod horses took them away from the White Eyes. As they went deeper into Mexico and the peaks and ridges of the Sierra Madre rose before them, hope for a better life filled the hearts of the free Apache. The Last Hundred.

Chapter Nine

Just after sunrise, Jock heard riders coming through the thickets of Cholla cactus. The boy led their horses out of the likely field of fire, and freed their weapons. The boy covered the right flank with the BAR and Jock behind the Lewis Gun covered the left flank. They would be rubbed out maybe, but they would kill many White Eyes first. Then they heard the owl hoot.

An old man mounted on a pinto pony led a party of Apaches into the camp. He was dressed in faded denim jacket and jeans, worn boots thrust into the stirrups; long white hair hanging below the grey wide brimmed hat. Stiffly he attempted to dismount.

Jock recognized him from the old days and got up from behind the Lewis Gun. "Silver. It's been many years; I am glad to see you. Thank you for training the boy. May I help?"

The old man grunted and accepted Jock's outstretched hand. Half way out of the saddle Jock caught Silver's arm and brought the hand to his shoulder. He felt Silver's weight then lightness as the right foot found the ground. "Thank you. We meet again, Jock; it is Ussen's will."

Jock knew that Silver survived the years as a prisoner of war at Fort Sill and had been released to the reservation at Rudioso where he'd been living in active retirement since nineteen thirteen.

"How is he?" Silver said, jerking his head at the boy.

"Good. He is a warrior and has done well. Miriam has watched over us. She came from the Happy Place and gave him a new name; He Who Fights Well."

Jock studied the boy with Silver's eyes. The boy was lean and hard from the life on the trail. The prominent cheek bones and chiseled features emphasized his strong nose, and there were faint lines etched on the corners of his keen dark eyes from crinkling against the sun; thick black hair bound with a red bandana hung below his shoulders, a faded blue calico shirt, long off-white breech clout and long moccasins.

"I am proud of you, son," Silver said. "Jock, you have made him strong."

Silver brought eight Chiricahua and six Mescalero from New Mexico. There were two elderly couples in the party, surviving prisoners of war from Fort Sill, grabbing this chance to escape from the reservation. The remaining ten were five young men and women. All of them yearned for the old way of life. Jock was glad that the men were strong and vigorous, the women of child bearing age. The thought of more new babies in the rancheria warmed his heart.

"I prayed to Ussen, and my power told me where to find you," Silver said.

The Apaches had left the reservation at different times by several routes, making their way across the desert to a rendezvous near the ghost town of Lochiel. Then Silver guided them to Jock and the boy in the Parjarita Wilderness.

The party rode good horses. The men wore wide brimmed hats, jeans, and boots, the women, calico or cotton skirts, and blouses. Their Colt pistols were hidden. Reservation Apaches, tame Indians, typically ignored by Americans.

"You have many guns," Silver said.

"I took them from Mexicans and White Eyes who tried to kill us," Jock said. "I would have destroyed these weapons, but Ussen guided me to keep them."

Jock and Silver sat a while, smoking thin, dark-leafed Mexican cigars that Silver had brought. "I used my power to bring you north, to lead us from the Americans. I sent the boy to help you."

"Yes, he told me. After he came, we killed Mexicans and many White Eyes who wanted to kill me."

The Apaches Silver had brought from the reservation would strengthen the band, but first they must get to the stronghold. "We'll have to look after the older people," Jock said, "help them to get to the rancheria."

"I am older than you," Silver said. "But do not worry about me."

The young people looked fit and capable, dressed now in traditional clothing. But could they fight? If the five young men and women were as fierce as they looked, then on the way to the stronghold, Jock could hit Hargan's force hard at a time of his choosing.

Silver guessed what Jock was thinking. "They are strong, and I trained them when I could. They shall not let you down."

Jock gave rifles and additional side arms to the young men and women. The old Chiricahua's approached Jock. "You fought at Cibecue when the soldiers killed *Noch-ay-del-klinne*, and so did we," one of them said. "Then we raided with Ulzana. We are old but younger than you, and our women can fight. Give us weapons."

The boy gave them rifles, Colt pistols and ammunition.

"Your wives teach the young ones to make small bows and arrows?" Jock said.

"We can do that," the women said.

The Chiricahua veterans helped the young men check the weapons. Jock and the boy removed the iron horseshoes from their mounts and smoothed the hooves with a file, and the women made buckskin boots for the horses.

When the work was done, Jock joined Silver, who had moved to a quiet place communing with the spirits and fortifying his power. Silver had packed his western garb for traditional dress; he wore his buckskin medicine shirt adorned with red and blue crosses and orbs, and an ancient buckskin medicine cap decorated at the front with a single eagle feather.

"My power is strong," Silver said. "I have seen enemies."

"Tell me," Jock said.

Hargan had patrols out looking for Jock and the boy. Neither Hargan or MacIntosh or the Mescaleros knew of the arrival of the runaway Apaches.

"The White Eyes shall look only for two men and the pack animals," Jock said. "They do not know that you are here."

The plan was that the new arrivals would split into three groups. Silver would lead one and the Chiricahua veterans would lead the other two. By night they'd cross the border for a rendezvous in Sonara and prepare an ambush in the Santa Cruz mountains. It was unlikely they would run into a patrol, but if they did, they would split again and make their separate ways to the rendezvous.

At first light, Jock and the boy started for the rendezvous, the pack horses weighed down with sand and rocks to approximate the load of the weapons now in the hands of the new arrivals. They would lead the pursuit into the ambush.

"I have been preparing for these days for many years," Jock said. "We have the initiative, can surprise them maybe."

Jock believed in this cause. Enemies had tried to rub out the boy and himself and failed. He and his young companion had shown them what it meant to engage in guerrilla war. And though weary from the pursuit, he had the reserves of power to finish this action. Soon their adversaries would learn what it meant to be ambushed. And later, Jock had more unpleasant surprises for them when they faced the warriors and fighting women on the field of Jock's choosing. Jock had adapted to fighting in the twentieth century, marrying classic Apache warfare to what he'd learnt observing and skirmishing when Villa and Pershing's troops had clashed. War, that fraught endeavor shrouded in uncertainty; but win or lose, Jock meant to give the White Eyes and the Mexicans a fight to remember.

The first patrol, as intended, saw Jock and the boy soon after they crossed the border for the Santa Cruz Mountains, straddling the frontier between Arizona and Sonora. Signals by heliograph were exchanged between the patrols. A second patrol joined the first. Soon, twenty men hunted Jock and the boy, Hargan in command, MacIntosh and the two Mescaleros tracking.

Four hours later, the patrol was closing in with Jock and the boy as they went deep into the Santa Cruz Mountains. Jock lay prostrate on the canyon rim, watching the patrol's progress through the long glasses. When the first rider started up the trail and the near vertical walls of the canyon narrowed, they fell into a single column, limiting the number of men able to engage the two fugitives to one or two at time. All was ready.

MacIntosh had been here in the eighteen eighties, and one of the Mescaleros had visited the canyon when out on a raid in the eighteen seventies.

"Opens out at the head of the canyon," MacIntosh said. "Should be water there."

The riders were tiring and ready for a short rest to replenish water bottles. "Send the Mescaleros to reconnoiter," MacIntosh said. "Don't want to get boxed in at the spring."

The Mescaleros reported signs of two riders and pack animals at the top of the canyon where it opened out. There was something not right about the tracks, the cut of the hooves in the sand different from earlier tracking. Something had changed and that made MacIntosh uneasy. MacIntosh, binoculars raised examined the steep trail at the end of the canyon, leading to the commanding heights of the ridge.

"They're close; up ahead," he said. "Three good men an' me and the Mescaleros; we'll get 'em."

Hargan hesitated, then shook his head. "No, we move in force or not at all."

"Water bad," one of the Mescaleros said and it was. The smaller of Jock's pack horses floated on the surface, blood flowing from its cut throat. No one could drink from the spring.

MacIntosh caught the mane of the horse, pulled it closer to the bank, and inspected the dead animal.

"It's lame." MacIntosh withdrew a small rock from the pack saddle. "Horse's carryin' rocks and sand. What the hell are they up to? Hauling guns and ammunition for days, one horse can't take the load of two; he ditches the loot? I don't think so."

Then the man next to Hargan gagged, choking from an arrow piercing his throat, staggered and fell. Two men fell dead from the steady fire pouring in on them. Horses screamed, went over and men hid behind them firing wildly at their tormentors. A few rounds thudded into saddles, fewer ricocheted off rocks. Some bullets killed outright; others wounded, shattering bones, tearing flesh. The patrol cowered behind the dead horses and what cover they could find around the spring.

Then silence.

Macintosh risked an upward look and saw Jock watching. Here and there along the canyon rim, other Apaches appeared. The Chiricahua veterans turned their backs and gleefully, insultingly, lifted their breech clouts exposing their bare asses to the enemy. Sounds of horses moving, cries of *Yii, Yii,* and the Apaches vanished.

"How many, Scout?" Hargan said.

"About fifteen or sixteen, probably, by the rate of fire."

Where the additional Apaches came from, no one had any idea. They couldn't have come from Jock's stronghold, and it was doubtful there was an additional band of holdouts anywhere near them.

"Breakout; come from up north," one Mescalero said. "Join with Jock."

Jock had hit them hard, but the dead and wounded would not halt the chase. Four dead and three wounded to be picked up later by the supply wagons. Hargan led the survivors up the trail to the canyon rim. He consulted MacIntosh and on the map chose a point for the command to assemble. He sent two riders back to coordinate.

"Eleven riders now, Cap'n," MacIntosh said. "We're outnumbered, but it's enough to chase while the command catches up."

"I agree."

The Apaches rode off the Santa Cruz Mountains, but once well ahead of Hargan's patrol, they stopped.

Jock cut a brass button from the Confederate Navy uniform jacket and handed it to one of the Chiricahua veterans, a superior rider who knew the terrain.

"Ride to the stronghold. Give this to Cherokee Jim, and he'll know I sent you. Tell Jim to meet us at the gates; leave some old men and boys to defend the stronghold, and bring down everyone who can fight. Do not forget the tools for digging, guns and ammunition."

MacIntosh surveyed the Apache position. The approach to it was across bare sloping ground; the scrub burned off. No Man's Land. The flanks were firmly anchored. The BAR secured the left flank, and on the right was the Lewis Gun. In the middle was a gate-like opening about fifteen yards wide. Behind rocky walls on either side of the opening, there was good cover. There was no way to get behind the Apaches. Jock had chosen a killing ground.

Hargan had expected to run Jock to earth at some point, pin him down, find the way to the Apache stronghold and, after disposing of Jock and his companion, make his way there, stage a surprise attack, kill everyone in it and raze the place to the ground. At the start of these troubles it had all seemed too easy, a short, straightforward campaign. Typically, Hargan had frequently underestimated Jock; the old man had repeatedly foxed him and out fought him.

"The old man led us here," MacIntosh said. "Apaches call it the Gates of The Sierra Madre, or The Way To The Blue Mountains. They say it appears only when Apaches are in trouble. Holy Ground. White men are never able to find it. Power's strong here."

MacIntosh looked back at the line of low hills to the rear, a perfect gallery from which to view the battle that would soon unfold. MacIntosh turned to the Mescaleros gazing into the distance. "Has Jock got riders behind us?"

"No riders," one said. The other Mescalero swept his arm towards the hills and the mountains. "Power, Apache power everywhere."

Yes. MacIntosh felt the potency from across the land, and he knew that the spirits of the Apache dead had come to witnesses this clash of arms. "Apache ghosts are watching" MacIntosh said.

"Ghosts, my ass," Hargan grumbled. "We'll whip these hostiles."

MacIntosh shrugged at Hargan's misplaced confidence. "You can't see 'em; don't feel 'em, but you'd be smart to be scared."

"No way around him?" Hargan said.

"None. He might push us back," MacIntosh said. "We need to get in and finish it before they retreat up the mountain; handful of warriors'll knock hell out of us."

"How many?"

"Hard to say; I reckon about forty; mebbe a few more. And there's them Apaches broke out that joined him. Women too; tough ones."

Hargan snorted.

"You go up against Apache women, you watch out, Cap'n."

"I thought Apaches liked to hit and run," Hargan said.

"Jock's given us plenty of that," MacIntosh said. "But one thing for sure, he'll have surprises for us. Frontal attack, Cap'n; only way."

"Yes," Hargan said.

"Two companies of Buffalo Soldiers or a battery of mountain artillery," MacIntosh said. "That might do it, if we had 'em."

"Yes, and a bombardment," Hargan said. "Soften them up."

MacIntosh knew that Hargan's position was far from hopeless. His men were not shy of fighting, and they outnumbered the Apaches, but they were not disciplined, professional troops. They had a good supply of grenades and rifles fitted with launchers. Determined riders or skilled men on foot could throw sticks of dynamite into the position. Several volleys from grenade launchers and blasts from dynamite would weaken the Apaches. But MacIntosh was not confident that Hargan's men would stand up to the sustained fierce fighting and the slaughter that must come.

"Me an' my relatives, might be able to get close enough on foot," MacIntosh said. "Throw dynamite. You hit 'em first with rifle grenades."

"You're volunteering?"

"Sure; we signed up for a fair fight. We just ain't assassins."

The Chiricahua had divided after the successful ambush in the Santa Cruz Mountains, confusing their pursuers, keeping well ahead, heading to rendezvous at The Gates. Jock had chosen the battleground carefully. The Gates were Holy Ground; Jock prayed for Apache spirits to come and he felt his power grow. It was his time. Here he would make his stand. Jock expected no mercy from Hargan, and he meant to give no quarter to his enemies.

The ground in front of The Gates was open and sloped down towards the place where Hargan had gathered his forces. The rock buttresses on either side, with the Lewis gun positioned to the left and the BAR to the right. Hargan could not get behind to attack from the rear, and there was nowhere to stage an ambush. There was good cover among the rocks for the warriors and fighting women.

By selecting The Gates to make his stand, Jock forced Hargan to deploy a tightly packed formation to breach the Apache lines. Hargan had to attack from the front. Jock reckoned Hargan meant to get his men inside the position and slaughter everyone in that rocky bowl. Any survivors he'd hunt down all the way to the stronghold. Then he'd massacre the women and children, the old people, and burn the place to the ground. But Jock had prepared for setbacks: if the battle went against them the fighters would retreat up the mountain, with one, or two warriors and women fighters delaying the enemy at fortified points to let the band escape. No matter what happened on the day, the band must survive.

Jock wasn't fazed by Hargan's larger force, but his stomach was a tightening knot. He walked around the position to ease his nerves, removed his neckerchief and dried his hands. Jock had had enough of waiting; he wanted the fighting to begin.

"You are ready?" Jock said to the boy and the warrior handling the Lewis Gun "We're depending on you to hold the flanks."

"Do not worry. We have everything we need for the BAR and the Lewis Gun." The warrior smiled and nodded.

Two warriors had reconnoitered the enemy camp. Hargan's men were experienced and well equipped; some of the National Guard had grenade-launching Springfield rifles. But Jock had given the force several hard knocks, blunting their fighting edge especially for close order combat. Jock knew that Hargan was aggressive enough once engaged, but he dithered when he should act. And the presence of MacIntosh and the Mescaleros had not lessened Hargan's innate caution.

Jock knew of the devastating effects of artillery on the Apaches at Apache Pass in 1862. The Springfield rifles didn't amount to artillery, but volleys of grenades exploding inside the position could kill and wound. Hargan might follow the barrage with an attack by mounted dynamiters or the hardest determined men closing in on foot.

Jock had the warriors dig slit trenches to the rear, about four feet deep, enough for men to crouch down. The women carried strong branches down from the mountain, placed them over the trenches and covered them with earth and rocks. Hargan would expect the grenades to kill and wound many Apaches, and the dynamiters to wreak greater havoc. Once his force got inside the position, they'd anticipate feeble resistance, but Jock had a surprise for Hargan. When the barrage was over, Jock's fighters would emerge unscathed from their holes and face Hargan's men.

A hand on his right shoulder startled Jock. "Come old friend; let us smoke a good Mexican cigar," Silver said. "We have prayed to Ussen and we shall pray to him again; you have made the plan and we know what to do."

For MacIntosh, who'd fought in the Apache Wars and loved his Mescalero wife, this whole thing was a tragedy unfolding. But at the same time, he was a participant in events at once savage and noble. As the frontier days faded away, old timers like himself knew of the handful of Apaches holding out in the Sierra Madre. Perhaps twenty or thirty, scattered across the wilderness in small groups. Sure enough, they rustled cattle, traded here and there with a few remote Mexican villages, survived despite threats from bounty hunters. But he'd never expected that a band of about a hundred wild Chiricahua thrived in the Blue Mountains.

And he found that he wanted them to be left alone. Macintosh wanted a truce, an understanding that these troubles could be ended bloodlessly. There had been enough killing.

With his binoculars Hargan searched No Man's Land, separating his force from the Apaches. "You think he'd parley, under a flag of truce, Scout?"

This was one of the few good suggestions MacIntosh had heard from Hargan. "He'll keep a truce. If he gives it, Jock's word is good. But what the hell terms you offering?"

"Let's see if we can leave him with some honor."

MacIntosh was surprised that Hargan had come around to his way of thinking and had done so with no prompting. To persuade Jock to return to his stronghold and end the fighting and in return, Hargan's force would go back to Samalyuca and disband. The killing would be over. It was much more than MacIntosh had hoped for.

Jock and Jim watched from behind the cover of the rocks that lay on either side of The Gates of the Sierra Madre. Two mounted men approached slowly. One, an officer of the Texas National Guard with the insignia and badges of rank removed from his uniform, carrying a flag of truce; the other, a Mexican officer, a lieutenant, the symbol of his government's authority. They halted about two hundred yards out.

"Find out what they want," Jock said to the boy. "Take two warriors."

The boy, flanked by the warriors, faced the two soldiers, rifle butts resting on saddles, but they were at an angle, leaving a clear field of fire for the automatic weapons behind them trained on the enemy. After a moment, the boy left the warriors behind and rode back to the Apache lines to confer with Jock.

"Hargan wants a parley," he said. "He will come with an escort of two soldiers."

"Do you trust them?" Jock said.

"No. He gets you out there, he'll try to kill you, maybe."

Jock wondered about what terms Hargan might propose, but he knew at once that the only thing Hargan wanted was his death and the destruction of the band. A surrender meant that the Apaches would be slaughtered; men, women and children. Only a fool would trust a man like Hargan, who would kill while protected by a flag of truce. Jock would meet them, but he wouldn't ride into a trap. Later, he'd take steps to ensure the safety of himself and his escort.

"You did well, son. Tell him I'll see him tomorrow at sunrise. Tell him to bring MacIntosh."

The boy walked his horse towards the waiting emissaries, delivered the terse message. Then the Apaches rode dressage, their mounts stepping backwards, heads high and reined in, rifles covering the American and Mexican until they turned around and rode back to their lines.

Hargan came at the appointed time, escorted by the Mexican officer and MacIntosh, carrying a flag of truce. Jock rode out with the Colt automatic pistol snug in its shoulder holster at his left arm pit and the saber hanging from the saddle. The boy rode on Jock's right, the flag of truce attached to the barrel of his Winchester. One of the Chiricahua veterans rode on Jock's left. Jock reined in his mount about five yards from Hargan, but the boy and the warrior slowed, passing Jock, forcing their horses between Hargan and his escorts, jostling their way through. The Chiricahua veteran gave MacIntosh a hard look. They turned and positioned themselves on either side of Jock, leaving a space of about two yards. Jock saluted MacIntosh. A long minute passed.

"Surrender and you'll get a fair trial for your crimes," Hargan said. "Then prison and maybe life on the reservation."

Jock saw the astonishment on Macintosh's face. "There's fuck all honor in that," MacIntosh said.

Jock waited, staring into Hargan's eyes. He'd been right not to trust this man. In No Man's Land, the breeze raised puffs of sand, and an eternity of fifteen seconds ticked away. "And my people?"

"I'll disarm your band and take you to the reservation at Redioso. The Apaches who broke out will be punished."

"You have the power, guaranteeing our safety?"

"I give my word, as an officer."

It was not the first time that Jock had heard White Eyes make promises. "I do not recognize your laws and I do not trust you. I did not look for this trouble, but Mexicans and White Eyes attacked me. Then you bring many men, hunt me down with the Old Jenny, try to rub out my friend and me. I say to you, leave. Take your men and go and it is over. No more killing."

MacIntosh moved his horse forward looking at Jock. "We leave, you'll go back to the stronghold and keep the peace?"

"I give my word."

Hargan dismissed MacIntosh with a wave of his hand. "Surrender, Old Man. Your days are over; you're finished." Hargan removed his campaign hat and wiped his brow with a flourish of his neckerchief.

Silence.

Jock looked at Hargan's flag of truce and shook his head. "You mean to kill me and all my people. You are the same old cavalry; it's past times all over."

She Wolf's howl came from deep in Jock's throat, intensifying, then stopping abruptly, startling Hargan and his escorts, their horses neighing, hooves skittering and raising dust. Jock and his escort, a tight rein on their mounts, remained still.

Jock raised his left hand. On either side of them a pair of Apache women dressed in calico blouses and skirts rose from hollows about two hundred yards away and came over, carrying Winchesters. A dark cloud of flies buzzed around calico wrapped balls carried by two of the women. They were strong women, walking confidently and silently in their moccasins. Jock nodded at the space separating them from the Americans, and the women rolled bearded heads out of the bloody shirts. The eyes were flat, and the lower jaws hung slackly, exposing discolored, lolling tongues and decaying teeth. Clouds of flies dropped on the bloody heads. Jock signaled to the women to return to the lines.

"Your assassins," Jock said. "Do you think I'm a fool? Last night I prayed and my power told me that you meant to kill me. Before dawn, our grandmothers found your sharpshooters. There can be no parley, no truce. But I will let you withdraw from Apache land."

"Hargan, you treacherous son of a bitch!"

"Shut your fuckin' mouth, MacIntosh!"

Again, silence. Seeing the heads of his killers evidently shook Hargan's confidence some. But Hargan wouldn't retreat, not now; not after coming so far. Jock had hoped, but looking into the man's eyes, he could see his offer was useless.

"I have many men," Hargan said at last.

"Not enough," Jock said.

"You fuckin' Red Niggah!" Hargan said. "You'll pay for your crimes and for murdering my mother and father. I'll wipe you out."

"Your father was a scalp hunter," Jock said. "He murdered my family and my friends for money. Soon, we shall meet here. Then maybe you start the journey to the underground from where no man returns; meet your mother and father there."

Jock gave the barest nod to the boy and the Chiricahua veteran, and while facing Hargan and the escort, they withdrew several yards.

"Thank you for trying to make a good truce, Joe," Jock said.

Jock sat rock-steady, controlling his horse with knee pressure and tension on the reins. Hargan's party turned and trotted back to their lines. The boy and the Chiricahua rode back to their lines.

But the Mexican lieutenant suddenly turned and galloped back towards Jock, who was still facing Hargan's retreating party. The Mexican's horse made little sound crossing the sandy ground; the Chiricahua and the boy did not hear; and the Apaches in the lines watched in dismay, afraid to shoot lest they hit their leader. The Mexican, saber held in both hands, closed with Jock.

Jock moved slightly to the right and drew his saber. The patent leather chin strap of the Mexican's cap reflected the sun, and salt glistened on his uniform. Closer now; and at the last moment, Jock veered to the left, caught the stink of him passing as his saber cut air. Jock swung the saber down, smashing through the cap and skull, mashing his brains. The Mexican toppled out of the saddle onto the sand, and the horse galloped back to the lines.

The sweat soaked Jock's calico shirt, and the reins slipped on his wet hands as he turned the horse, realizing how close he'd been to death. The horse went from walking to a brisk trot; and as his people yelled *Yii, Yii,* Jock breathed easily.

"You could have galloped back," the boy said. "Then we would have shot the Mexican."

"I didn't want you to shoot him," Jock said. "I let them see what an old man can do. Now we shall fight them."

Jock turned to find Jim grinning at him, very proud of his old friend. The band from the rancheria had arrived.

"Listen, good Cap'n; me and the Mescaleros'll have nothing more to do with you."

"I expected you to say that. You and that pair of savages got us here; you served your purpose."

Hargan waved his hand. A dozen men appeared, guns drawn, disarmed MacIntosh and the Mescaleros and bound their hands. MacIntosh resisted the hands pulling him away.

Dancers gathered expectantly. Jock agreed with Jim that some dancing and singing would lighten the somber mood on the eve of battle; and it would spook the enemy.

Jim handed Jock the concertina that was his since his days on the *Alabama.* "I brought it from the stronghold. It's good with the drums."

Jock opened and shut the concertina; dust had invaded the instrument, and he blew it away, held it up to the low firelight, cleaning the last stubborn patches on the bellows with a wetted finger.

Jock smiled at one of his veterans and jerked his head in the direction of the boy leading the guard, the handful of warriors keeping watch, their eyes staring into the darkness lest the White Eyes out there should try a surprise attack. The warrior relieved the boy, and as he joined the line of dancers, a pretty young girl urged on by her mother came forward and stood opposite him. She smiled shyly.

Jock fingered the buttons, then pumped the concertina, forcing air through the reeds. He hit the occasional wrong note, but very quickly his touch returned. He opened and closed the instrument in an elegant arc, fingers finding the true notes. The two lines of men and women faced each other, hands by their sides swaying in time to the beating of the buckskin drums. The singing started quietly, gathered momentum and in the low firelight the lines of men and women swept back and forth in a two-step, Jock's medley of jigs and sea shanties complementing the drumming. It had been a long time since the band danced and sang, and Jock was proud; the elegant steps, the sweet pure sound of the women's voices, and on the eve of battle, the calm faces and shining eyes.

The voices and hypnotic thud of drums drifted over No Man's Land. The Mescaleros, bound hands resting on their laps, swayed in time to the music; their shrill voices catching the rhythm of the songs coming from the Apache position. MacIntosh knew these songs. His wife, Her Voice Is The Sound Of Falling Water, had taught him. He knew that if the Chiricahua lost, all the survivors would be massacred. When the Apaches tried to make peace back in the eighteen eighties and had come onto the reservation, they had been cheated and betrayed, and the yelping citizens of Tucson had demanded their extermination. MacIntosh wished that he was up there with the Chiricahua. He began swaying and singing, adding his rich baritone to the falsetto singing of the Mescaleros.

Hargan stood over MacIntosh. "Stop that damned racket."

"They're getting ready," MacIntosh said.

The Mescaleros kept singing, and their voices filled the camp, spooking the Americans and the handful of Mexican soldiers.

"Goddammit! Stop that, I said!" Then Hargan did what he had so clearly wanted to since he'd set eyes on MacIntosh and the Mescaleros. He lashed out with his swagger stick, beating the bound prisoners until the hand of one of his officers restrained him. "That's enough, sir."

The Mescaleros gazed at Hargan, their shirt sleeves and shoulders cut to ribbons by the blows; blood leaking from welts on their heads and their black eyes pierced Hargan.

"If the Apaches don't kill you," MacIntosh said through bruised, bloody lips, "one of us'll do it."

Jock had done all that he could to get ready for the battle. Above the low hills that lay near the horizon to the front of the Apache position, thunder rolled and storm clouds piled up. Darkness crept over the land, occasionally breeched by sheet lightning that gave them moments of eerie light.

Miriam watched over her sleeping husband. Jock was drained and exhausted, preparing for the ordeal that lay ahead. He was racked by worry and feared defeat. A nightmare of the day his family was murdered haunted him, the bloody heads of the dead littering the ground, the knowledge that the battle lost meant the massacre of the band; survivors hunted down like dogs. Hargan ordering the mutilation of the dead, selling the scalps to the Mexicans.

Jock was a disciple of Ussen. Gifts of spirituality, acute sensitivity, and intuition bestowed on him meant he understood and felt more than other men. In the uneasy sleep and the agony of worry about his people, Jock sweated and his sweat turned to blood until droplets of red stained his shirt.

Miriam came near, a ghostly hand bearing a white cloth, rolled back the sleeves, raised his shirt, then dried his forearms and torso. Her beloved was so frail, and her hands caressed the bones that lay close to his skin. She was sad as she remembered the strength and vigour of their married life and recalled a handsome, even beautiful, slim, and sinewy young man, his fine abundant red hair, the gentle nursing when he saved her life and all the love and the affection he'd lavished on her in their life together. His love reached beyond death and warmed her very soul.

Only Miriam knew the depths of his worry and fear about the coming battle. She understood his doubt that he had done all that he could to prepare. Of course the band knew how seriously he took his obligations as leader, but only Miriam grasped how grateful he was to have been made Chiricahua, and the honor Jock felt when the followers came to him in the Parjarita Wilderness. She lifted him up and lovingly held his old body in her arms. Her tender embrace sent Jock into deep, deep sleep, to a place that made him stronger. She laid him carefully on his blanket and joined with him and when he convulsed with love for her.

"My love, my love, I am waiting for you," she whispered. "May you have more power."

Jock woke, refreshed, well before dawn and walked back up the line away from the position to pray for the safety of the band. Sitting cross-legged and quiet in a secluded rock shelf, he waited for the sunrise.

She Wolf laid her forepaws on his lap and Jock opened his eyes. Spirit flowed from her penetrating eyes, and he was glad that she had come to him. She Wolf nuzzled his hand.

"You are a great warrior," she said. It is your time."

Jock's hands sank into the vivid white coat, his fingers finding the red hairs flecking the white fur, his head cleared, and he felt the power that came to him from She Wolf.

"Old friend," Jock said.

"I am your Power," She Wolf said. "I am with you always." She Wolf vanished into the sunrise, and Jock made his way down the trail to the Apache lines. The spirits of his warriors and fighting women soared when they saw his new strength and resolve as he went among them.

"I rested well, Jim. We're ready."

Jim saw the blood stains on Jock's shirt; but the love bite bruising Jock's neck caught his eye. Miriam had come in the night and he knew that Jock was all right.

Jock and Silver sat cross legged on a blanket at the rear of the position, quietly praying and calling on their power. They opened their eyes. The air was moist, warm and sticky. Behind Hargan's lines, the sky darkened.

"The storm will come," Silver said. "Our storm. We will use it."

Jim and Silver sat on low rocks conferring with Jock. They moved to the rocky ramparts at the front and passing the long glasses back and forth watched the enemy. Fingers of sunlight crept above the horizon, illuminating Hargan, as he hectored his men. A hoarse cheering broke out from the massed riders and traveled across No Man's Land. Some of the newcomers to the band were uneasy.

Jock walked to the middle ground inside this natural fortress. "My power is strong." Jock spread his arms to embrace everyone there. "Together, we have the strength of twice our number. Ussen is with us and we are ready for them. They are bounty hunters come to fight us for money. There are few soldiers among them. Let them feel our power and the force of our spirit. We can beat them and take all their horses, all the weapons and supplies. You all know what to do."

Jock moved back to confer again with Jim and Silver. "I'll be at the front beside the boy. I'll handle the Lewis Gun."

"No Jock; farther back," Jim said. "Direct our forces."

For once Jock listened. Jim, his deputy, did not want his old friend killed or wounded in direct fighting. An experienced warrior would man the Lewis Gun. The plan demanded that a tough younger warrior act as Jock's bodyguard, protecting him while he concentrated on deploying the warriors and fighting women. Silver would attend to casualties.

Jock raised his arms and nearly everyone went into the slit trenches.

The storm rolled onto Hargan's lines and his men were enveloped in a fierce wind carrying sand and moisture, delaying the attack.

Jock sent the party of five warriors and five middle aged women fighters towards Hargan's men. They split into two groups of five, hidden by the swirling sand gathering at Hargan's rear. They were armed with Winchesters and Colt pistols, all the warriors carried a sturdy bow and arrows, and the women had slings attached to their belts.

"I'll signal with a dynamited arrow exploding overhead," Jock said to the Chiricahua veteran leading them. "Attack then."

The storm abated, and about a hundred and fifty yards out, six riflemen of the Texas National guard fired from cover prepared in the night. Four simultaneous grenade explosions, followed by two more detonations muffled the hearing of the Apaches; shrapnel hissed overhead, striking rocks and ricocheting dangerously. Jock lost count as the flood of incoming missiles rang out in a continuous blast. Explosions hurled stones upwards and they crashed down; spent grenade fragments hit the sandy ground. But the warriors and women fighters sheltered in the shallow pits were protected by the rocks and branches.

Silence fell. Jock gave the cry of She Wolf and the Apaches came out of their holes in the ground and hunkered down behind the low rock ramparts. The boy manned the BAR and a mature Chiricahua warrior took the Lewis Gun.

Now that MacIntosh and the Mescaleros were prisoners, there was no one with the field skills to come undetected and on foot in a surprise attack, hurling dynamite among the Apaches. Hargan ordered a mounted assault.

Ten horsemen came fast out of the dust of the retreating storm, forming a steep diagonal line, well spread out, each man carrying two bound sticks of dynamite, fuses smoking and hissing.

The sharp tack-tack-tack of the Lewis Gun cut down the rear of the line and the harsh bark of the BAR destroyed the lead riders. A hail of lead from both weapons butchered the middle. Horses screamed from shattered forelegs, torn flanks, and went down. Dynamite exploded, blowing arms and legs away. Dead and wounded men and horses littered the ground about thirty yards out. Methodically, the boy and the warrior working left to right fired into the heaps of dead and clusters of wounded flesh until the horses stopped screaming and the wounded lay still.

In the silence, Jock walked to the rocky bulwarks and through the long glasses he surveyed the carnage. He adjusted the range and saw Hargan wave his massed riders forward; he was committing his main force. The riders magnified, filling the long glasses threateningly. Jock walked back to his place of command at the rear of the position.

The White Eyes and Mexicans charged through the bodies of dead men and horses, hooves stamping on faces and scattering limbs severed by explosions and fire from the Apaches. Hargan was not shy and led his men in a spirited attack to smash the defenses, break in and overwhelm the Apaches.

A crash, and forty assorted repeating rifles discharged a volley, reloaded and fired again. Gaps appeared among the massed riders; dead and wounded men hit the ground, horses screaming, keeling over, dying.

Hargan led them on, waving a Colt automatic pistol in his free hand. A third volley hit them. Hargan's riders staggered, flanks ragged from the crossfire of the automatic weapons and the massed rifle fire.

Jock sat on a flat rock behind the main fighting; feet firmly planted on the ground. Silver was safe behind him, attending to the wounded carried there by a couple of the women. He looked for Jim; he was firing into the mass of riders thronging the Gates. Jock uttered a piercing owl hoot that rose above the clamor and the Apache fire eased. The lead dozen of Hargan's riders surged through the narrow Gates and shot into the position. But unexpectedly, another half dozen riders got through. Jock gave the second signal, the old Rebel Yell from long ago, and a small party of women stationed on either side of the Gates hauled up a rough net fashioned from rawhide lariats, binding it tightly to stakes hidden behind the rock buttresses, trapping the riders inside the position.

The Apache men and women were fighting in two sections: attacking the riders trapped inside The Gates, and at the entrance the majority fought to stop the more than one hundred mounted men trying to fight their way in. Jock meant to damage the morale of the attackers outside by making them watch the Apaches slaughter their comrades trapped inside.

Hargan dismounted and led a group on foot, Bowie knife in one hand to cut the rawhide ropes and get more of his riders inside; Colt pistol in his other hand, he shot at the defenders above him, trying to kill the boy and the Chiricahua firing the BAR and the Lewis Gun.

Jock gave the howl of She Wolf.

Jim broke off, leaving the defense of the Gates to a few crack shots, the BAR and the Lewis Gun, and led warriors and women into the hand-to-hand fighting. He blasted White Eyes and Mexicans with the Winchester pump action shot gun. The boy and the warrior barely held off the main attack. The magazines of the BAR and the Lewis Gun emptied simultaneously. The boy turned the BAR and drove the butt into the face of a man climbing, knocking him to the ground. In the lull, Hargan managed to sever one of the ropes and more riders almost broke through. Just in time, the Lewis Gun fired long bursts into them, and they wavered. The boy reloaded, and the combined fire of the automatic weapons drove Hargan and his men back a crucial few yards.

Too many riders had gotten in, and the fighting was now very hard. The Apache men and women were well disciplined. Fighting for survival, they found reserves of strength and courage, giving them a ferocious edge in the close-quarter fighting. A Chiricahua matron fell dead but not before she stabbed a Mexican soldier through the heart. An attractive younger woman was bowled over by a blow from a rifle butt. From a sitting position she shot her assailant, got to her feet and shot another target in the head. Jock grabbed a passing youth and sent him to get the boy's attention, then help the Lewis gunner reload. The rate of fire from the Lewis Gun increased. Jock made a turning motion with his left hand. The boy put the BAR on single shots and in the space of a minute or two had killed or wounded more than half a dozen Mexicans and Americans who had gotten through the Gates. The Apache men and women fought with renewed energy and further thinned the ranks of the attackers.

Jock's bodyguard fell, bleeding heavily from a chest wound. Jock was alone now and without protection.

Jock drew the Colt automatic from its shoulder holster and shot the man who had wounded his bodyguard. He shot at Mexicans and Americans when he was sure of hitting them. Jock ejected the empty magazine from the Colt, then dropped the full magazine and, as he bent over to pick it up, was rushed and knocked over by a Mexican who had just clubbed a woman to the ground. Jock was no match for this burly younger man; he went limp and the Mexican relaxed his grip on Jock's throat.

Jock pulled out the Derringer tucked into his belt and fired both barrels into his assailant's chin blowing away half his face.

As Jock got out from under the dead weight of the Mexican, he heard Jim yelling. "To me, to me!"

And the men and women gathered with him, forming a wedge that cut into the disorganized remnants of the attackers, pushing them back until they were hard against the ropes. None survived. As this slaughter unfolded, the warriors and women on the ramparts poured a murderous fire down on the main attack still trying to fight their way in. Hargan rallied the men near him for another charge. As the corpses of their comrades piled up, they withdrew in a tight defensive knot of milling riders and dismounted men.

Jock raised his hand and stayed the thinned ranks of his fighters from pursuit. Time for the final signal. Jock raised and then dropped his right hand. A young warrior, renowned for his archery skills drew a mulberry bow to its full power and loosed an arrow, a stick of dynamite fastened to the shaft, fuse smoking as it flew in a steep arc, exploding at the apex. The boom of the missile barely registered with the Apaches who expected it, but the detonation unhinged Hargan's men rallying again for another charge at The Gates.

In Hargan's rear and undetected, the Chiricahua women were up first, Winchesters slung across their backs, slings loaded with grenades. The warriors followed, lit the fuses on the dynamite, and counted the seconds; the women pulled the pins on the grenades and counted. The timing had to be right, there were sufficient missiles for only one volley.

The dynamited arrows fell first into the body of Hargan's men; and a few yards farther back, the grenades landed. The explosions cut down a swathe of men and horses. Slings and arrows, traditional weapons, delivered modern ordinance into the massed White Eyes and Mexicans.

Jock nodded and a small group of women cut the rawhide rope gate.

The warriors and fighting women came out of the wind and dust and closed in on Hargan's rear. Jock waved his fighters on, and the warriors and the women stepped over the dead and poured out The Gates. Fighting with cool ferocity, they closed the vice. Discipline gave the Apaches an edge; they selected their targets, the women with the small bows releasing arrows, the rest firing round after round into the tightly packed horsemen. From the corner of his eye Jock glimpsed the boy taking deadly single shots with the BAR into the knot of Hargan's men. Riders toppled out of the saddle; at the edge of the fighting Apache women flitted from cover, finishing off casualties with knife and pistol. The pitiful screaming of wounded horses rose above the pistol shots and rifle volleys. Apaches at their front and rear, the Americans and their handful of Mexican allies pulled into a tighter protective cluster. They could retreat no further. Hargan was on the ground, wounded. Firing eased, and one by one the survivors discarded their weapons.

"Let them live," Jock said.

The band paid for victory with six killed – four men, two women. Jock grieved for them as the boy tied the dead to mules. When they reached the stronghold, families would take care of their own. There were as many again wounded, and they were assembling near Silver, preparing for the ascent of the mountain. They would survive; Jock and Silver had attended to them. The women of child bearing age were unharmed, and the newcomers brought by Silver would strengthen the band.

The dead and wounded were a heavy bloody price, but the band had prevailed against a much larger force; maybe forty wounded, disarmed, and broken men of Hargan's command survived. They might die in the desert on the retreat to Samalayuca. Or they might not. That was up to Ussen.

Jock and Jim rested their arms on the saddle horns, reins gathered loosely in the right hand and let their weight settle into the saddle. Hargan lay in pain from gunshot wounds in his torso; an arrow was embedded in his right arm. Jock considered letting him perish alone among the dead of his command. He was a poor fool of a man.

The warriors and the fighting women moved among the dead and wounded, the creak of leather, the chinks of weapons and harness disturbing the silence, gathering loot, packing it on to mules and horses – weapons, ammunition, clothing, everything they could carry.

MacIntosh and the Mescaleros, bound hand and foot, had watched the fighting from the rear. Two warriors guarding them cut the rawhide binding their hands and ankles, helped them mount and tied their hands to the saddle horns. They said nothing, getting ready to die.

Jock approached slowly on horseback. He was shocked at their cut and bruised faces, the torn shirts. "Who did that to you?"

"Hargan," MacIntosh said simply.

Jock turned to stare at Hargan a moment, then faced MacIntosh and the Mescaleros.

"This is over, and I look ahead," Jock said. "Come south with us to the land of bananas and tropical fruits, to where the mangoes grow."

The Mescaleros exchanged a look. They wavered, and Jock was sure that they wanted to come.

"We have beaten them," Jock said. "There's work to be done. It won't be like the old days, but we'll have something."

They looked at the wreck of Hargan's command: the distressed flesh of the dead and the dying. The remains of the force that Hargan had led to destruction.

Jock must take the band beyond the Blue Mountains. This time, this last time, the Chiricahua had won a great victory and the weight laid on him by Hargan was lifted. When word of their triumph spread, carried to the border by rumor and story tellers, the Mexicans and Americans would send soldiers to kill them, maybe. But perhaps these men who wanted his people dead would pretend that the fighting was trouble started by adventurers and bounty hunters.

Jock could not afford to take chances: he would take the band south.

Jock had often been close to death in his long and dangerous life. When he was young, he'd been afraid of dying, but now as his ninth decade approached, he was ready. His work was almost done. The burden laid on him forty-three years ago when Miriam, Nalin, and Runs With Horses were murdered was lifting. At times in the phase begun a few weeks earlier when he came north, he'd wondered if he and the boy would survive. Once he'd brought the band to a safe place far to the south, then with Ussen's blessing he would leave this life and journey to the Happy Place.

Jock swept his arm around the scene of the battle. "The earth, the sky, and the winds hear us. The sun sees us. The spirits know that the Chiricahua came to this place."

Jock dismounted and crouched beside Hargan. He could have had Hargan killed riding at the head of his men when they charged, but he'd instructed his fighters to wound, not kill. And now…

Jock would not kill him. He would punish Hargan letting him live, to lead the remnants of his shattered force back to Samalayuca.

"Up there, let them know that the Chiricahua was here."

Hargan stared at Jock, his face a mixture of fear, pain and relief. Jock put his left foot in the stirrup and swung his right leg across the saddle.

Jock turned to the boy. "Lead the way son."

The warriors and fighting women mounted; mules and pack horses laden with booty. Jock nodded. The Mescaleros kicked their horses forward and he cut the rawhide bonds freeing their hands, moving his horse aside to let them pass and join the line of mounted men and women moving forward. Jock's smile of stained teeth and empty spaces deepened the creases around his mouth. He walked his horse across the space separating him from Macintosh and cut his wrists free. MacIntosh rubbed circulation into his hands.

"You belong with us, Joe. When it is your time you will find Her Voice is The Sound Of Falling Water waiting for you in the Happy Place."

Distant thunder broke the silence. The sun brightened the battle field.

"Can you see them?" Jock said.

"No."

"Look hard, Joe."

And MacIntosh heard the cries, *Yii, yii,*' and then saw many shadows moving on the low hills. "I see them."

Jock turned his horse and let Joe MacIntosh pass, and they followed the line of riders vanishing one by one through The Gates and into the vastness of the Sierra Madre.

* * *

We hope you enjoyed reading *The Last Hundred.* If you have a moment, please leave us a review - even if it's a short one. We want to hear from you.

Want to get notified when one of Creativia's books is free to download? Join our spam-free newsletter at www.creativia.org.

Best regards,
Jim Ellis and the Creativia Team

About The Author

Thank you for reading my novel. I write historical novels, the kind I'd read, and hope that my books attract readers who'll and spread the word.

I've made a living as a seafarer, production planner, personnel manager, and university lecturer.

I like to write. When not writing I'm reading. Then finding time for Jazz, and travel with my wife, especially New York City.

Books by the Author

One Summer
The Last Hundred
The Music Room
Westburn Blues

Made in the USA
San Bernardino, CA
03 January 2020